I0736293

LAST TIME WE LOVED

Timing is Everything Series, Book 1

CHRISTINE MILES

LAST TIME WE LOVED

Timing is Everything Series, Book 1

Published by Sealed With a Swoon Books LLC

Copyright © 2021, 2023 by Christine Miles

2nd edition

All rights reserved. Except for use in any review, the reproduction or utilization of this work in whole or in part in any form by any electronic, mechanical or other means, now known or hereinafter invented, including xerography, photocopying and recording, or in any information storage or retrieval system, is forbidden without the written permission of the publisher.

This is a work of fiction. Names, characters, places and incidents are either the product of the author's imagination or are used fictitiously, and any resemblance to actual persons, living or dead, business establishments, events or locales is entirely co-incidental.

Cover Design by The Killion Group, Inc.

To first loves and second chances.

Books by Christine Miles

ADULT CONTEMPORARY ROMANCE

Timing is Everything Series

Last Time We Loved (Book One)

First Time We Laughed (Book Two)

The Time We Met (Book Three)

This Time It's Forever (Book Four)

YOUNG ADULT

Pacifica Academy Drama Series

Me, Shakespeare and the Anti-Love Club (Book One)

The '68 Camaro Between Kenickie and Me (Book Two)

Teddy Brewster's Hold On Me (Book Three)

Silver Bells for Me and (Saint) Nicolas (Book Four)

You and Me Dancing to Gershwin (Book Five)

Summer in Winter Wonderland (A Cozy Mystery)

Chapter One

HER TENDENCY toward perfectionism hit overdrive as she stepped away from the wedding party's head table for the *third* time.

Alyson Douglas tilted her head right to examine the elaborate bouquet of deep red and bright white roses with a hint of green.

Dammit. That vase still seemed off center.

She sighed, returned to the table, slid the vase slightly right, and angled her head back.

Perfect. At least, perfect enough to move on to the final head table vase and call it a day and night.

The Friday evening wedding at the Boettcher Mansion in Golden, Colorado, happened to be on the "most romantic day of the year." Valentine's Day. The main reason the bride had opted for the red-and-white theme, but with a splash of black since they'd also wanted everyone to be in black tie attire.

As Alyson's eyes scanned the rustic Fireside Room—the place for the reception—she slowly nodded at the bride's choice in color scheme. Bold red roses. Spots of black. Bright-white tablecloths and napkins, that also complemented the other roses. Candlelight.

She smiled at the room glowing with warmth, romance, and love.

The perfect setting for a Valentine's Day wedding set in the foothills on a wintry, Rocky Mountain evening.

"Alyson, these arrangements are simply *breathtaking*!"

She turned toward the wedding planner, a heavyset woman pushing fifty, who had the energy of a small child on a sugar high. "Thanks, Deirdre." She pointed at the last vase on the metal cart. "I'm almost done. Is there anything else I can do before I leave?" And fight the oh-so fun Denver metro area rush hour traffic.

"No!" the woman chirped. "The bride and groom are nearly ready to go. As is the bridal party." She shook her head. "No one can get the mother-of-the-bride to stop crying, so that should be interesting." She waved her hand as if shooing an annoying gnat. "But I'll take nonstop tears over a mother-of-the-bride who wants to micromanage *everything* I do." She faced Alyson. "You get on home, my dear. I'm sure traffic will be particularly awful tonight."

Due to Valentine's Day. *Crap.*

Alyson swallowed a moan.

Deirdre leaned toward her. "Got anyone special eagerly awaiting your arrival?" She followed up her question with an exaggerated wink.

Alyson kept her smile in place. "Yes. His name is Thatcher and he's the love of my life."

The woman laughed. "I love it! Where'd you two meet?"

Alyson picked up the last vase and placed it on the table. "At the breeder's home." She again tilted her head right, while fighting the urge to reach out and turn the vase a tad to the left.

"The breeder's house?" Deirdre asked. "He must breed dogs for a living?"

She frowned, and reached out and "fixed" the vase.

Her perfectionism wasn't normally this bad. But for some reason edginess had engulfed her, probably because Valentine's Day was one of their busiest days of the year *and* her least favorite "holiday." Outside of the fact it brought in significant revenue to her flower shop, especially if they had a wedding.

"Alyson?"

Yes. Deirdre had asked about the love her life.

"Thatcher is my Siberian Husky."

Deirdre's smile slipped. "Oh. So he's a *dog*."

Alyson grinned. "Actually, he's *family*."

She squinted at her. "Alyson Douglas, *you're* breathtaking. How is it you don't have a man in your life?"

Because I don't need a man in my life. But Alyson held onto a sigh and said, "Deirdre, I have everything I could possibly want and need. But thank you for the compliment." She straightened. "I hope everything goes smoothly tonight. And that the mother-of-the-bride stops crying long enough to enjoy herself."

Deirdre nodded and brought back her enthusiastic smile. "Thank you. And you drive carefully." She stepped backward. "I'll see you in a few weeks for the Antonello wedding."

As Deirdre scurried away, Alyson's eyes skimmed the room one final time.

Each vase she'd placed on a round table appeared perfectly centered. Each vase she'd placed on the head table appeared perfectly placed. Except that one vase still looked—she needed to leave. In under five minutes, she was in her coat and headed out of the mansion.

The dry, below freezing air surrounded her and she paused long enough to pull on her black beanie cap and thick, matching mittens.

She breathed the frigid air deep into her lungs while walking toward her burgundy 4Runner that also worked as their second delivery vehicle. Her head instantly cleared of all things wedding and Valentine's Day…and Deirdre's question that had been loaded with a little too much "what the *hell's* wrong with you."

It's not as if she didn't put herself out there. She'd even, at her best friend's insistence, tried app dating. Nothing terrible had happened, but nothing extraordinary had happened, either. After her last, pretty brief relationship that hadn't been courtesy of an app, she'd simply decided to focus on herself and business, since she *didn't* need a man.

When she reached her 4Runner, she stopped and gave the Boettcher Mansion a long look.

Inside, there happened to be a room that glowed with warmth, romance, and love. If the young couple was lucky, it would be a long-lasting love. The kind of love that involved the words *soul mates* and *epic*.

She turned from the mansion and climbed into her SUV.

The kind of love that only existed for the lucky ones on this planet.

Once she'd started the engine, she removed her cell phone from her coat pocket. While she waited for her vehicle to warm up, she could finally check in with the shop.

"Happy Valentine's Day from Daisy's Bouquets!" Hayley McCowan practically sang.

"It's me," Alyson replied. "How's it going?"

Silence, followed by, "Umm…well. Something's up. I'll give you to Jillian."

Alyson squeezed her eyes shut as Hayley put her on hold, and Frank Sinatra singing "My Funny Valentine" drifted through her phone.

Oh, *God*. What could have possibly happened? The plumbing? The shop was in an older building located in the heart of the Highlands neighborhood. Or, worse, had the delivery van been in an accident? Or break down? It was a Toyota mini-van over a decade old with well over a hundred-thousand miles. Wouldn't that be just perfect? The van breaking down *today*.

"Hey." Her best friend and business partner, Jillian Castillo, sounded a tad out of breath.

"Hi," Alyson answered slowly. "What's going on?"

Silence, followed by, "Where are you?"

"I'm about to leave the Boettcher Mansion."

More silence, then, "I'll wait to tell you. Call me when you get home."

Alyson released an exasperated sigh. "You can't be serious. It'll probably take me close to an hour to get home. Please tell me what the hell's going on." She paused, then asked, "Did the van break down?" *Oh, please, please, don't be the van.* She wasn't entirely certain where she'd find the money to get it fixed.

"No," Jillian replied. "The van's fine."

She expelled a quick breath. "Good. And I consider that worse-case scenario."

"Al, Cliff made his decision."

She gripped her phone.

"He sent a letter that he's selling our building and the one next door immediately."

Alyson rested her head against the headrest.

No. *This* was worst-case scenario due to the negative possibilities for the small business she and Jillian had been diligently building for the last few years.

"He and his family decided to move back to Portland, Maine, as soon as they can."

Damn, damn, *damn*. And this news was just another reason to dislike Valentine's Day.

⬚

DAVID FOCUSED ON HIS FINGERS, rapid and energetic against the piano keys while he played his vigorous notes. He brought his solo to an end, and when he stopped, their drummer launched into his solo. Quick, rhythmic drum beats filled the club. Many people were dancing and several audience members started to howl.

He grinned as he tapped his foot in time with his bandmate's drumming.

The band had never played at the Blues Note on a Friday night and Valentine's Day. The place was packed, too. He'd told his family members they should arrive no later than eight and was glad they'd listened. By 9:00, there'd been standing-room only.

The Blues Note, a spacious, dimly lit club located in Lower Downtown Denver—LoDo—featured live blues and jazz every night of the week but Monday. They usually played Thursday nights, but because of their popularity the manager had asked them to play tonight.

His bandmate's drum solo started to end.

David waited, then slid his left index finger across the keys.

The rest of the band rejoined the song.

His fingers matched the rising tempo and, with expert precision from every member, the song ended.

Thunderous applause filled the club as he stared at his long fingers still on the keys.

And it was *these* moments that reminded him he was exactly where he belonged.

He straightened, released a quick breath, and exchanged broad smiles with the guys.

When the applause subsided, their lead vocalist, Lea, stepped up to the mic.

"Thank you!" she said while several people continued clapping. "You've been a fantastic audience. Let me introduce you to these amazing guys." She launched into the introductions.

David's eyes landed on the table where his family sat, diagonal from his place on stage. They, too, were still applauding, and his smile grew.

"And on *piano*," Lea began, "Mr. David Preston."

He waved to the audience, then heard his future brother-in-law's finger whistle above the noisy applause, which made him laugh.

"I'm Lea Olson, and we're Sixteenth Note. We're here every Thursday night!"

Still trembling a bit from the adrenaline rush he always felt before, during, and after their gigs, David stood. He grudgingly walked away from where he belonged and met his bandmates at the center of the stage.

Randy Hyatt said, "*Shit*, we were on fire tonight."

David shared a quick laugh with everyone.

"I think that was one of our best shows yet." Randy had co-founded the band with David, and looked more like a retired, defensive lineman than a jazz singer and saxophonist. But the guy knew his jazz and blues music. "Terrific job everyone."

David exchanged a few hearty pats on the back and "*See ya next week*" with the guys, followed by a quick hug from Lea, before he and Randy were alone.

"So, who was that finger whistle?"

David laughed. "Matt. My sister's fiancé?"

Randy nodded, and they turned toward his family's table and waved at his Aunt Eileen. Her tan face lit up with a bright smile as she waved back.

Randy faced him once more. "A family date on Valentine's Day? Man, you really need a woman. Didn't Lea say she had a friend you might like?"

He managed not to cringe before saying, "Yes. And I told her thanks, but no thanks. But I appreciate you two cupids taking an interest in my personal life." *Or serious lack thereof.*

Randy chuckled. "Point taken."

"I should head their way." David stepped back. "I'll see you Wednesday at rehearsal."

The trembling started to fade while he walked stage left. But *yes.* Randy had been right. They were always damn good, but tonight had easily been one of their best shows yet.

He jogged down the stairs and turned right into the hallway.

On nights like these, and with a fantastic audience, it was hard to stop playing and walk away. Especially since his daytime Monday through Friday looked nothing like this.

He strolled past the restrooms and made a sharp right into the actual club.

His aunt and uncle sent him huge smiles the moment they spotted him, which he returned. When he reached their table, his aunt stood and gave him a long, tight hug.

"Hi, Honey. You guys were wonderful! As usual. We saved you a seat." She pointed to a chair that would place him at the head of the table, his aunt on his left, his sister on his right.

"Thanks," he replied. *If only* this *could be his daily reality.*

His Uncle Hugh slid a glass of ice water toward him. It was in that moment David sensed the somewhat subdued mood.

His eyes landed on his his aunt and uncle, who were people watching. Then went to Matt, who wiped the moisture off his beer glass while reclining in his chair, his long legs half-hidden beneath the table. And finally his sister, who was unusually quiet considering most of their conversations lately had revolved around what he called "the most important day of the twenty-first century." Also known as her wedding day, August ninth of this year.

"What's wrong?" he asked his sister before taking a long swallow of his water.

Nothing.

He looked at his aunt. "What the hell did I miss?"

She paused, then quietly said, "Another day of unsuccessful wedding dress shopping."

At that moment, his sister's subdued mood made absolute sense.

David put his glass down and turned right. "Becs, look at me."

It seemed like eons before she finally lifted her deep brown eyes that were like his.

"I don't care what it takes or costs to find you the perfect wedding dress."

She sighed. "Oh, I've found many perfect dresses. It's just none of them have fit this"—she slapped her wheelchair's tires—"horrible thing."

Her actions hit him right in the center of his heart and gut.

"Rebecca," their uncle said, reaching across the table to squeeze her hand, "your dress is out there. I promise. It just hasn't found you yet."

Her shoulders slumped. "According to my planning countdown calendar, I should've found and ordered it three months ago. Now I'll probably have to settle for…decent looking." She picked at her pink fingernail. "Maybe I'm being too picky."

Matt wrapped his arm around her shoulder. "I don't care what you wear that day as long as you show up."

She cracked a smile. "Matty, every groom says that to his bride-to-be."

"We still have all this weekend," their aunt offered. "We'll find something. And I really wish you wouldn't take that countdown calendar quite so seriously. It's just a guideline."

"But what happens if we don't find a dress before you guys go back to Florida?"

David leaned toward his sister. "Then I'll take you."

Becs stared at him, her mouth inching into her first smile since he arrived at the table. "That's really sweet. But who's going to help me in the dressing rooms?"

Matt chuckled. "She's got a point."

David lifted his shoulders. "Isn't that what your maid-of-honor or bridesmaids are for?"

"They have helped," she answered. "*Numerous* times. But I can't keep asking them to give up their Saturdays or Sundays. They have lives of their own. Next Saturday is my birthday and party, and *wow*. I can't believe my birthday is already here."

Neither could David. He also couldn't believe she'd be turning twenty-six *and* was getting married in what would be six, very short months.

Those thoughts made him feel every bit of his thirty-one years of age.

"Becs, we'll figure something out if you don't find a dress this weekend," he assured her. "The point is I don't want you to worry about it."

"Okay." She nodded. "You're right. I can't and won't give up."

A breath of relief escaped at his sister acting more like, well, his sister—positive and determined—and he reached for his glass. But then she leaned toward him.

"Today wasn't all bad, and I really need to talk to you. Now. Possibly in private?"

That had to mean she was about to give him expensive news. Wedding expensive. At the same time, what could be more expensive than his little sister getting married at the Brown Palace Hotel? Also known as one of the oldest and priciest hotels in downtown Denver.

"I'm almost positive I found the florist I want to use," she continued.

"Okay." He eyed their aunt, uncle, and Matt chatting together. "Why do we need to talk about that in private?" He grinned. "I would think you'd want to be surrounded by family when you tell me how much *that's* going to cost."

She remained focused on him while wearing a tentative smile.

He sighed. "Becs, give it to me straight. Pretend you're ripping off a band-aid." He'd discovered over the last six or so months that seemed to be the best way to approach and deal with wedding news, expensive or not.

She leaned even closer and waved him forward, which he cautiously did.

Shit. How expensive could flowers be?

"I found *her*. Today. While looking for a florist."

He paused for a breath, then slowly straightened.

The chattering around them faded into a hazy fog as he pictured *her*, who could only be one person. A person he'd tried not to think about, and unsuccessfully, the last several years.

"David?"

He cleared his throat. "How can you be sure it's *her?* Her name isn't that unique." One reason she'd liked the nickname Al over Aly. But no way in hell could it be *her*. Plus, during moments of weakness, he'd tried to find her via social media over the years only to be led to women who weren't the one and only Al.

"There wasn't a pic, but the flower shop is in the *Highlands*," his sister countered.

Air left his lungs as he sat back.

Okay. Maybe it could be *her*.

"Why aren't you asking me questions?" Becs demanded. "Don't you want to know the name of the shop? And where it is in the Highlands? To see if it really is her?"

Oh, yeah. But with that came the desire, and for the first time in a while, for a *real* drink. To eradicate the nasty taste of guilt that wouldn't go away, no matter how hard he tried to forget.

MANAGING the financial side of Daisy's Bouquets was the toughest part of Alyson's job. But given her business degree and the fact the business had been her idea, she felt this tedious responsibility belonged to her.

Yes, the shop was definitely making a comfortable profit each month, but comfortable did *not* equal having enough left over to pay a higher rental fee if the new owners raised the amount. That was a reality they had to be prepared for, too.

She leaned back, gathered her long, thick hair, twisted it into a loose ponytail, and stretched her neck right, then left.

The business bottom line was they needed to be averaging two weddings per weekend, which ultimately meant more business exposure. *Big* weddings would be ideal, too.

The savvier website with everyone's name and pics of their work that she and Jillian implemented in the fall had helped, as had their Facebook page with customers' comments and glowing reviews. Still, most of their wedding business was only a result of referrals and partnering with a couple of wedding planners, like Deirdre, who specialized in coordinating smaller, intimate weddings. As happy as all of that made her, it wasn't keeping them busy enough. They needed something *big* to happen. Something along the lines of partnering with Felicity Mayhew big. As Denver's most sought after wedding planner, being one of her go-to florists—or *the* go-to florist—would cinch Daisy's Bouquets' future.

Alyson minimized the accounting program.

She just needed to find a way into the dream wedding world that Felicity Mayhew consistently created for her couples who had parents with extremely deep pockets.

"Get away from that computer and help me take down the Valentine's Day decorations. You've been at that way too long." Jillian stood in the backroom's doorway as she piled her shoulder-length dark hair into a messy knot on her head. "*Estás obsesionado.*"

Yes. She was obsessing. Still, she said, "The good news is that we're making money."

"And I love good news." Jillian leaned against the frame as Alyson stood. "Al, we're assuming the worst when we don't even know what's going to happen once the building is sold."

She met Jillian at the doorway and grudgingly nodded. Though, she preferred to think of her actions as a business owner being prepared for the worst-case scenario.

"Spring begins in a little over a month, followed by Easter," Jillian stated. "I decided to design a spring-inspired window, then all we'd have to do in a month or so is add Easter decorations here and there."

Alyson tried to focus on transitioning the shop into springtime. But the busy work failed to capture her full attention as her obsessive brain kept sifting through the what-ifs.

What if the new owners raised the rent to a market-competitive rate? Cliff, an absolute sweetheart and near-perfect landlord, had been charging them less than the market rate for this oh-so valuable spot on 32nd, near Zuni. He hadn't needed the money and been supportive of them as an emerging, local small-business when they opened a few years earlier. And what if, when the time came, they couldn't afford the new rate? There was no way they'd find another spot like this for what they were paying unless they relocated to well outside the Denver metro area. That wasn't an option, since their lives—including the shop—were based in Denver.

She stared blankly at the pink stuffed bear she held, holding a sign stating "Smooch Me."

Where would the business go? What would they do?

At that moment, Hayley burst into the shop, loudly weeping.

All thoughts of business left Alyson's mind as she dropped the bear and rushed to their young employee's side. "What on earth happened to you?" She wrapped her arm around the girl's shoulders, steering her toward the counter and tissue box.

"He's...he's *cheating* on me," she wailed as tears slid from her big blue eyes.

Jillian met them at the counter and reached for the tissues.

"I don't understand," Alyson said. "I thought you and your boyfriend had a romantic night planned on Valentine's Day."

Jillian handed Hayley the box, and she ripped a tissue free.

"He...t-took me to dinner right near the Buell." She wiped her nose with a loud sniff. "Then surprised me...with tickets to *The Lion King*. Awesome seats, too. I should have...known something was up with him. He's n-never been that romantic. I'm soooo *stupid*!"

She brushed several blonde locks off Hayley's soaked, red face. "It sounds like he did something out of the ordinary. And isn't that what Valentine's Day is all about?"

"Th-that's what I thought on Friday...until I saw him just now. On campus. He was walking across the quad." She lifted her head, and Alyson's heart reached out to the girl's anguish. "He had his arm wrapped around some *girl* with black and lavender hair."

The shop's little door bells tinkled.

Alyson looked at the door as a tall, somewhat dark, and striking man entered. He stopped just inside the shop when he saw their huddle.

Her eyes locked with the man's brown eyes, and she withdrew from Hayley and Jillian.

His eyes were ones she had spent innumerable hours gazing into what felt like ten lifetimes ago, and her breathing slowed almost to a stop as he took a tentative step forward.

The corner of his mouth—that she'd spent hours upon hours kissing and fantasizing about ten lifetimes ago—inched into a nervous, awkward smile.

"David," she said, barely above a whisper.

He hesitated, then said, "Hi, Alyson."

Chapter Two

A TAUT SILENCE settled inside the shop as David started to tremble.

He tore his eyes from Al's, and caught the two other women's gazes swinging from her, to him, to her, and back to him. The brunette's eyes even widened as her mouth inched open. Which had to mean Al must have told her all about the asshole back in college who'd chosen darkness over her *and* them, breaking her in half. He knew he'd done that, too, since he'd seen it in her eyes before she'd left him that night.

"I'm sorry," he said now. His gaze flickered from her, to the brunette, and lingered on the blonde girl obviously having a shit day. "I can come back later if this is a bad time."

Al remained silent, and as she continued to stare at him with wide eyes he realized she was no longer a girl. Alyson Douglas was now a woman who had, incredibly enough, become more stunning since the last time he'd seen her ten years ago.

She'd kept her auburn hair long and stayed in shape, based on how well her tight jeans fit. He couldn't help but wonder if she still ran every morning. She'd been a dedicated cross-country runner in high school and her first two years at CU. And her hazel eyes, still round with dismay, were favoring green.

What sounded like a back door slammed shut.

Al blinked, breaking eye contact with him.

A woman with dark-blonde hair marched into the shop and tossed a set of keys onto the counter. "There are crazy people all over this damn city. And this is the first day since I moved here that I really miss Durango." She made a sour face. "This *asswipe* cuts me off, then flips me off like I'm the bad driver. Then, we get stuck at the same light and he jumps out of his car, faces me, and starts yelling." She crossed her arms. "I know I'm the one who keeps volunteering, but I'm done doing deliveries today and for a while because I might end up committing a felony."

The woman's blue eyes registered him and she swiftly turned bright red.

"Oh," she murmured, looking at Alyson, followed by the other two. "I'm so sorry." She glanced back at him. "I don't normally talk like that. Especially in front of our customers."

He grinned. "Driving in this city can bring out the worst in a grandmother with her grandkids. I've seen it firsthand." He winked. "*That* was an interesting day."

She laughed, which he took as a good sign since Al still hadn't said a word.

The brunette stepped forward, extending her right hand. "I'm Jillian Castillo."

He grasped her hand. "David Preston."

"Campbell Grey is the one who won't be making our deliveries for a while. And this," Jillian continued, angling her head toward the distraught blonde girl, "is Hayley McCowan who should probably be excused today."

The girl gave him a half smile while swiping her nose with a tissue.

"And you know Alyson, of course."

Their eyes locked again, but his grin slipped. "Yeah, we're—we went to CU together." He managed not to cringe at his pathetic correction.

He'd spent at least ten minutes inside his SUV before finding the courage to get out and walk to the shop. But he'd almost turned back twice at not knowing what he'd be walking into. He'd expected her surprise. After that wore off, he'd half expected her to walk up to him, kick him in a place that would make him see the planets and stars, then tell him to get the hell out and never come back. So he didn't know what to make of her ongoing silence.

The other women's pointed stares made Al blink a few times, then she shook her head and cleared her throat.

He silently released a breath he hadn't known was waiting for release.

"Hayley," Al said, "Jillian's right. We'll see you on Wednesday."

"Thanks." Hugging the tissue box, she flew past David and out the door.

The shop's bells continued to jingle as the door slowly closed.

"What happened to Hayley?" Campbell asked.

"I'll tell you about it while we're gone," Jillian answered. "There are two bouquets that need to be delivered and then we'll grab an early lunch." She passed by Al and gave her left hand a quick squeeze. She then grabbed the same set of keys. "Can we bring you anything?"

"Um…" Al focused on Jillian. "No, thanks. I'm not hungry."

Seconds later, the back door slammed shut, leaving him alone with Al.

For the first time since he'd kicked her out of his bedroom. His apartment. His life.

Another heavy silence settled around them; the seconds ticked by at a painful pace.

Not knowing what else to do with his trembling hands, he slid them into his pockets. A handful of seconds later, he quietly asked, "Is the girl who looked like her world just ended going to be okay?"

She stared at him. "I believe so," she replied as quietly. "But I think a girl power movie and pint of ice cream will certainly help."

Point taken. *Yet another guy has brought a woman—girl—to tears for being a dick.*

He stepped forward, unable to fight the same inexplicable pull toward her he'd felt as a nineteen-year-old kid the day they'd met in that huge classroom. "You look amazing, Alyson. Really. And this" —he removed his hands from his pockets to gesture at her shop—"is great. Your own business? You did exactly what you always wanted to do."

"Thank you," she murmured.

"Did you choose the Highlands to be close to your grandparents?"

"Yes and no."

He frowned. "Are they still in that house nearby? Or…did something happen to them?"

She leaned against the counter. "My grandpa passed away from a stroke several years ago. My grandma didn't want to live in their house by herself, so she gave it to me and moved to Evergreen to live with my parents."

He leaned forward. "Al, I'm so sorry." *For more than you can possibly imagine.*

"Thanks." She lifted her shoulders. "But the move was exactly what she needed. She loves the quiet and watching all the wildlife."

Another round of silence surrounded them.

Burning questions circled his mind.

What else have you been doing the last ten years? Are you married? With kids? And happy? Other things she'd always wanted. Things they'd talked about having together once college was behind them. If she had married, she'd kept her last name. Something that wasn't at all unusual nowadays. Before he could stop himself, he glanced at her left hand. But due to the angle, he couldn't tell if she wore a ring.

"How's Becca?"

He lifted his eyes back to hers, now wide with genuine interest.

Of course her first question for him would be about Becs.

He brought back his grin. "She doing great. She's getting —*finishing* her doctorate in psychology at CU." The plan had been if he'd gotten this far with Al, not to give away anymore than he had to right at this moment.

She smiled softly. "That's wonderful. And she's happy?"

His eyes penetrated hers. "Extremely."

She released a quick breath. "This may sound silly, but will you please tell her I said hello. And that I've never stopped thinking about her."

The guilt, always hanging around the edges of his conscience, barreled through him and landed right in his gut. His vision blurred and he looked at the floor.

With her standing three feet away their memories, from the extraordinary to the excruciating, inundated his mind, all of it inter-twined with guilt.

For the second time in a while he wanted a *real* drink.

"David, how did you know I was here?"

He swallowed, quietly inhaled, and lifted his head. "It's actually the reason I'm here. I probably should've called first, but, to be honest, I wasn't sure if you'd be willing to see me."

She slowly nodded. "Then you must have found me—us—because you need flowers?"

"It's one reason I'm here, but yeah. Do you have a few minutes?"

She straightened. "Of course. We can talk in the backroom."

He followed her, and when they reached a work table, she pointed at one of two stools.

"Please. Have a seat."

Smiling, he sat and looked around at the many types of flowers in large, white buckets, in vases, ready to go somewhere, or lying next to a utility sink. "So this is what the backroom of a flower shop looks like." His eyes met hers once more. "It's impressive."

She moved the other stool at least a foot away from him before taking a seat.

He didn't know whether to laugh or cringe. But she *wasn't* wearing a ring. At the same time, that also didn't mean a damn thing.

"I appreciate hearing that," she said. "We love it here." Darkness flashed through her eyes as she leaned toward an immaculate desk to grab a legal pad and pencil.

The darkness vanished as quickly as it had appeared, so he asked, "How's your family?"

She smiled. "They're great. My dad's been able to slow down a bit in his electrician business since he has some really good employees working for him now. And my mom still works full time, but now she's a nurse practitioner, working in a women's health group."

Silence fell once more.

She eyed him while he racked his muddled mind for the right—

"So are you here because you need flowers for your…wife?"

He coughed on a nervous laugh. "I suppose that's a logical question, but no. I'm not married." He frowned. "And I would never do something like that to you—" He coughed twice into his fist. "I was married, though. But no kids."

Her hands dropped to her lap as her mouth drifted open.

"It only lasted a year. We didn't work that way. " He paused, then added, "And you and I know I'm far from perfect."

She continued to stare at him.

Despite the awkwardness her question had caused, she'd given him the perfect opening to ask, "What about you?"

She blinked a few times. "Oh, I'm not married. I never have been, either."

Relief rushed through him. And, yeah, it made him a total ass.

"But I have a boyfriend," she swiftly added. "We've been together several months."

Of course she did. No one but him deserved that reality check, too.

David smiled tightly. "I'm happy for you." He needed to get to the point behind his real reason for walking in here today. "I'm throwing a party at my house Saturday and thought having a lot of flowers would go over well. Are you available on such short notice?"

Please let this part go the way it had to. He couldn't walk out of here with nothing.

"It won't be a problem. Does your…girlfriend?...have a favorite flower?"

"*Yes*. Thank you."

She angled her head back.

He froze. *Shit*. He'd officially crossed into that special realm where asshole met jackass.

Al gave him a hesitant smile. "What's her favorite flower?"

He tried on what he hoped was his most charming smile. "No girlfriend. So that means you'll take the job?"

She narrowed her eyes. "Yes, but who's the party for?"

"Someone very important. I was told she really likes yellow roses, too. But I'd like to make it a little more interesting." Maybe if he kept the conversation going at this pace, Al would stop looking at him as if he'd morphed into an actual jackass.

"Then I would suggest a couple vases of yellow roses since they are her favorite, some sunflowers, and maybe some oriental lilies and gardenias that are also quite fragrant."

His smile deepened. "Sounds perfect."

She wrote down the names of the flowers. "How many bouquets were you thinking?"

"I don't know. What's your professional opinion?"

She glanced at him. "Where's the party being held?"

"The living room, but it's an open floor plan, so there's a lot of space to work with. And I'd like at least one vase in the foyer and the dining room."

"How does eight vases sound?"

"Make it ten." He stood. "The yellow roses can go in the other rooms."

"Good." She finished writing, and dropped the pad and pencil on the work table. "We'll work on the quote. Can we send it to you this afternoon?"

"No quote necessary. Just e-mail me the bill." He reached into his back pocket, retrieved his wallet, and withdrew his business card from the first crevice. "That has all my contact information, including my cell number."

She took the card.

"The party starts at five. When you send the bill, I'll e-mail you my address."

She nodded. "We'll only need an hour or so to deliver and set up."

"Then I'll see you at four on Saturday." He walked toward the doorway, but stopped after a couple steps when something occurred to him. "Could you add a few balloons, too?"

She lifted her eyes from his business card. "Yes. Yellow would look nice with the flowers. We also have a mylar, sunflower balloon I can throw in. Or is this a birthday party?"

He grinned. "What you suggested will work. And thank you. I appreciate you doing this." *More than you can possibly imagine.*

"Wait a minute!" she called before he reached the doorway.

He faced her.

"You're an architect?"

His grin faded as he slipped his hands back into his pockets. "It's a living."

"But what about your music?" she persisted.

He hesitated before saying, "I had to make some big changes after everything that happened." He huffed. "I can guarantee you graduated way before I did. But I still play. All the time." He gave her a half smile. "I have a jazz band. We've been together a while and have a great time. We even made a CD last year since we have a pretty loyal fan base."

She released a quick laugh. "David, that's amazing."

"Thanks." He inched his way closer to the doorway. "Have a good week. And Alyson?"

Their eyes snapped together.

"I'm really glad I came here today." He walked swiftly to the door and the jingling bells followed him from the shop.

Once he was almost to Zuni Street, he stopped his hurried pace long enough to breathe the brisk, February Colorado air deep into his lungs.

Outside of crossing into the realm of asshole-jackass for a brief moment, their meeting had gone better than expected. It gave him hope that Saturday—his phone began to vibrate.

He reached into his inside coat pocket. "This is David."

"Where are you? Vivienne Dunne has called *three* times already."

He continued walking to where he'd parked. "Good morning to you, too, Marjorie."

"She's driving me *crazy*."

"Welcome to my world," he muttered. "I'm on my way." He hung up before Marjorie, the firm's office manager who also answered the phones, could utter another complaint.

He sighed. Back to a reality he'd never envisioned until life had ripped his world out from underneath him and left behind the destroyed remains it had taken him years to rebuild.

RAPIDLY SNAPPING fingers appeared in front of her face.

Alyson jumped, and looked over and up to find Jillian standing at the desk.

"Where were *you* just now?"

University of Colorado Boulder, day one of the spring semester, in a massive classroom, where a super hot sophomore and music major sat beside her. Making the rest, as the saying goes, history. And somewhere she absolutely didn't belong.

"I was..." She focused on the laptop monitor, her memory returning to the present. "Doing some research." She spun the chair right. "Where's Campbell?"

Jillian settled herself onto the stool David recently occupied. "She's hard at work on the window display." Her friend stared at her. "You were thinking about *him* just now."

She sighed. There was no point denying her best friend's perceptiveness. "Guilty."

Had he *really* been here? Sitting a foot away from her at their work table?

Despite his moments of nervousness, especially while sharing the fact he'd been briefly married—a biting detail that hurt more than it should—he'd been David. The calm, affable, too-charming-for-his-own-good David Thomas Preston she'd met and fallen for almost immediately those many, many years ago in a lower division English class.

Since he appeared so physically and mentally healthy, so David, she'd wanted to ask him, *"How could you have waited this long?"* But she'd somehow managed to swallow the words.

He'd also looked incredibly good, too, in his khaki pants, emerald-green polo shirt, and black leather jacket. If anything, he'd gotten better looking the last ten years. More importantly, he no longer resembled the David from the last time she'd seen him. The visibly hurting boy who blindly turned to the wrong thing mere days after his world crumbled, his desperate attempt to numb the pain. But it had done nothing but make him angrier.

"Was there a particular reason he walked in here from out of nowhere, outside of the obvious wanting to see you?"

Jillian's question broke through her second, more painful visit to the past.

"He hired us to provide flowers for a party he's having on Saturday."

"And that's how he found you and the shop?"

Alyson nodded and shrugged.

"Well, I guess thank God for Google." Jillian's forehead formed a deep V. "Who's the party for? He wasn't wearing a ring—and, yes, I was curious and looked—so it can't be for a wife. He could be engaged, I suppose, since he's not exactly hard to look at."

Not even a little bit, which wasn't at all fair.

Alyson leaned back. "He's single. But…he did tell me he was divorced."

Jillian crossed her arms. "How long ago did that happen?"

She moaned. "I don't know, Jilly. I didn't ask. But he admitted his marriage was extremely brief." Saying the words "his marriage" tasted decidedly sour.

"How brief?"

It only lasted a year.

"He wasn't specific." She didn't want to hear Jillian's theories on that still shocking tidbit.

"Al, I know we need this job because of all the unknowns right now, but do you think it was a good idea taking it?"

She eyed her friend. "I'll admit I hesitated. But there was no legitimate reason to say no." And curiosity could be a pretty powerful motivator. Jillian probably suspected that, too.

How could she not be curious, though?

She glanced at his business card that she'd set beside the computer.

LWP Architecture + Interiors ~ David Preston, Senior Architect.

He'd become an architect instead of a *full-time* musician. Understandable, considering the unfair ugliness he'd been given those many years ago. And what about his brief marriage? Though he'd offered the reason he and his ex "hadn't worked that way."

As lovesick college students, they'd talked about their future, and always and forever had been implied since they *had been* a couple of the lucky ones.

But heart-breaking tragedy had a way of changing people forever.

"Self-preservation comes to mind," Jillian continued, "since, after everything you told me, and considering the way both of you couldn't take your eyes off each other earlier, it feels like you two could still have a *pretty* strong connection."

Her best friend never missed a thing. Regardless of that fact, she said, "It was a long time ago." She swiveled her chair back toward the computer, suspecting Jillian didn't believe her any more than she believed herself. "We're not kids anymore." At that moment, she remembered the tiny white lie she'd told him. "He might also be under the impression I have a boyfriend."

Alyson peeked at Jillian, looking at her through narrowed eyes full of judgment.

"Don't look at me like that!" she snapped. "I was nervous, he'd just told me about being briefly married, asked me if I was married, and it came out." And, in the spirit of hell hath no fury, she'd wanted to really get his attention. It had worked, too, when she saw the light fade from his…deep, soulful brown eyes. *It was also safer this way.*

Jillian leaned forward. "He was in here for, what? Maybe thirty minutes? And you resorted to lying to him about your personal life. *Eso parece un poco loco*," she mumbled.

Alyson glared at her friend.

"Al, him showing up here obviously rattled you and your sanity, which means you and Campbell can take the Fraser-James wedding in the morning. Hayley and I will take the party."

She gritted her teeth and said, "It'll be fine. I promise." *It absolutely would be, too.* Like she'd said earlier, she—they—were no longer kids.

Jillian arched her right eyebrow, but thankfully remained silent.

She forced her unexpected reunion with David Thomas Preston to the back of her mind. "We need to talk about something way more important. Like my idea for bringing in more revenue as another way to prepare for the unknowns. Can we please focus on that?"

Jillian sighed, then nodded. "I'm listening."

Alyson lifted her chin. "Two words. Felicity. Mayhew."

Her friend frowned. "One word. How?"

She faced Jillian and folded her hands on her pristine desk. "I'm glad you asked that, because I have a plan. A *reconnaissance* plan."

Jillian's frown deepened. "I'm not sure I like the sound of that."

"While you were gone, I called Felicity Mayhew's office and pretended to be a bride, considering hiring her for my big, expensive mountain wedding."

Jillian groaned and shook her head. "You really have gone *loca*."

"She has a typical, fantasy wedding coming up next Saturday at the Ritz-Carlton."

"But you're really interested in the flowers and florist."

"Yes." Alyson caught her friend's eyes. "We have to see the competition in action and their work in order to conquer them."

Jillian squinted at her. "Who are you right now? Because you sound like a general preparing for a defeat that will include total annihilation."

Her shoulders slumped. "It's called survival of the fittest, Jilly. As business owners, we have to be prepared for all scenarios, especially right now. And Daisy's Bouquets is ready to be a part of the fairy tale wedding world of Felicity Mayhew." She paused before quietly adding, "You know we need to do this." The business belonged to them. It was their labor of love and livelihood. They had to protect it, themselves, and their two employees.

Jillian released a quick breath. "Okay. You're right. What are you thinking?"

"Thank you." Continuing to keep the long-lost David Preston far from her mind, and right where he belonged, Alyson leaned forward to launch into her reconnaissance plan.

Chapter Three

DAVID LEANED BACK and rubbed his eyes.

"I've been thinking about this," Vivienne Dunne said during her third damn call of the day, "and the master suite closet needs to be a room in itself. I'm not loving the idea of it being accessible through the bathroom. I'd like it to resemble a dressing room. Big enough to hold *all* my clothing, shoes, accessories, but also have a chaise and small table. What do you think?"

That you have too much shit. And you're damn lucky we've barely started construction on the second floor.

"Shouldn't be a problem," he answered.

"Wonderful! Thank you so much, David. You're an absolute *darling.*"

He heard something that sounded like an air kiss before the line went dead. He then slammed the receiver down and stared at the master suite designs filling his computer monitor that was the size of a small, flat-screen TV.

When he met with Vivienne—the widow of a prominent plastic surgeon who'd died in his sleep from sudden cardiac arrest—last fall during one of her prolonged stays in Denver, he'd suspected she might end up being his most difficult client yet.

She had not let him down. Or anyone else in the office.

Upon her husband's death, she and their only child, a daughter, had inherited everything that included a sprawling estate in Cherry Hills Village that she'd sold to pay for the construction of a new, sprawling estate in Aspen.

He'd been hesitant to take the project for reasons that included Vivienne's challenging personality and the distance. He'd never managed a project outside the metro area. Temporarily relocating to the famous mountain town, about three-and-a-half hours away, during construction also hadn't been an option because of his life here in Denver. And everything had been going well until she'd moved into the Hotel Jerome in downtown Aspen in order to "monitor progress."

He swiveled his chair slightly right and stared out his office window.

Like everyone in this building, she drove Bob the contractor *crazy*. His hardhat had to be close to blowing off his head.

David couldn't help but imagine early retirement that would look something like him with his piano, band, and music sheets.

A smile played with the corner of his mouth.

His second story view of 22nd and Blake in LoDo always provided an entertaining, people-watching break. Most of who he watched worked in the immediate area. But it also attracted the baseball crowd due to Coors Field, home of the Colorado Rockies, so game days were particularly fun with their building being crawling distance to the field. At the same time, his slight view of Coors Field reminded him daily of a much happier time in his life that had involved *her* and a completely different *him* he couldn't believe had ever existed.

Someone knocked on his office door a second before it flew open.

Jackson, his closest friend and business partner, walked inside. "Zach and I are heading to play some basketball. You game?"

Considering the surreal way his workweek started yesterday

morning in the Highlands, a physical release like a hard game of basketball sounded great. But he said, "Not tonight." He did, however, have another long, therapeutic date planned with his piano. "What's up with you, though? You never leave this early on a Tuesday."

"I'm coming back later." He strolled toward his desk. "Marjorie, then Penny when she got here, were on my ass all day with one thing after another. I barely got any of my shit done."

Starting the firm had been Jackson's idea. As such, he owned a bigger piece of it than David and their other partner, Zach. With that came designing and managing the *big* projects, and managing the operations, meaning the money and their small staff of five that included an intern.

"And no matter what you and my family think, I'm not a robot who does nothing but work." He sat in a chair across from David. "I did decide at the last minute to go skiing with Laura and Josh last weekend. But Winter Park was packed. Way too many couples."

David grinned. "Meaning you didn't get lucky."

"Not one come and get me smile at the bar Saturday night. But the skiing was great."

He started to close all the programs he had opened.

Jackson sighed. "It's been weeks since Tami and I split, and I'm starting to feel the *pain*."

Because all he and Tami had done for five weeks was hook up, since his good buddy's first priority was this firm. But he said, "She wasn't your type." *Outside of the hook-up factor.*

"I'm not sure I have a type, but"—he shook his head—"how's Rebecs doing?"

"She's still upset she didn't find *her* wedding dress last weekend —" He stopped as his eyes locked on a picture of Homer Simpson choking Bart, and he laughed.

Laura, of Josh and Laura, must have changed his desktop picture when he was in a meeting earlier. Being the firm's lead interior designer also working with Vivienne, she'd started changing his desktop pictures to what fit their moods after conversations with their client.

This picture was the best one yet, considering Vivienne's *three* damn phone calls today.

"What's so funny?"

"Nothing." He shut down his computer. "Becs hasn't found her dress yet, and Hugh and Eileen have to work this week. Saturday's the party, then they're headed back to Florida on Sunday." He frowned. "Becs has been on the verge of a meltdown since Sunday night. I think the only thing keeping her sane is focusing on her dissertation. I told her I'd help her out, but we'd need a woman to go with us. And she now feels like she's bothering her friends."

Jackson became silent.

David stood and reached for his jacket hanging on the back of his chair.

"What about my mom helping out? She does call you two her 'other kids'."

He faced his friend who had, over their years of friendship, become more of a brother. They'd become instant buddies following Jackson's family's move to his Longmont neighborhood the summer before their sixth-grade year.

"That's not a bad idea." David shrugged into his jacket. "They'll be at the party, right?"

"No, they'll be up at the cabin with Will and his family. And Savannah's parents who will be up from Santa Fe."

He nodded. "Okay. I should talk to Becs first anyway. But I don't see why she'd say no to your mom's help. She really needs…" His mother's warm, smiling face appeared in his mind.

"I know she'd love to help," Jackson quietly replied. "She did get stuck with two sons."

David straightened. "Thanks for the idea. I'll see you tomorrow." He started to walk by Jackson when he heard, "Is there anything else going on with you?" His steps faltered as *her* perfect face flashed through his mind. But he faced him and asked, "What do you mean?"

"You've seemed a little distracted the last couple days."

He wanted to tell his closest friend about his impromptu meeting yesterday with Al so badly he could taste the words. But he didn't feel prepared for what Jackson's reaction might be to the news. He also wanted to keep their meeting private for as long as possible.

He brought back his grin. "I'm fine. Just a lot going on. And Vivienne isn't helping."

Jackson followed him from his office. "Laura told me Queen Dunne was in top form today. David, if you need help with anything I don't mind—"

"I know. And you have helped with your suggestion." He then headed down the stairs.

The second he was inside his SUV, he took a deep breath and expelled the air.

Shit. As hard as he'd tried not to think about yesterday morning and *her*, she really had looked as incredible as he remembered, but wary and unavailable for many reasons.

He started the engine and backed out of the parking spot.

When he recalled the last time he'd seen Al, he still couldn't believe she hadn't thrown *him* out of the shop. Although it had been ten years ago, profound heartache, as well as anger, had a way of permanently gripping a person to the point one couldn't breathe. Something he understood very well. That night in his bedroom he'd witnessed Al's heartache when he'd told her to get out and never come back. Anger with him must have followed soon after.

He braked at a stoplight, then shut his eyes, remembering her dismay when he'd confessed, as a result of her marriage question and his nervousness, he'd been married. That led to her disclosure she had a boyfriend. Which made him hit the accelerator a little too hard.

At the same time, he'd half expected her to be married with kids, so he wasn't sure why her disclosure was making him edgy. Taking it out on his piano edgy since he couldn't punch something. Or have a *real* drink.

The harsh reality was that he'd blown it. Pure and simple. That meant he had to say everything he needed to on Saturday before she left. Say what he probably should have yesterday, especially after her earnest comment about his sister never leaving her thoughts, even after all these years. But that hadn't been his plan when he'd walked into the shop.

For the umpteenth time, he thanked the universe that Al and her shop were available this Saturday *and* that she'd agreed to take the job. He'd already talked privately with Matt about showing up with Becs at least thirty minutes early. Between the big surprise and Al's pretty amiable actions, Saturday had to go *exactly* the way he imagined. For everyone. He also knew once he said what he needed to— what he long since owed her—he would have to walk away. All he could possibly hope for on Saturday was that she'd leave with more understanding and, if he was lucky, leave some forgiveness behind. But picturing that conversation with her caused him to tremble, and that reminded him of his numerous, pitch black days.

Yeah. He definitely needed quality time with his piano.

His fingers started to twitch the closer he got to his house. Then he felt his phone vibrate before bursting into the piano riff.

Keeping his right hand on the wheel, his eyes focused on the road, he used his left hand to reach into his coat pocket to retrieve his phone. "Hey." He accelerated through a yellow light.

"Are you sitting down?" his bandmate, Randy, asked.

"I'm driving."

"Perfect. I have unbelievably good news."

"I could use some of that right now. What's up?"

"Just as a heads up the news…well, it involves Sara."

Sara being Sara Channing, also known as his ex-wife and their former lead singer.

"How is she?" he asked, his curiosity sincere since he had cared for her.

"Really good. She's rarely in the city anymore, touring with that blues band she joined after…well, you know where she went."

Sara's eye-catching looks—tall, slender, dark eyes, and wavy hair that fell past her shoulders—wasn't all that ignited his attention after meeting her for the first time. Her sultry singing had fueled a small flame deep within him and, over time, replaced some emptiness.

"Her band has played at the local jazz fests, including Evergreen," Randy continued. "I guess they're in pretty good with these organizers."

But it had been Sara Channing the singer he'd loved.

"Evergreen, David."

Thinking about their doomed, whirlwind relationship only reminded him of that, as well as being an ass to his family and friends who had pleaded with him to slow down.

He sighed. "Randy, I'm not following you. Just spit it out."

"The festival. We. Are. In."

His mouth fell open.

The Evergreen Jazz Festival was in late July. And it was a *big* deal. Three days of nothing but jazz and blues in Evergreen, about thirty minutes west of Denver. Playing the local jazz festivals was something they'd always talked about as a group, but never had time to pursue. Everyone worked full-time day jobs, and all his bandmates, with the exception of Lea, were married with kids. Two of the guys even had young grandkids.

"How? I mean—" He shook his head. "What the hell did you do?"

"Kept in touch with your ex."

"Okay, then what the hell did she do?"

"Put in a good word when her band had to drop. I also had to send them our CD."

David joined Randy's laughter.

The Evergreen Jazz Festival. A festival he'd attended countless times while always imagining the *how-cool-would-it-be-if* factor.

"Holy shit," he murmured. "I can't believe Sara did that. That was really decent."

"Why wouldn't she? It's not like you two parted ways as bitter enemies. I also did something a little crazy. But I'm only telling you this since I don't want anyone to get their hopes up, because I'm sure our chances are pretty damn slim."

"Alright," he slowly replied.

"On a whim, I submitted an artist's kit to Jazz Aspen Snowmass several weeks ago."

He blinked a few times, uncertain he'd heard Randy correctly. "Are you shitting me?" Because the Jazz Aspen Snowmass Labor Day Experience was world-renowned and featured recognizable, first-class musicians. That prompted him to say, "You've lost your mind." Their band was damn good and perfect for Evergreen. But Jazz Aspen Snowmass was the Big Time.

"It's a long shot. But I figured we had nothing to lose. It also gets our name out there. Anyhow, I don't care what's going on with your job in July."

Randy was making it clear he still hadn't gotten over the fact David had traveled to Aspen a month ago to put out the flame between Vivienne and Bob before it turned into a raging wildfire. Trips like that interfered with their gigs, but hopefully that trip would be the only one. "Randy, I can promise you nothing will keep me from that festival." He pulled into his driveway, then waited for his garage to open. "I don't care who I have as a client then. And the project in Aspen that's *still* pissing you off should be done before late July." *If she stopped changing her mind every damn day.*

"I'm holding you to that. I need to call everyone else, but I'll see you tomorrow night."

David smiled as he ended Randy's call.

Feeling…buoyant…for the first time since yesterday morning, he sat at his piano and launched into Scott Joplin's "The Entertainer."

Chapter Four

JILLIAN STEERED their delivery van into the long, narrow driveway.

She turned off the engine, and they stayed seated, staring at David's classic, two-story beige-brick home in upscale Cherry Creek. His house also happened to be mere minutes from the Cherry Creek Mall, one of their favorite places to go for retail therapy.

"Didn't you tell me he was a musician?" Jillian asked.

"He was—is," Alyson corrected. "But I think it's just for fun now. He switched to architecture at some point after we broke up." He'd obviously achieved great success in a career he'd never considered pursuing. Architecture had been his best friend's passion.

"*Santo cielo*," Jillian murmured. "We chose the wrong careers."

Alyson opened the passenger-side door at the same time David walked out of his house.

He waved at her, which she half-heartedly returned.

In his jeans and bright white, untucked button-down shirt with the sleeves rolled to his elbows, David Preston looked, as usual, incredibly good. *It wasn't fair.*

She tore her eyes from him and met Jillian at the van's sliding door.

"You know," her friend said, grabbing a vase of oriental lilies, "if it weren't for the fact he still seems hung up on you, I might just—"

"Jillian, stop it," she hissed while grasping a vase of sunflowers. "He's not interested in me like that anymore. This is just business."

"You can't really believe that."

A part of her didn't really believe that. "He thinks I have a boyfriend and you better not tell him the truth." *It was safer this way.*

Jillian shook her head. "Truthfully, I think you need therapy for lying to a successful, *ridiculously* good-looking guy who's clearly still into you."

Alyson faced forward. She gradually approached him while taking slow, deep breaths of the cool, late-afternoon air to settle her racing heart.

She'd *never* admit this to Jillian, but memories belonging to their beginning, specifically their first date, had popped into her head throughout the busy workweek, no matter how hard she'd tried to vanquish them.

Dinner at a popular, college hangout on The Hill, followed by a long walk back to and around the CU campus that had been filled with endless, getting-to-know-you chatter. Their connection and attraction that night had been so electric, she'd longed for a kiss goodnight as they laughed and chatted their way through a lengthy goodbye outside her dorm.

"Hi," he said, finding her eyes above the flowers. "Can I help you two?"

But David the gentleman hadn't made a move until the end of their *third* date.

"No," she answered, crushing that thought train yet again. "We've got it. But thank you."

The fact she'd been mostly unsuccessful at shutting off the memories all week made her wonder if Jillian had been right about taking this job.

"Where would you like these?" She needed to focus.

"In the living room, just to your right."

She stepped into the foyer, her eyes locking on the staircase that gently curved up to the second floor. As her eyes registered the main level's massive, open space, her steps faltered on the dark wood floor.

"Al?" Jillian said from behind her. "First one foot, then the next."

"Sorry," she said, taking two steps right, which placed her in the living area.

David passed them and pointed at the coffee table. "You can set both there."

She set her vase down, as did Jillian whose wide eyes told Alyson her friend was equally bewildered by their lush surroundings. But she shot David a quick, hello smile, then turned and sauntered back toward the front door.

His dark, sumptuous furniture went well with the floors and warm, beige paint.

She turned her head left to glance at his dining room; a room featuring nothing more than an area rug, two wilting ficus trees, and a formal dining table. Just beyond was the kitchen, fully modernized right down to what looked like slate tile flooring.

When she brought her gaze back to the living room, her eyes settled on his grand piano that filled the right, front corner of the room. And another memory appeared in her mind.

The very first time she'd heard him play.

"That looks beautiful in here," she said, forcing her mind off yet another memory.

"Thanks. It's one of my most prized possessions."

Jillian entered with a bouquet of yellow roses. "Where would you like these?"

"Wherever you can find spots. Are you sure I can't help you?"

"We're good." She placed the vase on an end table nestled between the couch and loveseat. "This is the easiest job we've had in a while."

Once Jillian left, Alyson met his gaze. "Do you mind if we move your pictures on the mantle? I think two bouquets would look really nice there."

"Sure."

He held his hands out, and she handed him each framed picture.

They were all family pictures, one of which was formal and that she remembered being taken while she and David were together. She couldn't help but hold onto the photo and grin.

He and Becca were formal, yet cute, in their dressy clothes. In front of them sat their striking parents. The siblings shared their dad's deep, soulful brown eyes—Preston eyes—and their mom's wide smile. Noticing Becca standing in the photo, however, caused her grin to fade.

"I always really liked this picture," she murmured, handing him the frame.

He remained silent, but she felt his eyes while she turned, picked up a vase, then faced the mantle once more.

"Your house is beautiful, David." She smiled as she placed the vase on the ledge while recalling the dingy apartment he and his best friend had shared in Boulder. "You've come a long way from that horrible apartment."

He released a long, deep laugh. His laughter was so genuine she stopped turning the vase into the perfect position to look at him.

She could remember with distinct clarity the last time she'd heard him laugh like that.

"God, Jackson and I were such pigs back then." He walked toward his piano bench. "I can't believe we lived like that." He placed the frames inside. "And the house didn't look anything like this when I bought it two summers ago. The foundation was damaged and had to be repaired. It also took weeks of general renovation."

She blinked herself back to the present. "Being an architect, it must have been a fun project for you."

He strolled back toward her. "Yeah, but most of the project was handled by the contractor I hired. I also worked closely with my colleague, Laura, on the interior design."

Jillian reappeared with the second vase of yellow roses. "Table in the foyer?"

Alyson nodded.

When they were again alone, he asked, "So what made you choose the flower business?" He paused before adding, "Because I know baking isn't one of your strengths."

Another memory filled her mind. The Christmas cookie catastrophe at her childhood home in Evergreen their first holiday together.

His shoulders shook with more genuine laughter. "There was so much smoke in the kitchen," he managed to say.

She fought a smile. "At least half that disaster was your fault since you distracted me."

Their eyes collided.

The smoke alarm had jolted them from their salacious make-out session. Soon after, her parents had walked into the house to find the patio door and several windows open, the smell of burnt sugar cookies and smoke permeating the first floor while they cleaned up the mess.

Their eyes stayed connected as he said, "Flowers are way less dangerous than baking."

Remembering his question, and ready for a subject change, she responded, "A beautiful bouquet of flowers brings most people joy and smells incredible. I have the best job."

He grinned.

She went back to turning the vase, stopped when it was perfect, then began to fix the flowers that had shifted during the drive. "And my grandma made the point that a sour economy won't stop people from getting married, celebrating birthdays, anniversaries, holidays, and there's always a need for sympathy bouquets."

"Wise words."

"Jilly and I met while working at a bank downtown," she continued. "I was in the finance department. She was in HR. So I had no problem convincing her to be my partner. She was also bored and ready for a huge change." She paused to glance at him, closely watching her. "We did a lot of research and worked part time with a florist about a year while we became certified."

"All while still working at the bank?"

She nodded.

His smiled turned warm and he pointed at the vase. "Is it perfect now?"

Heat consumed her face at his question, a little too affectionate for her comfort level.

She took a shaky step backward, suddenly uneasy with his closeness and him remembering her perfectionism. *Uneasy with him in general.* "I need to help Jillian." She headed for the door. "We'll be done soon."

The second she stepped outside she took a deep, head-clearing breath, then marched toward the van. Determination to get through the next several moments once again her focus.

Over the next twenty minutes, she and Jillian, being uncharacteristically quiet, swiftly converted David's living and dining rooms into a mini-flower shop.

She was tying one of the four balloons to a vase when he stopped at her right side. Up until this point, he'd been in his kitchen, unwrapping paper plates, napkins, and the plasticware.

"It looks great in here."

She shifted slightly to her left, staying focused on her tying.

"But I'm suddenly wondering what I'm going to do with all these flowers once the party is over. Any suggestions?"

She looked up from the tight knot she finally achieved and scanned the rooms. "Let guests take one home." She straightened and glanced at him. "Treat them like a party favor?"

"That's a great idea. I don't know why I didn't think of it. You've got a…" He reached out and captured something on her cheek.

His touch had been brief. Two seconds at best. Nonetheless, her eyes widened, and she used both hands to frantically wipe her cheeks.

He extended his right index finger that held a tiny, green bud. "This looks like an occupational hazard."

She returned to adjusting the flowers. "Please don't touch me like that."

"Like what?"

She faced him.

He unsuccessfully fought a smile that could only be defined as devilish.

"David, stop being *you*. And stop smiling at me like that."

He gave her an exaggerated frown.

She crossed her arms. "You're not cute."

He released a long exhale through his teeth. "What do you want me to do, Alyson? Because, to be honest, you're making me a little nervous."

She leaned forward. "*I'm* making *you* nervous?"

A loud, unmistakable clearing of the throat caused her to look right.

Jillian stood two feet away, holding the strings belonging to the other balloons. She arched her right eyebrow. "I hate to interrupt, but where would you like these?"

David smiled. "How about both in the dining room?"

Jillian strolled by them.

"Look," he quietly said when she reached the other room, "I think we both need to take a breath and relax. This isn't supposed to be painful."

"That's a really interesting word choice, David." The snarky response tumbled from her mouth before the words even registered in her brain. Words she regretted since every trace of lingering light-heartedness left his face. She pressed her lips together for a few seconds, then said, "I'm sorry. It's just…I am a little nervous. And feeling completely out of my comfort zone."

His eyes pierced hers for what felt like an interminable amount of time before he stepped backward. "Alyson, you of all people don't owe me any apologies."

Her heartbeat reached her throat as they continued to stare at one another; the space surrounding them blurring. But then a couple quick car honks outside his house made her jolt.

He pulled his eyes away first to look out the living room windows. "Would Jillian mind moving your van?"

She absently nodded. "I'll send her out there. We just have the balloons left and then we'll be finished."

"Take your time. I'll be right back." He headed for the front door.

She turned to walk into the dining room.

Jillian smirked. "You two are generating enough chemistry to incinerate this house."

She eyed her friend, unable to dispute her observation. "I think guests are starting to arrive. He needs us to move the van."

Jillian handed her the remaining balloon string, walked around the dining room table and, as she rapidly passed Alyson, mumbled, "*Conexión fuerte.*"

Alone for the first time since they'd arrived, Alyson took the quiet moment to collect her emotions. And settle her accelerated heart rate with yet another deep breath.

Dammit. How was it ten years later he could still have such an effect on her? She had a successful business, a home with a dog, family, and great friends. The near-perfect life. But here she stood in her long-ago boyfriend's amazing house, sharing prolonged, emotional stares with him. And after spending the week recalling choice highlights from their relationship.

She needed to get a grip. She also needed to attach this last balloon to a bouquet, then walk away without a backward glance, no matter the questions she had for him; the how and when he'd pulled himself from the darkness being the prominent one.

She leaned forward and tied the balloon to a vase of yellow roses.

David seemed happy. He'd stepped up to focus on a future that must have included making his sister a number-one priority. His house alone demonstrated that, based on the open floor plan and hardwood floors. For that she needed to commend him, then leave.

Self-preservation was now the priority since Jillian had been right just now and the other day.

They still had a strong connection.

Without him standing right beside her, she quickly secured the balloon. She adjusted the flowers once…twice…three—she needed to stop. She forced her eyes away from the flowers to glimpse their work. Everything looked perfect, which meant it was time to say goodbye.

"*Alyson?*"

The shrill voice caused her to jump. She whirled from the table and found herself staring down into eyes that were deep, soulful brown, and shining with shock and excitement.

"Rebecca." She stared at David's little sister.

Her thick hair was a shade lighter than her brother's and now just above her shoulders. She'd worn her hair long years ago as a pretty teenager. But now she was a striking, dainty young woman who appeared undaunted by the fact she was confined to a wheelchair.

Becca Preston scrunched up her shoulders and freed a loud squeal. "I *knew* it was you!" She leaned forward and threw her arms up.

Alyson laughed and bent down to give her the hug she wanted. Becca's skinny arms were surprisingly strong. Or not so surprising considering they received a constant workout. As their embrace tightened, her eyes met David's.

He lifted his shoulders and mouthed, "Surprise."

She smiled and gently pulled away from his sister. "You are absolutely beautiful." In truth, that adjective didn't come close to describing the young woman, especially when Alyson recalled the last time she'd seen her.

That being one of the many memories from back then she wished she could erase.

A tall, lanky man with short brown hair walked into the house with Jillian and headed straight for Becca.

"Oh! This is my fiancé, Matt Ridley."

Alyson returned Matt's smile, unable to ignore his blue, almost transparent eyes. Wow. Little Becca's—her eyes widened. "Did you say fiancé?"

Becca, like many other brides she'd known, held out her left hand to present her engagement ring; a round, carat-sized diamond in a simple setting on a thin, white-gold band.

It looked perfect on her slender finger.

She leaned forward to give the young woman a second, tight squeeze. When their embrace ended, she laughed. "I can't believe you're getting *married*." She paused before adding, "I'm suddenly feeling really old."

"That makes two of us," David said.

Becca gave her brother an affectionate smile. "This place looks beautiful, by the way." She inhaled. "It smells wonderful, too. Like springtime. And the balloons are perfect! Thank you." She released a quick laugh. "I just hope nobody's allergic to flowers."

"I didn't think of that," David replied. "Someone may have to make a Benadryl run."

Alyson glanced at David, then back at his sister. "Today's your birthday." She eyed him as she added, "I forgot your birthday was in February."

Becca giggled. "I'm the big two-six today. And my brother is a total sneak, because I *told* him it was you. When I was searching for florists for the wedding?"

Alyson frowned at Becca, then David.

That's how he'd ended up in her shop on Monday?

He lifted his shoulders, his expression now a little too angelic.

The "total sneak" had always been annoyingly good at keeping secrets.

"Oh. My. God," Becca continued. "Can you do the flowers for our wedding? Please, please, please? It's Saturday, August ninth, 5:00 at the Brown Palace Hotel."

The question caught her by surprise, especially when all eyes became fixed on her.

She couldn't visualize their August schedule right now for many reasons.

"I'm pretty sure we'll be able to handle that," Jillian said, sliding in next to Alyson. "I'm Jillian. Her co-pilot at Daisy's Bouquets."

Becca's smile deepened. "It's nice to meet you. So we're all set?"

Alyson's eyes met Jillian's, and her friend added, "We'll have to double-check our calendar, but between you, me, Campbell, and Hayley, I think we could handle it?"

Actually, they'd have to, since she couldn't say no to beautiful Rebecca Preston, who was getting *married*, and had stolen her heart with the speed her brother had those many years ago.

Keeping her eyes off of David, who seemed content watching this reunion he'd planned unfold before him, she said, "When can we talk about what you want?"

Becca squealed, and the doorbell chimed, followed by a series of loud knocks.

"That's probably the food." David stepped toward her, keeping an eye on the others. "I need to finish up some last-minute things before people start arriving, but..." He angled his head down. "Is there any way we could *really* talk. Before you leave?"

Her cheeks warmed from his penetrating stare, as well as the other eyes watching them.

"Leave?" This from Becca. "No, no, no, no. You and Jillian have to stay for the party."

The doorbell chimed again.

David released a frustrated sigh. "I have to go."

"I'll give you a hand," Matt said, following him to the front door.

"Please, *please* stay? Unless, of course, you have other plans tonight?"

David opened his door, and two people carrying trays of food entered.

She stared at Becca's pleading face, oh-so tempted to say yes to the young woman she'd thought about many times the last ten years. Of course, she was also extremely interested in what David wanted to talk about. Still, she said, "Becca, I'm not sure that's a good idea."

Her face fell. "Why? It's *my* birthday party and I want both of you to stay. I won't take no for an answer," she added, her voice going up an octave.

Alyson hesitated for a second, then blurted out, "Okay." At the same time, Jillian said, "We'd love to stay. Where's the nearest bathroom?"

Becca clapped. "To your right. Just past the stairs that go down to the family room."

When they reached the bathroom, Jillian leaned toward her. "I would've found you a therapist if you'd insisted on leaving." She stepped back. "I'll be right back with my purse."

Alyson walked into the bathroom and closed the door.

This highly unexpected job had changed considerably in a matter of minutes. David's request aside, there was so much she wanted to know about Becca, the young woman.

Right before the darkness descended, she'd been a popular sophomore in high school. She'd also been a straight-A student and *fantastic* soccer player. She probably would have ended up with a soccer scholarship to college if not for—she stared at her reflection in the mirror; the memory of that awful, early morning call from David consumed her mind.

Death itself had taken over his voice.

She released a breath she hadn't realized was in her lungs.

That another memory she wished she could sever from her mind and heart.

There was a knock on the door before Jillian slid into the bathroom.

"Here." She handed Alyson her purse. "I have a comb and lip gloss." Jillian watched her closely as she grasped the purse's straps. "Are you okay with this?"

She nodded. "It'll be good. I haven't seen Becca since…" *A few days after the funeral.*

"I know," Jillian murmured. "I'll give you a minute."

Alyson concentrated on freeing her hair from the ponytail, then found Jillian's comb. She ran it through her long, thick locks, while examining her apparel, nothing more than a heavy, black sweater and pretty worn skinny jeans tucked into her black Ugg boots. Certainly not what she considered birthday party attire, but it would have to do. Releasing her hair from the ponytail and the lip gloss had helped, though.

While she waited for Jillian, a few guests entered the house. Then a very familiar song drifted from the living room.

She froze.

"Good Day Sunshine" from The Beatles. A beloved song from her childhood, because she and her mom would sing it in the car at the top of their lungs. A memory she'd shared with David during their first phone conversation, which had lasted over two hours.

Total sneak? More like total devil.

A group of young, loudly chattering guests entering the house caused her to blink. They were followed by a man who stumbled into the foyer with two large gifts.

She rushed forward. "Here. Let me help you."

"Thanks." He half grunted, half laughed, when she took the top present.

The man transferred the other messily wrapped box to his right arm, his bright blue eyes settling on her for the first time. That immediately became as round as hers already felt.

"Alyson?"

"Jackson?"

In college, Jackson had been attractive in a rugged, outdoorsy sort of way, with constant rumpled, sandy-blond hair. He stood a couple inches shorter than David, but appeared to still be in excellent shape. And, also like his best friend, had only gotten better looking with age.

"Holy shit—" He shook his head. "I'm sorry. But where did you —I mean…*what*?"

Jillian appeared at Alyson's side, her inquisitive gaze locked on Jackson who yanked his eyes from her long enough to settle on her friend.

He returned her blinding smile.

"I'm Jillian Castillo. Do you know Alyson?"

"Yeah." He glanced at Alyson, then back at Jillian. "I'm Jackson. Lovett. She and—I mean, we all went to CU—what the…?" He laughed and glanced back at her friend. "I'm usually more articulate than this."

"Hey, man," came David's voice from behind them. "Do you need help?"

She and Jillian turned to find David walking toward them, his eyes trained on Alyson.

"You're still here." He stopped inches from her. "Thanks for staying."

"And you're a complete bastard," Jackson articulated. "Where and when did you run into *Alyson*?" His eyes swung to her. "I can't believe it. I'd give you a hug right now if I wasn't holding this present."

A blast of late afternoon, cold, February air barreled into the foyer.

David walked around them and, avoiding Jackson's piercing glare, shut his front door. He then stepped toward her and pulled Jackson's other present for Becca from her arms.

"Nice wrap job," he said to his friend.

"Gracie insisted on helping me since one of the gifts is from my parents, Will, and Savannah." Jackson's still round eyes landed on her, then Jillian. "She's my six-year-old niece." His eyes returned to David. "But stop changing the damn subject."

"Flowers," Jillian interjected. "That's what brought all of us here together today."

"Are you staying for the party?" he asked Alyson, though his eyes drifted to Jillian.

Alyson nodded.

"We'll be back in a sec," David said.

They walked down the hallway, speaking quietly together.

"*Awkward*," Jillian quietly sang. "And Jackson is…?"

"David's best friend from childhood. He's great, too. We always got along really well."

"Huh," her friend murmured.

"Alyson! Jillian!" Becca waved them forward. "Come meet people."

She watched David and Jackson until they reached the dining room, and couldn't help but wonder what other *surprises* the evening would bring.

The day had gone in a direction she never imagined when she woke up this morning.

Chapter Five

DAVID SET the gift on the dining room table. "Stop looking at me like that," he muttered.

Jackson continued glaring. "No," he quietly shot back. "You're a dick for not telling me about Alyson. It also explains why you were distracted this week. So you're a dick *and* a liar."

"Look, can we talk about me being a lousy-ass friend later?" He couldn't deal with this right now. He had a party to host. People to greet and talk to.

His eyes found *her* by his piano with Becs, Matt, Jillian, and some of his sister's friends from CU. Based on Al's smile and laughter, she didn't appear ready to bolt for the front door at any second. Which meant his sister must have sweet talked her into staying.

A little thrill mixed with a fair amount of nerves shot through him. The same combo he always felt right before one of the band's gigs.

"You also have to be," Jackson said, "the luckiest sonofabitch in this city. And by lucky I'm only referring to Alyson."

"I figured. And Denver's not *that* big."

He crossed his arms. "No, but the metro area sure as hell is." He shrugged. "She could've gone anywhere. Especially after that night—"

"Don't go there." David walked around him. "We're not doing this right now. So go be a pain in the ass somewhere else in this room."

He headed toward the one person he really wanted to talk to when one of his sister's friends, and the bridesmaid he'd been paired with as a groomsman, stepped in front of him.

She gave him a bright smile.

He held back an exasperated sigh.

"Hi, David." She laughed. "Your house is *unbelievable*."

He smiled tightly. "Hey, Lainey. And thanks. I'm glad you were able to make it today." He was, too, because she happened to be one of Becs's closest, oldest friends who'd he'd known since she was fourteen-years old.

She stepped closer. "I don't suppose you'd give me a...*private* tour later?"

And decided at some point she liked him as more than her close friend's older brother.

Shit. He couldn't deal with this, either.

He stepped left. "Not sure I'll have time for something like that, but since you're practically *family*"—he took another step left—"feel free to look around. I'll talk to you later."

Her face fell, and he darted passed her.

He liked Lainey. He always had. And, yeah, she'd become a good-looking woman. But his sister's friends, especially the ones from high school and farther back, would always feel like having more sisters. He shuddered at the thought of seeing them any other way.

David again headed for Al—only to be stopped by Zach and his wife, Erica.

He gave her a sideways hug. "How's the mom-to-be?"

She rubbed her stomach. "Only eight weeks and two more days to go."

"She started the countdown two weeks ago." Zach gave his wife a quick kiss on the cheek. "I'm going to grab a drink. Can I bring you two anything?"

Scotch. Neat. That would sure as hell take the edge off. But he said, "Bottle of water."

"Same," Erica replied.

Zach joined Jackson and Matt at the makeshift bar he'd set up where his living room met the dining room.

"I'm so looking forward to drinking a glass of good white wine," Erica murmured, then focused on some nearby flowers. "These flowers are absolutely gorgeous. My cousin is getting married in September and she hasn't found a florist yet."

He smiled at the possibility of sending more business Al's way as he replied, "Well, it just so happens the florist is here." Maybe it would score him some nice-guy points? Points he desperately needed when he thought about everything he had to say to her before she left. Returned to her life in the Highlands where she probably had someone waiting for her.

Something he didn't want to think about at this moment. Or ever, for that matter.

"Her name's Alyson Douglas." *Alyson Catherine Douglas.* "She's with Becs and Matt by my piano." Erica's gaze followed the direction he'd angled his head. *The stunning woman with auburn hair.* "The name of the shop is Daisy's Bouquets. They're in the Highlands. Her business partner is also here." He scanned the room until he found Jillian, now at the makeshift bar. And standing close to Jackson while they laughed together.

David narrowed his eyes.

Wouldn't that be fate's screwed up sense of humor at work if his best friend, and her best friend, ended up dating? Knowing Jackson, it'd only last a handful of weeks because Jillian would probably get tired of his workaholism, too. But shit. Really? How would that be fair?

Zach walked up and handed him his bottle of water.

"We need to go talk to the woman with Becca and Matt," Erica told her husband. "You know Gina is still on the hunt for a florist and these flowers are *perfect*." She grabbed Zach's hand and dragged him toward where Al was still deep in conversation with his sister and Matt.

Getting caught up. Re-acquainted after ten years. All because of his rotten choices.

He opened his bottle and nearly drained it.

His aunt and uncle walked into his house at that moment and headed for the birthday girl.

His eyes drifted back to Al, now chatting with Erica. Only this time she caught his gaze, smiled warmly, and mouthed, "Thank you."

He returned her smile, not certain what exactly she was thanking him for. The possibility of another wedding job? Hiring her for this job, which reunited her with Becs? Who hired Al for her wedding. Or maybe all of the above? But no matter. He'd take whatever he could get. He also needed to talk to her before she disappeared from his life a second time.

Her attention then turned to his aunt and uncle, staring at her with wide eyes and mouths.

He finished his trek toward the group and stopped beside Al, smiling at Eileen and Hugh.

"You two are so tan," she said to them. "Are you retired now?"

Hugh chuckled. "Not even close. We now own properties in Sarasota, Florida, and have been here the last couple weeks to spend time with David and Becca, and help with the wedding. We also needed to check on the properties we still have here in Denver." Hugh frowned at him. "I can't believe you didn't tell us about Alyson."

Al focused on him.

David glanced at his sister who started to play with the hem of her shirt.

Why was he taking the fall for this when Becs had been the one to actually find her? He opened his mouth, about to say as much, when Jackson and Jillian walked up.

"That feeling of shock is going around today, Hugh," Jackson said.

Becs tilted her head back to look at Jackson.

He smiled, hooking his fingers on the back of her wheelchair.

"Jackson," she said as he pulled her back and pushed her forward, "don't you think it's time you found a new family to infiltrate?"

"I love you too, Rebecs." He stopped and glanced at Jillian, smiling at their exchange. "David and I have been buddies since we were eleven, making the Prestons my second family for longer than they'll admit."

"That's for certain," Becs threw at him.

"Don't you have a roomful of guests who need your attention?"

"As a matter of fact…*everyone*? Let's get this party started!" Her singsong statement skipped through the room, causing almost everyone to laugh and watch her go right for the remote to David's speaker system he'd set on a table.

"Have I mentioned lately how charming your sister *isn't*?" Jackson asked him.

"Alyson, we're going to grab some food and drinks," Eileen said as Hugh grasped her hand. "Please come find us, because I would absolutely love to catch up with you."

Jackson smiled at Jillian. "I guess that means you're stuck with me. Are you hungry?"

Jillian's smile became almost blinding. "I think there are worse things. And yes. Very."

They fell into step together, leaving David and Alyson alone.

At that moment, the classic rock playlist he'd started, and with a very special song, went up several notches in volume.

He faced Al. "And *I think* we may have inadvertently created a love connection today."

She released a quiet laugh. "Could be."

Noticing her near-empty wine glass, he asked, "Do you need me to top that off for you?" He couldn't help but think she may want and need her glass filled before they talked. Or more accurately, he tried not to embarrass himself by begging for forgiveness.

"Oh, no thank you." She peered at him. "You're not drinking."

Of course she would have noticed that. But he said, "No, not anymore." He tried on a smile as she continued to stare at him. "Though I'll probably have a glass of champagne on the most important day of the twenty-first century."

She tilted her head right.

"The wedding," he swiftly clarified. "That's what I call it."

She laughed. "Yeah, she is *pretty* excited."

Silence descended, outside of the music, and chattering and laughter around them.

His eyes reached hers. "Can we go somewhere quiet and—"

"Yo, D-Man!" Matt's raised voiced reached where they stood. "We need more glasses."

His shoulders fell and he mentally went through every swear word in his vocabulary.

"David, I'm not going anywhere," Al assured him. "Go do what you need to do."

He stepped back. "Thanks." It was all he could think to say, since everything that needed to be said would have to wait a little longer.

And as he watched Al bend down to give Becs a goodbye hug that felt like two *days* later, he expelled a quick breath of frustration. Being pulled in five directions all night had not been how he pictured the party going. But true to her word, Al had stayed.

"Let's have lunch next week," Becs said to Al.

His sister and Matt, on the other hand, were preparing to leave, since he and Matt had finished loading up their SUV with all of her gifts and the yellow roses.

"Hmm," Al replied. "What do you have in mind?"

"Come to our house in Boulder. Say Wednesday afternoon? It'll be a working lunch for you. We'll talk flowers."

She hesitated, first looking at Matt, then him.

"Please?" his sister continued. "I won't take no for an answer."

Becs had said it in her *I'm-right-you're-wrong* voice that, depending on the day, could be fairly maddening. Al, however, laughed.

"Okay. I'd love that."

Becs quietly clapped, then looked up at Matt. "Can I have my phone?"

He withdrew it from his back pocket.

"Give me your number so we can decide on a time. I'll also text you our address."

Al rattled off her number.

David looked away as envy shrouded him.

Though he was relieved his party plans had been successful, more so considering she'd accepted his sister's invitation to stay, tonight would probably be the last time he'd really see Al. As heavy as that reality was, he had to be okay with it.

"Excellent." Becs laughed. "It's official. This is so not goodbye."

David followed them out of his house.

Once they reached their Cherokee, Matt scooped Becs out of her wheelchair and subjected her to a series of fast spins.

He quietly laughed with his sister's cackling that could probably be heard throughout his neighborhood. He folded up her wheelchair, carried it to the Cherokee's trunk door, and carefully placed the heavy item in the spot he and Matt had left empty.

Matt carried her to the passenger-side door, and David met them there.

She gave him a long look before leaning forward to give him a hug. "Thank you." She held him tight. "Today was so awesome."

David nodded, returning her tight squeeze.

Becs leaned back, letting her arms fall from around his neck. "Don't look so serious. This isn't goodbye for you, either."

He frowned. "She has her own life...that includes a serious boyfriend."

She simply smiled. "By the way, we're all set for next Friday. I have appointments at three more bridal shops scheduled. You'll let Nancy know?"

"Yeah, I'll give her a call on Monday."

David stayed outside until their Cherokee disappeared from sight.

Although he was ready to talk to Al, he was nowhere near ready for her to leave. Which reminded him, he hadn't seen Jackson or Jillian since helping Matt load the Cherokee.

In spite of the irony, he smiled. Talking to Al also had to be now or never, since she and Jillian had arrived together in their delivery van.

He walked into his kitchen, but stopped at the sight of Al at his island counter, stacking the remaining paper plates, followed by straightening them. Then she did the same thing with the napkins. That she set on the plates. Then she gathered what had to be crumbs, swept them onto her hand, which she brushed off into an empty aluminum pan that had held food.

Fighting a smile, he asked, "Did you have a good time?"

She looked over at him. "Yes. It was wonderful seeing your aunt and uncle again, too. And Jackson, even though I didn't see much of him tonight."

They shared a quick laugh.

"Where are those two?"

She grinned. "They were still talking so she walked him to his car."

David ambled forward, stopping right across the counter from her.

"And you're right. Becca's extremely happy. I can't believe she's getting married. Little Becca. And Matt seems like such a great guy." Her grin grew. "Thank you for planning this. Our seeing each other today."

He lifted his shoulders. "It was the least I could do for you both."

She kept her gaze level with his.

Shit. He needed to do this. Now. But how and where to begin?

"How's it going with your music?"

He froze at her question.

Okay. It wouldn't hurt to prolong the inevitable by talking about his music.

"Great." He released a quick laugh. "Better than great, actually. In the craziness of everything that's been going on, I haven't had a chance to tell anyone we're playing at the Evergreen Jazz Festival this summer."

Alyson leaned forward, her mouth dropping open. "David, that's *beyond* incredible."

"Thanks. We're *beyond* excited." It seemed perfect Al was the first person to hear this.

While a couple, she'd been his biggest and most constant supporter. Even when his parents had started pressuring him to have a Plan B. An idea he'd fought, and angrily at the end.

"How are you not telling everyone you know about this?"

Her question slammed through where his thoughts had gone.

She continued to stare at him, her eyes filled with…pride?

"It's what you've wanted. What you talked about."

He cracked a smile. "Life's been a little unpredictable. Especially this last week." Their eyes locked. "I've been swamped at work, too. The festival's not until July, so there's plenty of time to let everyone know."

Her grin came back. "Okay. I guess that's fair. But it's amazing news. Really."

He returned her smile.

"I've been meaning to ask what made you switch to architecture? Was it Jackson?"

He stayed silent for several seconds, formulating a concise answer, since her question brought back too many foul memories to count. "The summer following the accident I came to some significant realizations. One of them was knowing I had to put Becca's needs first. To take care of her properly." Her eyes became dim, but he continued. "The only way I could do that was by making really good money. I talked to Jackson a lot, researched the salaries and what it would take to get to where I needed to be, then made the switch and never looked back." He paused, then added, "While I was scrambling to get through the program in a shorter amount of time, and with Jackson's help here and there, Becs was living with Hugh and Eileen since they, according to my parents' will, were to take custody of her—us—if anything happened."

She slowly nodded. "So you have no regrets?"

"None," he replied, knowing exactly what she was asking. "There's no way I could've supported us if I *had* gone into teaching." Also known as the Plan B his parents had wanted, even expected him to pursue. "My music is still a huge part of my life."

A heavy silence descended, and he began to search for the right opening. But his mind failed to produce anything beyond those two little words.

"When we were talking about your house, and that apartment you and Jackson shared, you laughed." She absently pushed a lock of hair behind her right ear. "It was so genuine, too, and really nice to hear. It reminded me of the last time I heard you laugh like that." She leaned forward. "It was that day we *pulled a Ferris Bueller* and came into the city."

He laughed at her quoting him almost exactly from that day. "And ended up at a Rockies game." Ironically, just like the characters in the movie had ended up at a Chicago Cubs game.

"With everyone else in the city playing hooky that day because the weather was absolutely perfect." She grinned. "You bought me a stuffed Dinger."

He returned her soft grin at the memory of him surprising her with the toy version of the Rockies' mascot. "That was the best time I've ever had in this city," he quietly said.

Her smile slowly faded, leaving no doubt in his mind where her thoughts had gone. Because their day in the city had been one day before the huge fight he'd had with his parents, and two days before the equally huge fight he'd had with *her*. The same day as the accident.

Their perfect day in Denver had, essentially, been their last day as a real couple.

This harsh recollection gave David his much-needed opening. "Alyson, I…" He sighed. "I know this is too many years too late, but I'm so…sorry." He frowned.

After spending years carrying the way overdue apology, he'd expected the heavy load on his shoulders to lighten significantly. However, standing across the counter from her, watching her expression turn cautious, he felt little difference. At the same time, how could he begin to make amends for his despicable behavior all those years ago? She'd loved him, and he knew she would have stayed by his side during the long period of pitch blackness that had consumed him.

But it had also turned him into a reckless asshole.

If the right now were different, and she was willing, he could spend time showing her how much he had changed from that guy in the bedroom. That, however, was *not* in the stars.

"Those words sounded more meaningful in my head."

She opened her mouth, paused, then said, "David, I'm not looking for an apology."

"It doesn't change the fact I needed to say that to you. I know it will never be enough, either." He cringed. "When I think about that night. What I said to you? I…it wasn't me."

"I know that."

"I don't know who that guy was." He recalled his last phone conversation with Al, the morning he'd told his sister about their parents. "I should've listened to you, and my aunt and uncle, that morning. I never should've gone into Becca's hospital room by myself because…" He released a shaky breath. "Her reaction *hurt*. On every level."

She pressed her lips together while nodding.

"I'll spare you the details of what happened, but that was when my descent to the rockiest bottom imaginable began." He shook his head. "And you got caught in the fall."

Silence followed his confession, but she continued holding his steady gaze. A gaze that seemed full of questions rather than understanding. Though a part of him wanted to share the entire, ugly story from that morning, as well as the equally ugly details of the numerous weeks that followed, he knew nothing he shared would ever condone his treatment of her.

Plus, a much bigger part of him—the part still battling the shame—didn't want her to know the entire story, either.

"David, I—" She seemed to be searching for her words. "I... really appreciate what you did today." She stepped back from the counter. "Becca radiates happiness. I have no doubt you're a huge part of that, too. It's clear what you've created here, for yourself and her." She gestured toward his house. "It's remarkable."

He managed a quick smile.

"My next question is completely trite, but I need to know the answer before I leave."

Those last few words caused his breathing to slow.

"Are *you* happy?"

He squinted at her, and his mind went blank for several seconds.

Happy?

That was a question he hadn't thought about in, well, ten years.

Two months after the accident, it ceased being about him and all about Becs. Making sure she would always have everything she ever needed and wanted. As soon as he began making enough money to support himself, he'd started contributing to her care. Now he was beyond comfortable, and no longer needed financial help from their aunt and uncle. Though they were helping here and there with the wedding, but only at their insistence.

Happy.

Such a small word to describe a positive emotional state.

He was half a world away from that guy in the bedroom who'd shoved aside the girl who'd made him a believer of "love at first sight." His sister's happiness made him proud, as did his career success and, without question, his music. But none of that equaled *happy*.

"I'm without complaints," he finally answered, though it was untrue. He did have one, enormous complaint. And he had no one to blame for it but himself.

"That doesn't really answer my question."

He grinned. "Okay. Then how about you try me again? Let's say after the wedding?" He winked, and Al's mouth inched into her mischievous smile that had oftentimes been his undoing.

"I'll check back with you," she replied as he took a mental picture of her mouth. "How does August tenth sound?"

"It's a date." The flirtatious response slipped out before he could stop it.

Her smile slipped and she took another step back from the counter.

David damned his former self for the zillionth time in what felt like as many years.

"I—we—should go. My dog's waiting for me."

It took a moment for her statement to register, since he'd expected her to say something different. And with the word *boyfriend* in it. But he asked, "What kind of dog do you have?"

"He's a Husky."

When they reached his door, they stopped, she faced him, and he wished to hell he was wearing a pair of pants with pockets he could shove his hands into. Because, right or wrong, all he wanted was to pull her into his arms, bury his face between her neck and hair, and hold her until someone pried them apart. Which meant a third therapeutic session with his piano this week wouldn't hurt a damn thing.

He forced his mouth into a smile. "Have fun with Becs on Wednesday. Just send me the damage after you two get everything figured out."

As she said "Okay," his door popped open.

Jillian poked her head inside, wearing a huge, shit-eating grin, which told David his buddy must have been on his A-game all night.

"Hi," she said to him. "You ready?" This in Al's direction.

"Yes." Al opened the door wider. She paused on the threshold, turned, and said, "I'll…see you." She then walked away.

Once their van cleared the curb of his driveway, he shut his door a bit too hard, locked the bolt, and went straight for his piano where he dropped to the bench.

He stared out his living room window, sifting through his extensive knowledge of piano pieces until his memory stopped on one by George Gershwin. "Rhapsody in Blue."

Also known as one of his parents' favorite songs.

He placed his fingers on the keys, cleared his mind of everything but the notes he'd memorized years ago as a college student, and lost himself in the music.

Chapter Six

———————

"Jilly, Cliff left me a message earlier."

"*Just calling to let you know the building is now owned by that big company, Marsden Enterprises. They told me they'd be reaching out to you and the tenant next door about the sale and their plans for the buildings. Please know I did put in a good word for you guys, being such good tenants the last few years. Good luck with that flower biz of yours.*"

Alyson hung up and rolled her head left. "The building's been sold. Cliff's out and a company called Marsden Enterprises is now in charge. According to him, they'll be in touch with their *plans for the buildings*." Something that sounded a tad on the ominous side.

Jillian stopped at a light. "Nothing surprising. We move forward with your *reconnaissance* plan."

Alyson stared out the windshield. "Crashing a Felicity Mayhew wedding." She cringed. "When I say it like that, I do sound insane." But who she used for all of her fantasy, fairy tale weddings was not info posted on her website. Alyson had also, technically, been "invited" to the wedding as a potential client, so could it really be considered *crashing?*

Jillian accelerated through the intersection. "It's like you said, her weddings never have less than two-hundred-and-fifty guests. We get in, get the pics and info we need, then get the hell out. We also have all next week to psyche ourselves up for it." She laughed. "I think it'll be fun."

Alyson joined her friend's wicked laughter, which felt nice, considering the seriousness she'd walked away from moments ago.

I'll spare you the details of what happened, but that was when my descent to the rockiest bottom imaginable began.

She'd always known something terrible had happened between David and Becca that morning. Right after that, he'd officially shut down and permanently shut her out.

You got caught in the fall.

"Are you really going to make me ask what you two talked about?"

Jillian's exasperated question broke through her thoughts.

She faced her friend. "I could ask *you* the same question."

"I asked *you* first."

Alyson lifted her shoulders. "He apologized." Though she'd meant what she told him about not wanting one, it had been somewhat fulfilling to hear. Still, she couldn't shake the disappointment and irritation it had taken him so long to—it's not as if he'd been the one to find her. If not for his sister getting married, their paths would most likely have remained uncrossed.

David being the one to demolish *her* heart, and during a time that had not been easy for her, either, she'd never been compelled to search for him on the internet or social media.

"That's it?" Jillian glanced her way for a second. "You can't be telling me everything."

She sighed. "We also visited an old memory."

That was the best time I've ever had in this city. She'd almost said, "Me, too."

It had been a perfect day *and* night. The calm before the storm. Hurricane. F-5 tornado.

"Well, how do you feel?" Jillian persisted.

"Fine. Why?" Not exactly true when she zeroed in on his continued refusal to tell her what happened that morning with Becca. Considering the passage of time, it shouldn't matter to her anymore. Unfortunately, it did still matter, since that night he'd told her to get out and stay away she'd lost so much more than a college sweetheart.

"You're lying," her friend countered. "When are you going to see him again?"

Alyson whipped her head left. "Probably the day of the wedding." For some reason, that thought tugged at a place deep inside of her. A place David Thomas Preston did *not* belong.

"He still thinks you have a boyfriend. *Estas loca*," Jillian muttered.

"Of course he does!" she snapped. "It will stay that way, and I'm not crazy." *It was simply safer.* She also had much more important things to focus on, like preparing Daisy's Bouquets for whatever would soon be thrown their way. "Let's talk about *you* and Jackson." How utterly strange would that twist be if Jackson and Jillian ended up as *something*?

"He definitely has the three S's," Jillian admitted.

"Which are?"

She flashed a naughty grin. "Smart, successful, and sexy."

Alyson laughed. "And there's the whole *Jack and Jill* cute factor."

She groaned. "Not going there. But David has the three S's, too. I know you've noticed."

Of course she'd noticed. She wasn't dead. But she wasn't about to admit that out loud. So she asked, "When are you and Jackson seeing each other again?"

Jillian carefully parked the delivery van in front of Alyson's house. "I don't know. We did exchange numbers."

When they climbed out, she immediately heard Thatcher's excited barking from inside her house.

"Is there anything I need to know about Jackson in case we do end up on a date?"

They stopped beside Jillian's Subaru parked in Alyson's driveway.

"Jilly, I knew him ten years ago."

"And what do you remember? Seriously, Al." Jillian frowned. "He seems a little too good to be true, because on top of having the three S's, he's funny." She giggled. "*Really* funny."

Alyson grinned. "I remember that. He was also a really hard worker, but knew how to let loose and have fun." She paused, then added, "I don't remember him ever having a serious girlfriend. He was focused on his classes. I think the architecture program's pretty intense."

David had admitted throwing himself into his studies to get through it faster, so he could eventually take care of himself and Becca. Actions she couldn't help but admire, especially when she remembered how he'd looked and sounded that night before she'd left his room.

Angry. Despondent. Distant. Cold. Barely able to stand upright.

He'd walked away from alcohol at some point, too. Something else to admire.

More questions swirled through her busy brain. The main one being, how had David gone from that boy she'd left at his almost cruel insistence to the David currently in his big, beautiful home that had probably been renovated to accommodate his little sister's unfair reality?

"None of that sounds awful," Jillian slowly said. She shook her head. "I guess we'll see what happens. See you Monday."

As Jillian drove away, Alyson walked into her house.

Thatcher greeted her with his usual doggie dance at her feet, followed by a quick turn; his gray and white fluffy tail flapping wildly.

She bent forward and vigorously rubbed his white, fuzzy face. "Ready for a walk?"

He barked, and went up and down on his hind legs.

She grabbed his leash off the nearby table and fastened it to his collar. He then sprang from the house, but she held him back long enough to close the door.

On Wednesday, she'd be traveling up to Boulder to spend quality time with Becca. In addition to discussing flowers for her wedding, maybe they could talk about other things. If, of course, Becca was willing. She'd never push the young woman to go back to a time that had been incredibly horrendous for her if she didn't want to go there. But if she was willing to talk about those bleak, dark days, Alyson had a feeling all of her questions would be answered.

Thatcher led them toward the sidewalk and veered right.

That had been what hurt the most and held on to her all of these years. Never knowing the *what happened.* Beyond the alcohol he'd turned to, she'd never understood why he'd really done what he did to her. To them. No, it shouldn't matter, but she had to understand; her way of making peace with *him.* He'd needed to apologize, and she needed answers. Then, with him bringing Becca back into her life, perhaps she and David could move into… a friendship?

She inhaled the cool, night air.

Pleasant acquaintances might be a little more realistic and nothing more, despite Jillian's opinion to the contrary. Yes, she and David still had chemistry after all of these years. But now she was a woman, and he'd been careless with her heart which was no longer easily available.

The only male she needed and wanted in her life happened to be taking *her* on a walk at this moment. There was nothing at all wrong with that, either.

DAVID STOOD with Jackson on their gym's basketball court. They had it all to themselves with it being 8:00 on a Sunday morning. It was his ball, but Jackson had yet to relinquish it from his stance behind the side line.

"The luckiest jackass when it comes to fate and Rebecs ended up with her number?"

"Would you pass the damn ball?"

Jackson shot the ball at him, then jogged toward where he stood.

David dribbled in place for a few seconds before darting around his friend. "And stop calling me *lucky.*" Because that's not at all how he felt when it came to the one and only Al.

He made it to the three-point line as Jackson caught up with him.

"You're referring to the boyfriend."

David responded by taking a hard shot right from the free-throw line, the ball bouncing off the rim and into the wall. He rounded on Jackson. "I don't want to talk about this."

He gave him a hard appraisal. "She stayed for the party."

"That had nothing to do with me." *Not entirely.* "Becs invited them to stay."

"I also," Jackson continued, "couldn't help but notice she wasn't the first one out the door when the party was over."

He refused to disclose the fact he'd indirectly asked Al to stay after because, frankly, it was none of Jackson's business. He said instead, "True. But then she was waiting for *Jillian.*"

Jackson fought a smile. "Okay, asshole. So, that's it?"

"Yes." The simple, one-word response hadn't come out as forcefully as he'd hoped.

She'd said, *I'll...see you.*

David walked to where the basketball had landed. "That has to be it. I caused enough damage years ago. The least I can do for her now"—he picked up the ball—"is leave her the hell alone." He headed back toward Jackson. "I connected her with Becs. That's what's important." And that he'd achieved what he needed to last night, though it still didn't feel as freeing as he'd hoped it would.

His friend burst into laughter.

"What's so damn funny?"

"Listening to you," Jackson managed to say, "convince yourself that's it. You didn't walk into her shop *just* to order flowers and connect her with Becca."

"Okay!" he snapped. "What the hell do you suggest I do? She's happy."

Jackson's amusement faded. "How could you know something like that? You, what, talked to her for an hour? I'm actually feeling a little bad I didn't really talk to her last night."

"Well, you were busy." But David had to reluctantly admit Jackson made a strong point. Maybe he should have posed the "happy" question to *her*? Though she appeared to have almost everything she'd ever wanted. Things she talked about when they were together.

"She has her business, friends, family, and a…personal life. There's no reason to think she's unhappy."

Jackson watched him carefully. "It's not like she's engaged or married to this guy."

He stared at his friend for several seconds, then said, "Do you hear yourself right now?" David handed Jackson the basketball. "This conversation is over."

He frowned. "Stop looking at me like I'm a piece of shit you can't get off the bottom of your shoe. You know if she was any other woman on this planet I'd be the first one telling you to walk away. And if she and this guy were *clearly* committed to each other, you know I'd kick your ass first, then tell you the same damn thing. But she's not any other woman." He leaned forward. "It's Alyson, and I think you might be assuming too much about her." He dribbled the ball. "That's all I'm going to say about it. Let's play."

Which they did until a group of guys walked onto the court over an hour later.

David was sifting through everything his buddy had said when they silently left the gym together a half hour later, still damp from their quick showers.

He knew Jackson was trying to be supportive. He had been the first person to hear Al's name all those years ago. At the time, and on the heels of David declaring she was the "hottest girl he'd ever seen in his life," Jackson had given it two weeks. *Tops.* But once it became clear David was crazy for Al, and she felt the same way about him, his buddy had grudgingly retracted his original response. Because the only word that could accurately describe David at that time, and throughout his two-plus years with Al, was happy.

As if anything he'd wanted in life was possible.

Jackson had made a strong argument; his advice clear. But it wasn't that simple. No matter his feelings for Al that would *not* go away, he wasn't a relationship wrecker. That thought took him to last night as they said goodbye without saying the word, seconds before Jillian resurfaced. The true fact of the matter was that he had no choice but to walk away.

And he had to be okay with that.

They reached their vehicles, parked side-by-side, and David stopped. "Are you going to tell me about Jillian?" He hadn't been able to ask earlier due to the conversation revolving around him and Al. "The few times I did see you last night, you were grinning like you did after Brooke Michaelson agreed to go to Homecoming with you senior year."

Jackson smiled. "I probably was. Jillian's…wow."

David raised his eyebrows.

With the exception of Brooke, his friend, in all their dating years, had never used "wow" to describe a woman. He also seemed to be searching for the right words to continue.

"I sure as hell wasn't expecting a few things when I walked into your house yesterday, least of all her." Jackson's smile doubled in size. "We definitely hit it off."

"Al and I somehow picked up on that. What were you doing outside all that time?"

"Just talking and laughing. A lot."

David couldn't help but also grin. "So you're seeing each other again?"

Jackson leaned against his SUV. "I hope so. I'm headed to the office right now, but was thinking about texting her when I got home later. Seeing how that goes first." He focused on David. "Or is today too soon to text?"

He laughed. "You're asking me? How the hell would I know?" He shook his head. "You're the one with the most recent relationship." *Because he had no business dating* anyone.

Jackson frowned. "Yeah, but Jillian's completely different from Tami. She seems more sure of herself. And what she wants." He released a quick laugh. "She doesn't strike me as a woman who would take anyone's shit."

Which probably meant if his friend pursued something with Jillian, it would last even less time than Jackson's other relationships. But he said, "Well, tell me how it goes."

Jackson eyed him. "If Jillian and I end up dating, it won't be a problem? Right?"

The fact his long-time buddy appeared genuinely wowed by Jillian was significant. At the same time…he suppressed a sigh. "It would have nothing to do with me or Alyson."

Jackson smiled. "Thanks, man. See you tomorrow."

They climbed into their vehicles.

As Jackson backed out of his parking spot, David stared at his steering wheel.

His friend had looked and sounded like *he* must have over twelve years ago, after sitting next to his dream girl for the longest fifty minutes of his teen life. Especially when he'd found out, via a note he'd passed her, she was single. All he'd wanted was for class to end so they could keep talking. Which they had as he walked Al to her next class that had been nowhere near where he'd needed to be at that moment.

He would never begrudge his closest friend a meaningful connection with a woman. But David still felt tempted to damn the fact Jackson had connected with Alyson Catherine Douglas's best friend and business partner.

Chapter Seven

ALYSON'S PHONE burst into the old-fashioned ring tone. Keeping one eye on the road, she picked it up, hesitated, then answered, "Hi."

"Hi, Sweetie," her mom answered. "Did I catch you at a good time?"

Dare she tell her about David and reconnecting with Becca as she headed west on the turnpike toward Boulder?

"I'm on my way to have lunch with a new client." She cringed, even though it wasn't at all a lie. "What's up?" She just couldn't articulate the truth as this moment.

"Fondue Fun this Saturday night." Her mom laughed. "Bring wine, Jillian, and Thatcher."

As much fun as those nights always were, she and Jillian already had plans. "We can't this Saturday." *We have a wedding to crash.* "Maybe next Saturday night, though?"

"Oh," her mom murmured. "Bummer. Do you have an evening wedding?"

She focused on the Flatirons, rock formations synonymous with Boulder. "Yes." Also not a lie, but Campbell and Hayley had been put in charge of delivering and setting up the flowers while she and Jillian attempted to cinch their business's future.

"Okay. But you'll be free for certain next Saturday?"

She definitely would be, but considering how much Jillian and Jackson had been texting this week, she couldn't speak for her friend. "I'll talk to Jillian and get back to you."

"Sounds good. Everything else alright with you? You sound a little distracted."

Total understatement. But now wasn't the time to tell her mom about the building being sold and their uncertain future in the Highlands. Or about where she was really headed and how that had all happened. And she could never know about the wedding crashing. Alyson didn't want or need her family worrying. "I'm fine, Mom. I'll call you tomorrow after I talk to Jilly."

She took a deep breath, then slowly released the air as her memory once again revisited the past.

Her family, like his with her, had embraced David. They'd been stunned by the horrific accident, Becca's reality, and highly concerned for David. But their concern had shifted solely to her when she'd spent half the summer at home, after slogging through the final weeks of school, weepy and withdrawn. Their concern had been grave to the point her mom came into her room on a July afternoon, sat beside her on the bed, and suggested she consider talking to someone who wasn't family or a friend. Her mom's implication clear, she'd managed to yank herself at least halfway out of the despair for the summer's remaining weeks.

Following his harsh actions toward her, their fondness for David had dwindled.

She'd figure out an appropriate time to come clean with her family about reconnecting with the Prestons. As for the building, she and Jillian knew next to nothing, so telling them about that could wait until they *did* know something.

She needed to focus on the right now—lunch with Becca and, hopefully, getting answers. But her tummy began to flutter as she parked her 4Runner in the driveway of Becca and Matt's charming, taupe bungalow located a handful of miles from the CU campus.

She turned off the engine and her eyes drifted to her surroundings.

They had a quaint front yard with a single tree, and two small bushes planted along the house's exterior, right below what had to be the living room window. They also had a wide, tiled path that led straight to double wood doors featuring windows with simple grid work. The little house had old, twentieth century charm meets modern, twenty-first century elegance.

She expelled a quick breath, grabbed her purse, then the bouquet binder.

As she approached the front doors, her memory went to the evening long ago when she'd met David's family. Maybe because this meeting with Becca felt similar to that moment in time, since she didn't know *this* Becca she was about to have lunch with. She'd met her when she'd been fourteen; an eighth grader. Now, she was a twenty-six-year-old woman getting married.

When Alyson reached the doors, she found the right one slightly ajar. She pushed the door open, stuck her head in the opening, and tentatively called Becca's name.

The young woman immediately appeared in the living room, from what looked like the direction of the dining room, and gave her a huge smile.

"Hi!" she said, placing her hands on the wheelchair's tires, coming closer. "You just missed Matt who left the door open for you. Come in, come in," she added, waving her forward.

Alyson smiled and closed the door, her eyes settling on the bungalow's sophisticated and noticeably updated interior.

She met Becca inside the living room painted a richer taupe than the outside. "This is really beautiful."

The living room held a chocolate-brown, L-shaped sofa that looked comfy, and perfect for watching television on the flat-screen hanging above the fireplace flanked by two, bright-white shelves, holding many books and pictures. Between the sofa and fireplace sat a square, chocolate-brown oversized ottoman holding a light wood tray with their various remotes. Like David's home, all the flooring in their house was hardwood, only several shades lighter.

Alyson laughed. "It's also very tidy."

"It wasn't an hour ago. Between Matt working, me working to finish my dissertation, and all the wedding planning, I hate to say this place kind've looked like a hurricane and tornado hit it all at once."

Alyson's eyes slid right, toward the dining area, which had a northwest facing window and was offset by more bright-white, built-in shelving. A small dining room table sat in the center and atop it sat the bouquets of yellow roses, as well as sandwiches and lemonade.

"The house was actually an engagement gift from my aunt and uncle since Matt and I love living in Boulder. And my brother"—she widely displayed her hands—"helped us with all this. The house had to be gutted and redesigned to comfortably accommodate me."

Alyson's smile dipped as she remembered the pretty teenager who sized her up during their first meeting, all while lazily walking down the stairs.

"All of you came up with a beautiful house," she said.

Becca grinned and backed up toward the dining room. "Are you hungry?"

"Yes." She'd eaten very little for breakfast due to nerves.

"Matt made us sandwiches and lemonade. He makes the *best* sandwiches, too. Oh, and you can put your stuff on the couch."

She sat across from Becca at the table. After several scrumptious bites of Matt's roast beef with roasted tomatoes sandwich, and not quite ready to test the waters of discussing the past, she said, "You know, it occurred to me I never had a chance to ask you on Saturday about how you and Matt met?"

Becca swallowed her big bite. "We actually met through David. Because of the firm."

Smiling, Alyson lowered her sandwich.

"As they were forming the firm," Becca continued, "they hired

Matt to help them design their business logo and marketing materials. He does some web designing, too, and he helped them with that, which led to him being their sole website administrator." She grinned. "And the way we met was at a party the guys threw for everyone right after the firm opened at the Lovett's cabin in Estes Park. I know you've been there."

She nodded. Yes, she'd been to that beautiful cabin a few times. David had surprised her one Saturday night by taking them there. Her first visit. And the most unforgettable one.

She set down her sandwich, then reached for her lemonade.

"David and Matt have become such good friends the last few years, Matt asked him to be a groomsman in the wedding." She giggled. "I'm *so* excited you'll be my florist, too."

She buried the Estes Park memory. "Me, too." *Another place she didn't belong.*

"So…David mentioned you have a boyfriend?"

She put her glass down a little harder than she intended. "Yes. I do." She would surely rot in hell for lying to innocent Becca Preston. But she had no choice. *It was safer this way.*

"How did you two meet?"

Crap. She hadn't expected these kinds of questions. She also wasn't comfortable with the knowledge David had made it a point to mention her "boyfriend" to his sister. But she couldn't focus on that. Right now, she needed to come up with something believable—the last guy she'd dated for a little while popped into her head, followed by how they'd met.

She forced her mouth into a bright smile. "We crossed paths at his co-worker's wedding. We were hired as the florists, and he was a guest."

Becca eyed her. "That's cool. What does he do?"

Alyson again reached for her lemonade and took a long swallow. She needed to get them off this topic. "He was a high school math teacher, then became director of admissions and tuition at a private school in Denver." At least, that's what he'd been doing when they parted ways months ago. And now for that subject change.

"He sounds pretty important. I respect anyone who decides to be a teacher." Becca smiled softly. "My parents were teachers. Do you remember that?"

Alyson froze, since she'd given her the opening she needed. "Yes, of course I do."

Becca went back to her sandwich.

She stared at the bright yellow roses that had wilted a bit since Saturday. She had to do this before the subject went to wedding flowers. *It was now or never.* "Becca, I need to ask you something. Before I lose my nerve."

Becca straightened. "Sure. Anything." She leaned forward. "Sounds serious, though."

She picked up her napkin and folded it in half. "It is. Very." She smoothed the crease she'd made in the napkin, then chanced a glance at Becca, now frowning.

"You want to talk about my brother."

Alyson folded the napkin again, creating quarters. "Yes. But only if you're comfortable?"

Becca eyed her cautiously. "What do you want to know?"

She smoothed the napkin's creases, took a quick breath, then said, "I want to know what happened that morning David told you… about your parents." *A few days after the funeral and when Becca had come out of her coma.*

The young woman's eyes doubled in size. "He never told you?"

She stopped her obsessive napkin smoothing, since that had *not* been the reaction she'd expected. Discomfort with talking about it, definitely. But not shock she didn't know.

Becca sat back. "I shouldn't be surprised he never told you." She paused before adding, "He probably hasn't told anyone." Their eyes met. "Are you sure you want to know? It's awful."

Everything from that time had been awful. Horrific. So incredibly *painful.*

"I'm asking you because I know he'll never tell me." *And I need closure, too.* "I know I'm asking a lot, but I have to know what happened that morning."

Becca nibbled on her lower lip for several seconds, then said, "I'm almost positive I'm the reason you and my brother broke up."

Her breath left her chest and she remained silent.

"I don't remember a lot from that time," she continued. "I was recovering from so much and they had me on various medications. But I do remember *that* day. Very clearly." She lowered her eyes. "I said *terrible* things to him."

Alyson leaned forward. "Becca, he was already a huge mess before that day and pushing everyone away." But what little she'd admitted already explained so much.

Becca pushed her plate aside. "I didn't know that at the time, though. I wasn't even thinking about what he was going through, especially that day he told me." She lifted her eyes back to Alyson's. "He came into the room, all alone, and I remember thinking how awful he looked. I knew what he was going to say, but..." She sighed. "The truth, especially that kind of truth, physically hurts. And that was a truth so incredibly horrible and agonizing I didn't want to believe it. Which I didn't, at first." Her lower lip quivered. "I was crying so hard I could barely see David. He was standing right beside the bed, too."

Alyson slowly nodded, not certain she wanted to hear any more.

"Then I became so *angry*." Becca picked at the plate with her fingernail. "Not knowing any better, because I was only sixteen and in shock from everything else, I needed someone to blame." She hesitated before adding, "Someone to hate."

Alyson pressed her lips together as the puzzle pieces came together.

"That person," she softly admitted, "was my brother."

Becca's damp eyes met Alyson's for a handful of seconds.

Oh, no, no, no. But it also explained everything. And it never occurred to her that what happened between brother and sister that morning would have been even more painful. They had, despite their sibling angst, always been close. He'd been her protective big brother and Becca, though she never would have admitted it at the time, had adored him.

Becca sniffed. "The fact he—both of you, I think?—were supposed to be with us that night made me angrier and I…started *screaming* that it was all his fault and that I hated him."

Alyson stared at her lap as it became a wet blur.

She and David, like every couple, had experienced their fair share of arguments. But the day of the accident they had their first yelling match about attending Becca's big, play-off soccer game that night. David had backed out at the last minute because of another fight he'd had with his parents about his music and teaching. She'd tried to reason with him, but he'd, and not nicely, dug in his heels. Then she'd slammed his bedroom door on her way out. The next time she'd talked to him was when he'd called her before dawn about the accident.

"I said I hated him over and over," Becca continued, forcing Alyson back to the present. "I was crying and screaming so loud that a nurse and a doctor came into the room. I think our aunt and uncle ran in, too, and then I…went blank. They gave me something to calm me down." She twisted her fingers together. "I didn't see David again for months."

Alyson's mouth inched open.

That was when my descent to the rockiest bottom imaginable began.

"Aunt Eileen and Uncle Hugh tried bringing us back together for weeks, but I refused." She swiped under eyes. "I didn't even want to hear his name."

Alyson could only imagine how David had spent that dark time, too.

"You're not drinking."

"No, not anymore."

"I had no idea you were gone, too," she mumbled. "To be honest, I didn't care what was going on with him. I didn't care about anything after that morning." She peeked at Alyson. "That's when I started seeing a psychologist, because I was pretty…depressed."

She blinked her eyes clear and straightened. "That's completely understandable."

Becca absently nodded. "The woman I was seeing was the one who brought us back together. She had him come to a session." She frowned. "Without my knowledge. It made me angry, and the session didn't go well. But," she slowly continued, "I do remember he looked physically better than *that* day. But…lost. By that time, I hadn't seen him for four months."

Alyson's eyes widened while her heart took the full impact of Becca's declaration.

Four months? And during a time when they'd needed each other? Oh, my *God*.

"It took a couple more sessions for us to finally talk." Becca's eyes met hers once more. "That session also allowed us to grieve together. And for the first time since…" She released a slow breath. "I have no idea what went on with him during the time we were estranged. He's never talked about it, and neither have our aunt and uncle. But when he admitted, not long after that session and only after I asked about you, that you two had broken up months earlier, I somehow knew it happened that day." She leaned forward. "Alyson, whatever David said or did after that morning wasn't his fault."

She frowned at Becca implying David's decisions following that morning were her fault. But she also understood her loyalty and reasons why she'd think herself responsible.

David hadn't been entirely honest Saturday. His sister's reaction could not have "hurt" him. It probably destroyed him until…when? What had happened to get him back on the physically and mentally healthy road, far from the crutch that had made everything worse? Had his aunt and uncle intervened at some point?

During that time, she suspected he was battling survivor's guilt on top of everything else. Still, what if she and David *had* been with them in the car? It was a difficult question she'd asked herself numerous times, only to arrive at the same conclusions—she had been lucky, while fate had intervened on David's behalf, knowing Becca would need her big brother.

You got caught in the fall.

"Thank you for telling me what happened that morning. I know it wasn't easy for you." She took a deep breath and soundly released the air. "No one was thinking clearly back then, least of all—and understandably—you and David." She stared at a spot on the table. "When I really think about it now, his state of mind at the time, I honestly don't think anything different would've happened between us." Her getting caught in his fall had been unavoidable.

She still couldn't help but wish he would have treated her as his other best friend that night in his bedroom. Just like he had the night, twenty-four hours after the accident, when he unexpectedly showed up at her apartment, straight from his comatose sister's side, and unleashed his anguish while they were curled up together on her bed.

Alyson's eyes blurred at the memory and now knowing what happened that morning.

Her drive back into the Highlands would allow her plenty of time to digest everything Becca had shared. *Painful* information David hadn't wanted her to know to possibly protect her? And could it be all these years later he was still struggling with the ugliness of ten years ago?

"It actually felt really good *to* talk about it." Becca sent her an affectionate smile. "Especially with you, since I always thought of you as a big sister." Her smile turned shy. "Al, David's not the only one who's missed you."

Alyson's mouth formed an *oh*.

"Because of that," Becca slowly added, "and being so thrilled you're here again, can I ask a favor of you? It's a big favor, but I'd love it if you said yes."

Alyson squinted at her, still on the missing her comment. As well as everything else.

"I know you're super busy with your shop, but do you think you could go wedding dress shopping with me? This Friday?"

She blinked several times, not certain she'd heard her right since she'd spoken swiftly.

"I know. You can't believe I don't have a wedding dress by now. I can't believe it, either." She pointed at her wheelchair. "But it's been very challenging trying to find a dress that goes with this rotten appendage. They've been either way too long, way too poofy, way too short, right skirt with the wrong top portion…" She nibbled her bottom lip. "Aunt Eileen and Uncle Hugh went back to Florida on Sunday, and I've surpassed desperate. I need a woman to go with me, and I can't keep bothering my girlfriends. Will you go with me?" She folded her hands and placed them under her chin. "Please, please, *please*?"

Alyson shook the shock of Becca's request from her head, which instantly revealed her answer. She could also clearly envision what Jillian's reaction would be to all of this.

"Are you too busy?" Becca asked. "I have three appointments. I can't spare any more time or I'll be getting married in one of my sun dresses. But if you can't go, we'll figure—"

"I'll do it." The three little words came out in a jumbled rush. "I'm honored you asked me." She smiled. "It'll be a lot of fun."

"Thank you, Al." Becca returned her smile. "My first appointment is at 9:30. We'll plan on picking you up at your shop around nine?"

"That'll work. And we meaning you and Matt?" They did, after all, need a strong man to move Becca from wheelchair to car and vice versa. But she felt confident she could, with a saleswoman's help, get Becca in and out of whatever dresses she wanted to try on.

Becca's smile slipped a notch. "Actually, it won't be Matty."

Alyson stared at her.

"But everything will be *fine*. I swear."

She narrowed her eyes at the fact she'd just been hoodwinked by the little bride-to-be. She also knew if Becca had told her that piece of info first, she still would have said yes to her request, since the young woman had been like having a little sister.

David's not the only one who's missed you.

Alyson had missed her, too. Or more accurately *them*.

Chapter Eight

DAVID YAWNED, tears hitting his eyes, while he saved the newest round of changes to Queen Dunne's custom compound. He blinked the wetness away, then dropped the enormous file into the Dropbox folder that Vivienne and Bob could also access.

He'd definitely hit a wall this morning and the wall seemed to be winning.

The past week had been the custom compound by day, and band rehearsal, two basketball games with the guys, and the weekly Blues Note gig by night. They also had a new gig at a place in Evergreen tomorrow night.

Despite his busy schedule, he hadn't been sleeping well. Because at night, alone in his silent bedroom, his thoughts centered on one person. Adding insult to injury, she'd taken over his dreams, too. His conscious and subconscious seemed determined to relive their first moments.

Their first phone conversation that lasted for hours. Their first date. Their first kiss, a scene from a movie, "Whoa" moment. The first time she'd met his family and vice versa. The moment he'd given her his heart and she'd given him hers as they stood on campus, and right after a stupid misunderstanding. But she'd needed to hear the words, and he'd needed to say them. A little over a week later, he'd taken her to the Lovett's cabin in Estes Park.

His phone started to vibrate and burst into the piano riff.

She'd been surprisingly confident that night. And unforgettably irresistible.

He glanced at the screen, then swiped it off his island counter where he'd been working on his laptop since 7:00. "Hey." He yanked his brain back to the present.

"We're pretty close," Becs said. "Is Nancy there yet?"

"No. But I'm expecting her any minute."

He forced himself to concentrate on his work. There was one more thing he needed to do before shifting his focus fully to wedding dress shopping.

"I'm feeling really good about today. Finding *my* dress." There was a long pause on his sister's end, then, "I sort've forgot to mention something the other night. It's not a big deal, though. We just need to make one quick stop before heading to my first appointment."

He propped his phone between his ear and shoulder in order to type and send a quick e-mail to Vivienne and Bob, letting them know the designs were now available. "What do you need to do?" More hesitation on her end, which prompted him to stop typing. "Becs?"

"We just need to swing over to the Highlands and pick up Alyson."

She'd spoken rapidly. To the point he wasn't sure he'd heard her right, since Al had been consuming his thoughts quite a bit.

He grasped his phone, suddenly alert. "What the hell did you say?"

"She's going with us today. Alyson? I know I should've mentioned it a couple days ago, but with everything else going on it just kind've slipped my mind."

Like hell it had. They had talked late Wednesday afternoon about her flower meeting with Al. "Becs, what did you do? Does she know I'm going? And what about Nancy?"

"Of course Alyson knows you're going. And Nancy won't care." She laughed. "I say the more the merrier. It'll be fun!"

He swallowed a groan. Clearly he and his sister had entirely different ideas on what was considered fun. "And she still agreed to come along?"

"Well, actually, I—ouch!" It sounded like the phone had been jostled as he could just make out the words, "I'm *telling* him, Matt." More phone jostling, then, "I may have mentioned the fact you were going…after she said yes."

He straightened, his jaw turning to steel. "Rebecca Elizabeth Preston—"

"Ooh, Matt needs to talk to me. We'll see you in a bit. Bye!"

The phone went dead, and as his hand dropped to the counter he fought the strong compulsion to squeeze the device. To see if it would turn into dust.

"Shit." What the hell had his sister been thinking? Was she trying to torture him?

His phone began vibrating and riffing. It was the office.

He debated answering for two more riffs before tapping the green dot. "Hi."

"It's Marjorie. Vivienne Dunne is insisting that she needs to talk to you. Can I transfer her to your cell?"

Fantastic.

"No. My sister and Jackson's mom will be here any minute."

"Then you should tell her that so she doesn't keep you on the phone too long."

"Marjorie, don't you—"

Silence, followed by, "Hello? David, are you there?"

His shoulders slumped. "Yes."

Marjorie would pay for this one. Maybe he'd swipe her stapler from her desk?

"Your receptionist said you were out of the office today, but I *had* to talk to you."

Marjorie Bradshaw never missed a damn thing. She'd not only

notice the bright-red stapler missing from her spotless work area, but would tear the office apart looking for it.

"What can I do for you, Vivienne?" he managed to politely ask. "Have you already looked at the new designs? I just dropped them into the file."

"Oh. No. Not yet. I'm calling because I was watching something on HGTV last night and I have an idea."

Shit. He started to count backward from ten.

"This house had a beautiful, grand staircase in the foyer that divided into two sections of stairs, leading to the second level. It was just *gorgeous*, really, and it made me second guess the duel staircase we came up with. This staircase I saw last night made the lower level so open. What do you think?"

That you're a lunatic. And have too much damn time and money. But he said, "Vivienne, the staircase you chose months ago is already up. I don't recommend making that big of a change at this point." Bob's hard hat would definitely blow to the moon over a change that substantial, too. "It would also be a huge strain on everyone's time, as well as a significant waste of materials," he added, failing to mention the money aspect since that didn't concern her one bit. Nor did anything else he said. But he had to, for everyone's sake, at least try those tactics.

"But it was so…grand. I can't help but wonder what it would look like."

And here it came.

"Do you think you could come up with a design for me to look at? I think that would be fair, don't you? That way I'm not making any hasty decisions."

David sat back and stared as his laptop, trying to recall where he'd put his passport. Because a one-way ticket out of Denver to another country—he'd always wanted to see Scotland—where no one could find him sounded more appealing than what he was facing right now.

"I'll work on those designs this weekend," he answered.

"Wonderful! I'll take a look at what you put in the file earlier and give you a call if I have any questions or concerns."

Or changes.

"You're an absolute *darling.*" She followed that up with an air kiss.

He tapped his red button, then expelled a long, heavy breath.

Early retirement was looking better and better every day he dealt with Mrs. Vivienne Dunne and her custom compound in Aspen, Colorado.

He reached out to shut down his computer—screw the e-mail since he could give Bob a quick call—when his phone, once again, started vibrating and riffing.

He looked at the display, tapped the well-used green dot, and said, "David Preston's party line where the fun never stops. What the hell do *you* want?"

Jackson chuckled. "Busy morning?"

"You're my third call in the last ten or so minutes. I just talked to Queen Dunne."

"What does she want now?"

"She *thinks* she wants a different staircase, but I'll use my charm to talk her out of it."

"Good luck with that. Hey, can you give me Hugh and Eileen's e-mail address?"

He paused in the middle of closing his programs. "Sure, but why do you need it?"

"I'm..." His friend's voice faltered, followed by a pause, then, "Jillian asked for help on something having to do with the shop and it occurred to me they'd be an even better resource."

That caught his somewhat jumbled attention. Then the envious pang from Saturday, while Al and Becs exchanged phone numbers, shot through him. He also couldn't stop himself from saying, "Okay. But what do they have to do with it?"

"Jillian wants to know everything she can about the real estate investment company owned by that pompous dickhead, Keith Marsden." Silence, followed by, "She asked me about it the other night while we were talking and wanted more info after I told her what little I'd heard."

"Well, pompous dickhead was a nice way of describing Marsden." David shut down his computer. It was none of his business, but he asked, "Do you know why she wants to know about Marsden Enterprises?"

Jackson sighed. "No. She wouldn't tell me. Asked for help, then changed the subject. But me calling Marsden the definition of jackass, according to the Urban Dictionary, bothered her. She seemed distracted after that."

He narrowed his eyes. "Sounds like something's going on." He huffed. "Not sure my uncle will have anything nice to say about Marsden, either."

In a matter of time David would, and very unexpectedly, be seeing *her* again. And in her shop where it sounded like something questionable was brewing.

Becca's behavior was unacceptable. He'd be telling her as much. At the same time, he couldn't ignore the burst of adrenaline he'd always experienced when he and Al were a couple; anticipating being with her. Even when they weren't getting along because of school stress.

"Are you going to send me their e-mail address or not?"

His front door opened, followed by, "Yo, D-Man. We're here! I'm bringing her in, then I have to get the hell out of here."

He said to Jackson, "Yeah. Of course."

No doubt if he casually asked Al about any of this, she'd shut him down before he could blink. That meant he'd have to indefinitely shelve his curiosity.

"Thanks, man."

"Yep." He stood. "So I need to go wring my sister's neck. They just got here."

Jackson laughed. "I warned you little Rebecs would turn into a Bridezilla."

"That's not the problem. I'll tell you about it later." He ended the call.

The moment Becs and Matt were in his kitchen, he settled his eyes on his sister, conveniently focused on her fiancé.

"I'll call you as soon as we're back here," she said to him.

He tugged his eyes away from Becs to give Matt the same displeased look.

"Don't look at me like that, Piano Man," he said. "I had nothing to do with any of it. I just want your key so I can get out of here before your head explodes. I'm also running late."

Reluctantly, David reached into his right jeans pocket to remove his key fob.

The only reason he was handing over the key to his Audi, a brand new, black, custom-designed SUV, was because the back would only accommodate Becs's wheelchair if he put the seats down. Which he couldn't do because of Nancy going with them. And now Al. They had to take the Cherokee, and Matt needed a vehicle.

"If anything happens to my car, I can promise you both there won't be a wedding in August." He tossed the key to Matt, who grinned.

"You know I have insurance."

He didn't return Matt's grin.

Matt bent down to give Becs a quick kiss. "Have fun today. Remember to breathe. And I'll see you later. I hope," he swiftly added, then gave her another, longer kiss.

Matt made a bee-line for the front door. Before it closed, David was focused on his sister.

"Oh, stop it. You're not really mad about this."

He crossed his arms. "That isn't a bet I would take if I were you."

She rolled her eyes.

It was something he'd seen her do hundreds of times. But this was the first time he understood their parents' extreme irritation with the action. "Dammit, Becca, don't roll your eyes! Did you even stop to think about the position you put her in? She has a boyfriend."

"God, you sound just like dad," she muttered.

"Good," he shot back. "You manipulated this situation. How could you do that? Especially to her?"

"Fine!" She threw up her hands. "I'm sorry. I didn't mean any harm. But if she was really that uncomfortable, she would've backed out by now."

He leaned forward. "Whatever fantasies you're having about me and Alyson getting back together need to stop. Right now. Do you understand me?"

Her eyes widened since he had, indisputably, channeled their dad. The doorbell then rang, indicating Nancy had arrived.

Her surprise eased into something resembling innocent confusion. "I'm not sure I know what you mean, but" —she nodded once — "okay. Whatever you say."

Bullshit. But he straightened and stepped backward. "Becs, I know how much having Al back in your life means to you." *More than you can possibly imagine.* "But for your sake, you better not pull anything like this again."

Thirty-minutes later, his steps wavered as he approached Daisy's Bouquets.

Luckily, he'd found a parking space a few buildings down from hers, allowing him time to formulate his thoughts. Reign in his emotions that were an uncomfortable mixture of apprehension, excitement, and embarrassment because of his sister's actions.

He took a deep breath of the cool, morning air and opened the door. Their door's bells jingled as he cleared the threshold. His eyes then landed on Jillian.

She stood behind the counter, right near the computer-register. Beside her stood the pretty woman with dark-blonde hair who had walked in that Monday, complaining about the city's traffic. But for the life of him he couldn't remember her name.

Jillian gave him that same, shit-eating grin from Saturday night after spending all that time with Jackson. "Hi." She turned toward the backroom. "Al, David's here."

Something about her phrasing felt too…right. Too comfortable.

Al strolled out, adjusting her purse strap on her shoulder.

Their eyes snapped together.

All he could think to say was, "Hi there."

She gave him a tentative smile, then walked fully into the shop.

He tried not to stare. But she looked too…incredible…wearing tight jeans. She also wore a thick, beige sweater that matched the color of her shoes. And, just his damn luck, she had her hair pulled into a long braid that fell past her right shoulder. A hairstyle he'd always liked. *A lot*.

He looked at the floor.

Shit. This was going to be a long damn day.

"Campbell, I'll see you in the morning," she said.

He committed the woman's name to memory just in case he, for some unknown reason, needed to remember it. He also was, right or wrong, genuinely interested in Al's business.

Al smiled at Jillian. "And *you* have fun tonight."

Jillian laughed as she looked in his direction.

"Feel free to give my buddy all you've got," he said at the same time Al headed for the door. "I promise you he can handle it."

"Will do. *Have fun*," she practically sang.

He followed Al out of the shop, then veered right.

"I would think," she began, "that after twelve years, you would've come up with something to replace '*Hi there*'."

He laughed at her attempt to mimic his voice and that she'd remembered those were the first words he'd said right after he sat beside her in the classroom.

When they were two cars away from the Cherokee, he stopped, which made her do the same. "Well, I firmly believe in the statement 'If it's not broken, don't fix it'."

She fought a smile.

"I'm sorry." His grin became a frown. "I didn't know you were coming with us today until Becs dropped it on me about an hour ago."

She shrugged. "It's fine. Really. As long as you're okay?"

His frown deepened. "I'm still pissed about her behavior, but I'm fine." *But not really.* That thought prompted him to ask, "Is your… boyfriend okay with this?" He couldn't lie to himself. He was a *little* curious about the guy's reaction. He also felt somewhat obligated to ask since his sister had put them in this slightly awkward situation.

"Of course he is," she quickly answered. "Why wouldn't he be?"

Something about her fast reply told him she wasn't telling the truth. Then again, he couldn't blame the guy for being upset.

"Who else is in there?" she asked, squinting at the Cherokee.

"Nancy Lovett. Jackson's mom?"

She whipped her head in his direction. "What are you talking about?"

He sighed. "I asked Nancy last weekend, with Becs's okay, to come with us today. Which my *charming* sister obviously didn't tell you on Wednesday. I still want to wring her neck because of all this." He stepped toward her. "Al, I really am sorry."

She took a huge step backward. "Oh, no worries. I'll just go back to the shop."

She turned, probably about to make a run for it, but he gently grasped her upper arm and pulled her forward. "Oh, no. You, like me, made a commitment, and we're in this together."

She glanced at his fingers, and he released her arm.

"David, she doesn't need three of us helping her choose a wedding dress."

"I'm not here to help her choose a dress. I'm simply the driver. And the muscle," he added, then flexed his right bicep that, unfortunately, was underneath his fleece pullover.

She released a series of long, deep giggles; the same laughter he'd been hearing in his dreams that he knew so well.

Grinning, he lowered his arm. "I knew it. You *do* still think I'm cute."

She held up her right hand, now back to fighting a smile. "Don't get too full of yourself. I'm also laughing at this *ridiculous* situation." She laughed again, then shook her head. "You were right years ago when you said your sister could be sneaky."

"I'm pretty sure I also said she could be a pain in the butt." But thank God Al wasn't pissed at Becs. If the boyfriend was upset about today, she didn't seem bothered by that, either. In fact, she seemed to be in a great mood.

"You're glowing today," he said as they continued to walk toward the Cherokee. The last time he'd seen her like this was their hooky day in the city.

"Am I?" She shrugged. "I guess it has been a pretty good week. We've been really busy with weddings and soon it will officially be wedding season."

Everything sounded a-okay with her business. So why would Jillian be interested in learning more about Marsden Enterprises? It didn't make sense.

"How was your week?" she asked.

He shot her a quick smile. "Busy." Complicated by the fact he hadn't been able to stop thinking about *her*. He stopped them beside the Cherokee. "I'm really proud of you, Alyson." *More than you can possibly know*. He could only hope her shop was doing as well as she said.

Her cheeks flushed and she gave him a shy smile, reminding him of the day they met.

Oh, yeah. This was going to be an extraordinarily long day.

Chapter Nine

THEY SILENTLY EMERGED from the bridal shop, the final stop of the day.

Alyson chanced a glance at Becca, her forehead stuck in a deep frown.

"That's it." Becca's voice cracked on the words. "I'm just being too picky." She stopped when they reached the parking lot. Her face crumbled. Then tears exploded from her eyes.

Alyson's heart cracked as she stepped toward the distraught young woman. But Nancy Lovett, a constant source of positivity all day, knelt in front of Becca and grasped her hands.

"Rebecca, honey," the older woman murmured, "you have to keep a clear head."

"I know, but I...hate this *stupid* chair! It's...r-ruining everything."

Alyson pressed her right hand to her mouth before her eyes connected with David's, wide with shock and helplessness.

Nancy continued to hold Becca; her body shuddering as the tears came fast and hard.

"Is there another place you want to try today?" Nancy calmly asked.

"N-no," she said, swiping her wet nose. "You…know you usually h-have to have an…appointment. And I…I think I've been to every b-bridal shop…" Her words became lost in more heart-wrenching sobbing.

David ran a hand through his hair which made the short strands stick up.

That's when an idea hit Alyson. It would be expensive, but probably Becca's only hope in having her perfect wedding dress. "Okay." She removed her hand from her mouth. "Nobody panic just yet." She glanced at David. "Is it safe to assume that at this point money is no object?"

He blinked a couple of times, then nodded. "Absolutely."

"I have an idea." She refocused on Becca. "I know a place. I've referred a few brides to this shop. They're located in Cherry Creek North. You probably overlooked them in your search for bridal shops because they don't sell wedding dresses." She paused before adding, "They specialize in helping brides design their perfect dress, which is then made by a local team of seamstresses. Two of those women are sisters and own the shop."

Becca's sobbing subsided and she sniffed twice. "Really?" she squeaked.

"I probably should've mentioned it sooner," Alyson continued, "but the shop caters to brides whose budgets are…nonexistent." She eyed David, who nodded. "And the process, from beginning to end, takes months. Your wedding isn't until August, so you might be okay." She glanced at David and Nancy. "We can head there right now. I'll call the manager, who's a good friend, to give her a heads up. But I obviously can't promise this will work."

Becca released her grip on Nancy. "I understand, but I'd still like to try because that place sounds perfect." She wiped her wet cheeks. "I wish I would've known a place like that existed three months ago. But I was just so excited to go wedding dress shopping, you know?"

Alyson gave her a warm smile. "Yes, because it is *all* about the dress." She faced David, whose face had relaxed since Becca stopped sobbing. "Do you remember my roommate, Tricia Emerson? Well, she's Tricia Albright now. She married Ethan. The pre-med student?"

"Yeah, of course I remember them."

"Tricia manages the shop I'm talking about. She also does all their photography for their marketing materials and is really talented. I have some of her freelance work hanging in my house." She glanced at her watch. "We better head that way now." Hopefully, Tricia could help her work this into a perfect-wedding-dress miracle for a special and deserving little bride-to-be.

"Wouldn't that be a lovely and fortuitous twist?" Nancy dug through her purse. She pulled out a package of tissues, removed one, handed it to Becca, and stood. "If it all works out, you'll *really* owe Alyson a debt of gratitude. Considering how she ended up with us today?"

Alyson smothered a smile as Becca's face flushed.

Nancy grinned. "I think *all* of us will owe you our gratitude."

"Definitely." David walked behind Becca and tugged her ponytail.

She tilted her head backward. "Does this mean you're not mad anymore?"

He shrugged. "For now."

Alyson and Nancy followed the siblings to the Cherokee.

"The tension between these two this morning before we picked you up," Nancy mumbled, "was awful. It reminded me of Will and Jackson's fights when they were teenagers."

When they reached the SUV, Nancy clasped her hand and leaned forward.

"Despite how you ended up on this shopping adventure, I'm so incredibly happy you're here with us today."

Warmth spread through Alyson. All she could manage was an affectionate smile for the woman who had, like David and Becca's Aunt Eileen, immediately taken on the role of surrogate mother following that dark, horrible night so long ago. That had only been the beginning of the darkness, too, when she remembered everything Becca had told her on Wednesday.

David gently lifted Becca from her wheelchair.

Watching him, his gentleness with his little sister, she couldn't imagine the two being estranged for as long as they had been. Four months. It must have felt like four years for him.

Nancy opened the passenger door, and he carefully placed Becca on the seat. Once the older woman had climbed into the backseat, he returned to the back of the SUV.

He folded Becca's wheelchair.

She stepped forward to help him put it inside, then a question appeared in her mind.

"I got it," he said around a laugh.

"David, I don't mind helping."

He closed the door. "You already have." He grinned. "Thank you for what you're doing."

She hesitated before asking, "How come you haven't invested in a van with a lift?" She held her hand out toward the trunk. "It's none of my business, but it seems like it would be a little easier than..." Her voice trailed into silence as his eyes dimmed.

"We suggested it, but Becs didn't want to have anything to do with the idea." He lifted his shoulders. "She wants as much normal as she can have for as long as possible. And she likes sitting in the passenger seat like a *normal person*. That's how she put it," he swiftly added.

Alyson managed a soft smile. "That makes perfect sense."

He stepped toward her. "Al, thank you. Really." He brought back his grin. "Because you probably saved the day."

Their eyes connected.

"Just call me Superwoman." She took a wobbly step backward. "If this does work out."

His grin turned decidedly devilish. "I think I could do that."

Between his smile and deep, soulful brown eyes, her head became a tad foggy.

What were they talking about?

"We should probably go," he continued. "It'll be nice seeing Tricia again."

She blinked and turned from him.

Dammit. Or more like damn him for being the real *David.*

"I wouldn't thank me yet," she tossed over her shoulder. Though she'd definitely take the real David over the David who'd kicked her out of his life ten years ago. "If this goes the way we're hoping, you may be wishing I hadn't helped quite so much when you see the bill."

He followed her to the driver's side. "I somehow doubt that."

She opened the backseat door. "Remember, you haven't seen *my* bill yet."

He laughed, and she couldn't help but grin at the sound.

Once they were on their way, she called her old friend and roommate.

After she finished explaining the situation, Tricia said, "We're actually booked from now through August."

Crap. Her shoulders fell.

"But," her friend continued, "this is a really special circumstance."

She gripped her phone. "Without question."

"So when you get here, I'll sit down with her, see what she has in mind, then talk about the timeframe. We do have to factor in fittings and adjustments."

"I understand."

"And if we can work this out," Tricia warned, "it will cost a small fortune."

She cringed, but said, "They understand that." David had agreed to price being no object. Surely Eileen and Hugh were helping with the wedding expenses? "We'll be there soon."

As soon as she hung up, Becca asked, "Everything's okay, right?"

She sounded a tad on the anxious side, which made Alyson reply, "Definitely." She followed that up with a huge smile.

Becca's face relaxed and she faced forward.

Tricia's shop absolutely had to work out, since no bride on the planet deserved this more than beautiful, radiant Rebecca Preston.

It was a plea she tightly held to, as well, until the moment she and Tricia followed Becca and Nancy out of her friend's spacious office a couple hours later. Between the four of them, and under Becca's lead, they'd designed almost exactly what the young bride had been imagining, but was unable to find during her exhaustive search.

After Tricia took her petite measurements, Becca had chosen an A-line, silhouette style with a sweetheart neckline, adding simple, sparkly beadwork throughout the gown. For the material, Tricia had suggested diamond-white silk crepe. It was lightweight, soft, and would, most importantly, drape, allowing Becca to sit comfortably in her wheelchair, this being her biggest challenge throughout her search. They'd also decided, again for comfort purposes, the gown's length would stop below her calves.

Alyson stopped Tricia, then threw her arms around the woman. "You saved the day." They squeezed each other. "Thank you so much."

"It was a team effort." Tricia laughed as they released one another. "Now for the really fun part. Giving David the bill."

"That Eileen and Hugh will help him with," Nancy said over her shoulder. "I'm going to call them tonight. The 'really fun part' will be having you ladies on Eileen and Hugh's side, since David will put up a fight. But if we do this right, he'll have no choice but to acquiesce."

Becca giggled, long since back to glowing like a bride-to-be should.

Alyson thanked the Heavens yet again for all of this working out. There was no way she could have watched the young woman have another heart-breaking meltdown over anything wedding related. Recalling David's deer-caught-in-headlights expression, she suspected he couldn't have watched his little sister go through that again, either.

"So how's it been?" Tricia softly asked as they re-entered what was referred to as the design floor. "Being back in touch with David after all this time?"

Tricia had been around the last year or so of her relationship with David. She'd also been the one who'd intercepted Alyson that night upon her return from David's apartment.

"It's been fine." She'd then stayed up with her all night, trying to console the broken-hearted girl that had taken Alyson an embarrassingly long time to shed. "It's amazing being reconnected with Becca." *Absolutely the truth.* The first part hadn't really been a lie, either.

Her moments with David had been nothing but fine. Except when he'd stared at her with those deep, soulful brown eyes. And smiled as if he'd suddenly joined forces with the devil.

He'd always been really good at smiling like that.

Tricia peered at her. "Good. I'm glad to hear it hasn't been…tense."

Alyson gave her a bright smile. "Not at all." She then found herself searching for David in the spacious design area. But her smile faded once she found him.

He sat on a white, curved sectional sofa, talking easily with one of Tricia's co-designers, an exquisite, slender blonde wearing a short, yet professional skirt that showed off her equally slender legs. She then laughed at something he said.

Jealousy hit so swift and hard, her breath stalled.

She looked away, but caught Tricia watching her closely.

Alyson brought back her bright smile. Still, where had *that* come from?

Tricia linked her left arm with Alyson's right. "Let's go give David the good news."

What was wrong with her? They hadn't been together in ten years. Hadn't even seen each other in that long. Yet, here she was, a grown woman, reacting to him clearly flirting with a stunning woman as if she were still that girl he'd pushed away.

All of this meant it was time to bring the day to an end. She'd obviously gotten caught up in weddings and dresses and shopping and devilish smiles and…deep, soulful brown eyes.

A long, hard run with the *real* love of her life was exactly what she needed tonight.

Becca and Nancy arrived at the couch.

As she and Tricia approached, David handed the woman a business card, which she took with a blinding smile. They then stood.

"I'll definitely give you a ring," the woman said. In an elegant, British accent.

Alyson narrowed her eyes.

He smiled, then faced his sister while the woman excused herself. "So, you look pretty happy. Can I assume you have good news?"

"Your sister does," Tricia answered. "For you, not so much."

He laughed. "You have a dress."

Becca scrunched up her shoulders and giggled. "*Yes*! Or I will once it's made." She glanced up at Tricia. "You said the first fitting would probably be in May?"

"Yes." Tricia looked at David. "Putting a slight rush on it added to the overall cost. Which reminds me, can I have one of those?"

He frowned.

Tricia pointed at his wallet he still held. "You just gave Victoria a business card, and I'd like one, too."

Victoria. Naturally she'd have a beautiful name to match her beautiful self—Alyson pummeled that thought and concentrated on Becca's radiant face.

David was a grown man, single, and way too good looking for his own good. He could do anything he wanted with whomever. His personal life was none of her business.

He removed another business card from his wallet before returning it to his back jeans pocket. "Do you need an interior decorator, too?" he asked, handing Tricia the card.

"Eventually," she replied. "But first we need the house, meaning you, Mr. Architect. We own some land down in Elizabeth. And you're going to want our business after you see this."

She handed him the invoice she'd printed before they left her office.

Alyson looked at the women, watching him closely as he scanned the paper. The moment his eyes widened it was clear he'd reached the total amount.

"For *one* dress you'll wear *one* day?" he asked his sister.

Becca gave him a tight smile. "We did everything we could to keep the cost down."

"You're killing me, Becs."

"Honey," Nancy said, "you know your aunt and uncle will help."

"I do know that, but no. They're helping enough as it is, so please don't tell them."

Nancy turned her firm stare on Alyson, Becca, and Tricia.

"David," Alyson began, "no one expects you to pay for everything. They want to be a part of this, too."

"Not financially. No. I can handle—"

"They are the aunt and uncle of the bride," Tricia interjected.

He opened his mouth, but Becca said, "You've paid for all the other big stuff." She looked up at Alyson. "He bought the Cherokee, brand new, when Matt and I told him we wanted to go on a long road trip for our honeymoon. Even though the other SUV wasn't *that* old."

Alyson smiled, and focused on David, concentrating on the invoice. Her smile grew at his face turning stop-sign red.

"You also know Aunt Eileen and Uncle Hugh will never take no for an answer," Becca added in her high-octave voice.

He released a quick breath. "Fine. I'll call them tonight to talk about it."

Nancy smiled. "Excellent. But I will be calling them to make sure *you* talked to them."

He shook his head. "Let's get this over with before the reality of this number really hits."

"You only pay half now," Tricia said, gesturing for him to follow her. "You'll pay the rest when Becca takes the dress."

Alyson's phone began vibrating inside her purse. She withdrew it. When she saw who was calling, she said to Becca and Nancy, "I'm going to take this outside. I'll be right back." She pushed through the street door, stepped into the sunshine, and answered, "Hi." She headed right to be out of view from the shop. "I know. This took way longer than expected, but—"

"Al, we have a *huge* problem," Jillian stated.

She frowned, not only at Jillian's statement, but the distress in her voice. "What happened?" Maybe the van had finally died?

Crap. They didn't have the money for that kind of expense, especially right now.

"Some *asshat* from Marsden Enterprises was just here," Jillian continued.

Her frown deepened. "Okay." She walked to a nearby bench and slowly sat. "What did the asshat say?" But dread consumed her, since whatever happened could *not* have been good.

Silence, followed by, "We have thirty days to vacate. As does the tenant next door."

Alyson froze.

"They want us out to combine the spaces and turn it into some bar and restaurant." Jillian released a bitter laugh. "That's what the Highlands needs, right? *Another* bar and restaurant."

Her mind went blank.

"Jackson warned me about Marsden Enterprises, too. Basically said this Marsden guy is a *complete* asshole."

Jackson actually knew of this company?

"Considering the soulless asshat who just left, I'd say Jackson's description was too kind. *Hijo de perra,*" she muttered. "What the hell are we going to do?"

She stared blankly at the sidewalk.

"Alyson, are you there? *Hello?*"

She burst into laughter.

Silence again fell on Jillian's end, followed by, "Where are you right now?"

She continued laughing, but managed to say, "I have no idea."

"You have no idea where you are?"

"No. I'm in Cherry Creek North with David, Becca, and Nancy." Had she really been lost in wedding dress shopping all day as fate prepared to dump this crap into her lap?

She started laughing once again.

"Alyson, you're worrying me."

"Because I don't know what to do, Jilly!" she snapped, suddenly stone-cold sober. "*Thirty days*? How could they do that? How is that even possible?" Was that even possible? Her mind was incredibly jumbled. She couldn't picture that realistically happening.

Panic then replaced her insane mirth as she struggled to catch her breath.

"Do you want me to cancel with Jackson tonight?" Jillian asked. "I can come over to your place, and we'll sit down and figure this out."

She closed her eyes and took slow, steady breaths.

They had to vacate in *thirty days*. They'd considered the possibility of leaving if the rent increased to a number they couldn't pay. But being kicked out?

"Al, what are you thinking?"

We were stupid to not be prepared for something like this.

She opened her eyes. "Go on your date. Have fun. I'll see you tomorrow morning at the shop." They still had a wedding and a wedding to crash.

"Are you sure? Jackson and I can reschedule."

"I'm sure, Jilly." But she wasn't sure she could deal with all of *this* clearly tonight.

"What are *you* going to do?"

For some reason, Jillian's question filled with concern caused her eyes to become wet. "I'm…going to go on a run with the love of my life. I'll see you tomorrow." A run that she needed now more than ever.

After she hung up, she stared at her phone.

She'd gone into the day focused on all the positive things happening in the shop. And getting to spend the day wedding dress shopping with little Becca Preston. And *him*.

You're glowing today.

Of course David had noticed. Then he'd quietly said he was proud of her, knowing little about her as a small-business owner.

Dammit. She should have seen this coming. Done some research on Marsden Enterprises. Cliff had given no indication they should have expected something like this. But how much would a buyer tell a seller about their business plans?

She swallowed a moan at the answer.

They had to vacate in *thirty days*. Searching for a new space would probably be the best, smartest way to spend her evening. Only after her run, though, that would surely clear her head?

A warm hand landed on her shoulder. "Alyson?"

She spun in the direction of the familiar voice and stood.

David's eyes radiated confusion and some concern. "Is everything okay?"

"Yes." But she felt the sudden urge to yell at him to stop looking at her like that.

He continued staring at her. "You're lying."

She dropped her phone back into her purse, also not liking the fact he knew she was lying. "You're right. I need to get back to the shop. Now."

He frowned. "We're ready, but what the hell happened? You were fine minutes ago."

She walked around the bench. "It's none of your business." She stopped when she saw Becca and Nancy outside the shop, watching her—them—with wide, curious eyes.

"We'll meet you at the car," David said to them.

They slowly nodded and headed in that direction.

She started to follow, but he caught her left hand.

"Alyson, talk to me. What happened?"

"*Stop it*," she hissed in an attempt to not draw attention to their heated exchange. "Stop acting like you care. We're not a couple and we're definitely not friends!"

He dropped her hand as if it had turned scalding. Then his face became an emotionless mask. "Fine. I'm sorry. It won't happen again."

She gave him a curt nod, then swiveled left and marched toward where he'd parked.

David really hadn't deserved any of that when she recalled how amazing and patient he'd been today with all of them, especially his sister. He'd never liked shopping. Ten years ago it had been his definition of torture. If that were still true, today had *not* been his idea of a good time. But he'd done it for his little sister who'd needed to find her perfect wedding dress.

Still, something about lashing out at him like that had been... satisfying. Old, painful wounds coming back for vengeance. After they dropped her off, she had no idea when she'd see him again and maybe he hadn't deserved her outburst. But no matter what had happened between David and Becca that morning in her hospital room, *she* hadn't deserved what he'd done to her afterward. And what the hell had she done to deserve the soulless Marsden Enterprises taking over her beloved, *perfect* spot in the Highlands? A spot they would probably never replicate.

Tears hit her eyes and she furiously blinked them away.

After the long, hard run with Thatcher, she'd take a hot bath and free *all* her emotions.

Chapter Ten

NANCY'S contagious laughter usually made David laugh, but he couldn't get there tonight. As such, he was the only person sitting at his unexpectedly full dining room table not laughing.

Nancy had insisted on making dinner for him, Becs, and Matt. It was also the reason Will Lovett, Jackson's older brother, and his wife, Savannah, had ended up at David's house instead of at a restaurant in nearby Cherry Creek North.

"That firework was so loud and seemed to go on forever." Nancy paused to release another round of hearty laugher. "In fact, it was still going off when Jackson burst into the house looking like he'd just been shot out of hell. And I knew he'd been involved."

Everyone but David continued laughing.

Though it was definitely nice to have a home-cooked meal for a change and spend time like this with his family and *second* family, he hadn't expected his house to end up as the place to be tonight. He also couldn't stop thinking about Al and what had happened with her earlier.

"Jackson tried putting all the blame on his new little friend, David," Nancy added.

"Of course he did," David mumbled.

"Well, that firework was at *your* house," Will said while focused on him. "Jackson's also said you were the one who took him to the garage."

"It's true." Becs wrinkled her nose. "I remember because *you* wouldn't let me go with you guys."

David stood and picked up his empty plate, then Nancy's.

She said, mostly to Matt who'd never heard this story, "After I gave Jackson an earful, I went over to the Prestons' house to not only introduce myself as the parent of their son's accomplice, but also to apologize."

If Al hadn't done that crazed three-sixty after leaving Tricia's shop, he had a strong feeling she'd be here, too. He wondered for the umpteenth time what the *hell* had happened in those few minutes she'd been outside, on the the phone with…who? The boyfriend?

Nancy gave him and Becs an affectionate smile. "Your parents were so nice about it, too. But also very embarrassed."

David dragged his thoughts back to the present. "This story has also become one that Jackson and I will *never* live down." But at mentioning his buddy's name, an idea hit.

"Not while I'm still breathing," Nancy replied.

"Never, ever," Becs threw in as as her fiancé continued to laugh.

Al had said she needed to get back to the shop. If something big had happened there, chances were Jillian had told Jackson. She had asked him about Marsden Enterprises. Yeah, they were on their first date right now, but the curiosity would kill him if he didn't get an answer to Al's unexpected change in attitude.

"I can assure you," Nancy continued, "there was never a dull moment when Jackson and David were kids."

"*And* pyromaniacs," Matt replied.

Will smiled. "Truth. They were always in trouble."

Savannah stared at her husband. "And, what, you were a little angel back then?"

"He did worse stuff." David headed for his kitchen. "But the bastard never got caught."

Will's maniacal laughter followed him to his island counter where he set the plates down.

"Do you know what your brother's up to tonight?" Nancy asked.

"He's probably *working*."

David swiped his phone off the counter and headed for the French doors that opened to his patio and backyard.

Becs laughed. "Actually, he's on a date."

A date that was about to be interrupted. But he'd keep it brief.

Nancy's "Really? With who?" followed him outside into the brisk, night air.

He shut the door and walked several steps from his house. He could only hope Jackson would answer. Which he did after David called him three times in a row.

"This better be an emergency," Jackson answered.

"I know you're busy—"

"Yeah. A little bit."

"So I'll get to the point," David finished. "Did Jillian maybe mention something happening at the shop today?"

There was a pause, then, "Yeah. She did. And it's not good."

He sighed and shook his head.

"Let me talk to him." Jillian's voice barely reached him through the phone, followed by phone jostling. "Hi, David. It's Jillian."

"Hi," he slowly said.

"You need to go see Alyson. Preferably tonight. As in leave your house right now."

He frowned. "But what about—"

"I promise you she's at home. *Alone.* Here's the address." She rattled it off, but he'd been to Al's grandparents' house enough when they were together he still knew where it was located.

"Don't be scared. She won't bite. But I can't promise Thatcher *won't*," she added. "I'm hanging up now. Please don't call Jackson again tonight."

The line went dead, and he stared at his phone.

What the *hell* had just happened?

You need to go see Alyson.

Jillian had also made it clear she'd be *alone*. Which meant the boyfriend wouldn't be there. But why? If the guy was worth a shit, he'd be with Al, since something bad had happened with her business. Something so bad she'd become a different woman in a span of minutes.

"David?"

He turned toward Nancy, standing in the doorway.

"Do you want some help with the dishes before I leave?"

Right. *All those dishes.* He'd spaced that Nancy Lovett's excellent cooking always came with a cost—a huge mess afterward that included almost every pan and dish in the kitchen.

"No, I got it." He headed toward her.

"Are you sure?" she asked as he followed her into his house. "I made quite a mess."

He guided her out of his kitchen and to the front door where Becs, Matt, Will, and Savannah were shrugging into their coats.

He smiled. "You cook, we clean it up. That was always the rule." A rule Jackson and Will's dad had implemented when they'd been kids.

The three of them had spent a good portion of their youth cleaning the Lovett's kitchen.

Will laughed. "Have fun with that, D-Man." He hustled his wife out the door.

You need to go see Alyson.

"David, you're the best brother *ever*." Becs smiled at him. "Today was so amazing. And I know you were upset with me about Alyson, but it was actually a good thing she came today."

He narrowed his eyes. "You lucked out, Becs. I meant what I said this morning."

She wrinkled her nose at him before heading out of his house with Matt behind her.

Jillian had implied Al needed someone tonight. A someone who wasn't her boyfriend. So had they broken up at some point the last couple weeks?

A jolt of excitement shot through him and a smile played with the corners of his mouth.

Nancy wrapped him in her arms. "Your sister's right, you know." They squeezed each other. "You are the best brother *ever*." She released him and placed her hands on his face. "I know you, like Jackson, are ridiculously busy. But come out to Longmont and visit us. Okay?"

He smiled. "I promise."

"I'd also love to hear more about this friend of Alyson's he's on a date with." She turned, but then stopped and added, "Try to fit in some real fun, too. You deserve it as much as everyone else." She hurried toward her SUV parked in front of his house.

He closed his door after she'd climbed into her vehicle.

Fun.

He ambled toward his piano, something that was more than fun. That probably wasn't what Nancy had meant by fitting in some fun. But still. His music was one of the few things in his life that made him genuinely happy.

He lowered himself to the bench and stared at the keys.

Shit. What if he did go over there? What would she do? Slam the door in his face? Mention the mysterious boyfriend? Possibly tell her dog to attack his parts that made him a guy?

He flinched at that image, then placed his fingers on the keys.

I promise you she's at home. Alone.

He stood and raced toward the staircase.

No, he had no idea what the hell she'd do when she opened her front door. But—with the exception of her dog attacking his male parts—being there, with her, alone, sounded a whole hell of a lot better than being in this big empty house with only his piano as a companion.

He darted into his bedroom, yanked off the shirt he'd been wearing all day, and went right for his closet.

As much as he loved his piano, he wanted and needed something much more tonight. He wanted and needed a certain someone. Based on what Jillian had said, there was a damn good chance Al wanted and needed the same thing. Yeah, he was taking a huge chance. But what if this moment was the only chance he'd get?

His heart pounded his chest as he shrugged into a black, fleece pullover.

He'd be an idiot not to try.

ALYSON SIPPED her perfectly chilled glass of rosé, eyes trained on her T.V.

Sydney Bristow from *Alias*—an older female-power show she'd discovered on a streaming app—was thoroughly kicking some bad guy's ass.

If only real life could be like television for one, even two days out of the year.

Thatcher, sprawled next to her on the couch, had his head in her lap. As he quietly snored, she gently rubbed his head.

She'd taken them on a grueling run the moment she returned home and changed clothes, her emotions needing an instant outlet. The run, followed by a hot bath, had certainly relieved some of her frustration. Still, she couldn't shake the agitation over the *what now?* And the coldness of Marsden Enterprises.

They had thirty days to vacate.

She really needed to be on her computer right now, searching for empty spaces. But sitting on the couch with her near comatose dog, while drinking wine and watching Sydney Bristow kick serious ass, was about all she could manage at this moment.

She continued to stroke Thatcher's head.

Tricia had been worried about her abrupt departure from the shop to the point she'd texted her, wanting to know if something had happened with David.

David Thomas Preston.

Something had happened with him alright. But she hadn't shared that info with Tricia.

No longer quite as upset with Marsden Enterprises, she couldn't ignore the slight guilt at taking her shop's bad news out on him. His confusion and concern had seemed genuine.

She sighed, recalling the way he'd dropped her hand as if he'd been stung by a wasp. But then he'd given her that horrible blank stare. It had actually been the same stare he'd given her years ago, minus the anger embedded in his eyes, right before he'd annihilated her heart. If she hadn't been so upset about Marsden Enterprises, she would have really caught it then.

And, in the spirit of Sydney Bristow, probably would have smacked it off his face.

His out-of-the-blue presence had become unsettling and a reminder of unforgettable times, like falling in love with him the moment she'd read the cute note he'd dropped on her desk...to the moment he'd told her to leave and never come back. All the memories, from the amazing to the appalling, she didn't want or need to be reliving. She had more than enough going on in her life. David had his chance, and she'd let go of all the "what-ifs" years ago. She needed to put him back where he belonged—buried deep into her past. He would have nothing to do with maintaining her renewed connection with Becca. It's not as if he lived with Becca and Matt; the siblings had their own lives. She'd absolutely be able to avoid seeing David very easily.

Okay. She had a solid David plan. Though she hoped Jillian and Jackson were having a good time on their date, she was beginning to wish she'd taken Jillian up on her offer to come over here instead, so they could start to work on the *what now*? Or drink wine and watch *Alias*.

The doorbell ringing caused her to jolt. Then Thatcher sprang to life, jumped off the couch, and barked twice. His normal routine when it went rang.

She placed her glass on the coffee table and stood. After glancing at her watch, she frowned. It was just after 9:00.

Maybe it was Jilly because her date with Jackson hadn't gone well?

Thatcher trotted swiftly to the front door.

She followed him, where she paused to surreptitiously peek out the front window. Her frown deepened, though, at seeing some fancy SUV she didn't recognize parked in her driveway. But the moment she looked through the peephole she froze.

No. It couldn't be the one person she had just been thinking about.

She rubbed her eyes, took a couple of deep breaths, then looked again.

Yes. He really was standing on the other side of her front door.

She sighed. What was he doing here? And at this time of night? She also had no choice but to open the door since it was obvious she was home.

So much for her David plan.

She glanced at Thatcher who wagged his tail. She then raised her head, grasped the handle, and whipped the door open.

David smiled. "Hi there."

Thatcher barked three times.

He cautiously eyed her pet. That's when she noticed how different he looked.

She squinted at him. "You wear glasses now?"

He adjusted the thin, black frames. "For the last six years."

Of course he still looked so incredibly good, if not even *better*.

She leaned against the doorframe. "It's late. What are you doing here?"

His smile faded. "Can I come in? Please?"

Thatcher sat and quietly growled.

She shrugged. "Sure. If it's alright with Thatcher." She walked back to the couch where she picked up her wine glass from the table, took a sip, and watched the two stare at each other.

Surprisingly, David brought back his smile. "You're enjoying this."

She tilted her head right. "I have no idea what you're talking about."

He now leaned against the doorframe. "Fine. You want to let in all the cold air, go for it. I'll be perfectly comfortable just like this."

Alyson narrowed her eyes while his smile favoring devilish grew.

Damn him, that smile, and looking so unbelievably good in glasses.

"So," he began, "what are we watching?" He squinted at her T.V. "Looks like a *hot* woman who knows how to fight." He nodded. "I can definitely handle watching that."

Her shoulders drooped and she snapped her fingers.

Thatcher turned from David and trotted toward where she stood.

Once he was inside her house with the door closed, she said, "I'll ask again, what are you doing here?"

He walked toward her. "I was worried about you. Because I do care." He grinned at her, then Thatcher now seated right beside her. "He's a good-looking dog. And *really* well-trained."

She sat and took another sip of wine. "Please stop smiling at me like that. Obviously I'm fine?" She gestured at herself with her left hand.

David sat beside her. Then Thatcher jumped up and settled himself between them.

"Have you been training him in anticipation for this moment?"

She smiled. "No." She scratched Thatcher's head. "He just doesn't like you." Her eyes locked with his lit up with humor behind his insanely sexy glasses. *It wasn't fair.* But seeing him here, and so casual, made her memory drift to earlier in the day at Tricia's shop. "Why is it you're here, checking on me, late on a Friday night?"

He frowned. "What do you mean?"

She released an exasperated sigh and cleared her throat. "I'll definitely give you a ring," she repeated. In her best impersonation of a British accent.

A smile teased the corners of his still-perfect mouth. "You're pretty damn cute when your jealousy comes out as a funny British accent. I'm also not interested in her."

"Well, I'm not jealous." She faced forward and sipped her wine. "You really didn't have to come over here and check on me." Still, something about his familiar, strong presence, soothing voice, deep, soulful brown eyes, and devilish smile *was* helping her to feel more calm.

He'd also just admitted he hadn't been tempted by the stunning *Victoria*, which made her fight a smile.

"Al, I'm here because I know something tough is going on with your business."

Of course he did.

She said, "Let me guess. Jillian told Jackson, who told you?"

He shook his head. "Not exactly."

"It doesn't matter." She sat back and sunk into her couch cushions. "It'll be fine." *And it would be.* "That's what tomorrows are for and I've decided to put my business's problem into the category of tomorrow." She eyed him. "So you can join me in the now or leave with your tomorrows." She frowned. "I'm not sure that made sense, but it sounded good."

He removed his glasses and rubbed his eyes.

"By the way," she quietly added, "you look *really good* in glasses."

He raised his eyebrows. "Thanks." He returned her soft grin before saying, "Since you don't want to talk about your business, can I ask you a question?"

She hesitated, then replied, "Okay."

"Where the hell is your boyfriend tonight?"

Oh. *That* little white lie.

She winced. "I don't have a boyfriend." He was bound to find out the truth eventually.

He angled his head back. "So you broke up? When?"

She faced him, pursed her lips, then said, "I think it was about six months ago? I can't remember now."

His eyes widened. "You lied about having a boyfriend that day I came to the shop?"

"Yes. I did." He stared at her with such round, shocked eyes, she added, "I'm sorry."

"Why did you do that?"

She released a heavy sigh. "David, do you really need me to explain it?"

He fell silent.

She focused on her T.V., but the show's scenes became nothing but fast-moving images.

The silence between them lasted long enough for her to almost finish her glass of wine.

"Okay," he breathed. "I get it."

Alyson peeked at him. "It seemed like a good idea at the time." *It had been safer*.

"Right." He stood. "Are you going to be okay?"

She sat up. "You're leaving? Already?" Then it fully hit her she wanted company tonight. Human company. Him being here as *her David* was only fueling that want, too.

He stepped back. "I need to go home and wash off this rotten feeling called jackass."

She set her glass down, stood, and grasped his hand. "Marsden Enterprises bought our building last week from the nicest man you could have as a landlord."

He slowly nodded. "Keep going."

She gripped his fingers. "A total, soulless asshat from the company came by the shop today, when we were with Tricia, and told us we had to be out in *thirty* days, because—" Her voice broke on the word. Hadn't she gotten all of the irritation and sadness out during her bath?

He pulled her into his arms right as her dam shattered.

Chapter Eleven

AS AL SOBBED into his chest, David mentally called Marsden Enterprises every foul name he could think of since Keith Marsden was more than a pompous dickhead—he was the Satan of Denver's real estate investment world.

He gently pulled away from Al, cupped her face, and met her dim, wet eyes. It took every bit of willpower he possessed to not kiss her forehead. Then her damp cheeks. Then her—

"Oh, my *God*," she groaned. "I'm acting ridiculous tonight." She scooted Thatcher off the couch and dropped to the cushion. "All of this caught me completely off guard."

She reached out and straightened a small stack of magazines on her coffee table until they were perfectly aligned. She switched to adjusting a couple of candles, followed by reaching for a framed picture of her dog as a puppy.

David sat beside her and clasped her hands. "Al, it's going to be okay."

She raised her wet, weary, defeated eyes to his.

He wanted to hunt down Keith Marsden, rip out his black heart, and feed it to him. But he said, "You're upset. It's understandable. But you'll find a new spot for your shop."

"In *thirty* days?" Her mouth inched open. "It's less than thirty days. And we have to pack up the shop. Change the utilities." She moaned again. "Change all of our business cards, marketing materials…" Her lower lip quivered as a few more tears slid from her eyes.

He squeezed her hands. "Where do you keep your tissues?" He had to do something useful right now.

She sniffed. "In a nook right off the kitchen. Can you bring me a bottle of water, too?"

David stood, turned right, and headed into the small kitchen that, like the rest of the little house, had been modernized at some point the last ten years.

He went for the stainless steel fridge where he grabbed the water, then spotted the narrow nook she'd turned into a mini office space. The desk held the box of tissues. But as he grabbed the box something else on her desk caught his attention. A familiar piece of now very worn notebook paper folded into a square sat beside her laptop…along with his business card.

Had she really kept *that* all these years?

He reached out, hesitated for a few seconds, then picked up the folded paper that he quickly opened—she had kept the note all this time. And *damn*. He couldn't stop his soft grin, even though she'd just confessed to not having a boyfriend these last couple weeks. Yeah, he still felt like a first-class jackass when he thought about all the time he'd wasted thinking and talking about someone who was a lie, but now wasn't the time to focus on that part.

Al was single, she hadn't told him to get lost, she'd opened up to him about her business, *and* she'd actually kept that note all these years.

Though he still needed to tread very carefully, a flame called hope ignited inside of him as he went back into the living room.

He handed her the bottle of water, which she opened, and he again sat beside her. Only this time a couple inches closer since her dog had settled himself into his nearby dog bed.

After taking several sips, she looked at him. "How'd you know I'd be here alone?"

He handed her the box. "Instinct?"

"Thanks." She grabbed a tissue, then swiped her nose and eyes. "Instinct named Jillian?"

He smiled. "I'll never tell."

She sighed, sat back, and slumped down until her head rested on a cushion.

He copied her actions. "Al, maybe I can help you." *You can trust me.*

She rolled her head left. "Are you also into real estate investment? On top of being an architect *and* musician?"

He rolled his head right. "No. But you know my aunt and uncle are."

She shook her head. "I—we—can't ask for their help."

He frowned. "Why not? I know they'd love to help you guys."

"Jillian and I started this business on our *own*," she enunciated. "We were preparing for something big when Cliff, our former landlord, announced he was selling his properties and moving back to Maine." She picked at the couch's fabric. "Just not something *this* big."

"Because of that, let me reach out to my—"

"*No*," she insisted. "Jilly and I will figure this out."

"Shit, you're still stubborn. And the only reason you're saying no is because of me."

She faced him. "Not everything is about you, David Thomas Preston."

He faced her. "Then let me call my aunt and uncle, Alyson Catherine Douglas."

She narrowed her eyes, now favoring green, and he couldn't help but smile. Her eyes had always done that when she was pissed off. Especially at him.

"David, stop smiling at me like that."

"That's the third time you've said that to me in the last couple weeks." He continued smiling. "Which means you must still like it. By the way"—he reached into his back jeans pocket—"I saw *this* when I grabbed the tissues from your desk." He presented the note.

Her eyes widened and she snatched it from his fingers."So you went snooping, too?"

He exhaled through his teeth. "It was right next to your computer."

She lowered her eyes to the note.

He paused, then said, "I can't believe you've kept it all this time." That had to mean something significant.

"I can't either," she murmured, then lifted her eyes back to his. "I probably should've burned it *that* night when I got home."

Or maybe not. *Shit.*

He nodded once. "Right." He stood. "I deserved that." What else could he say? "I should leave." What else could he do? She'd stopped crying and been honest with him about her business. *At least she'd been honest about that.* "Al, will you please call me if you change your mind about my aunt and uncle?" He didn't exactly like the fact she'd refused the help. At the same time, he couldn't fault her for wanting to figure all of this out on her own.

But there had to be a special place in hell for the Keith Marsdens of this world.

"Yes," she quietly answered, still staring at the note he'd given her that day during class.

In that moment, he became aware of Alyson Catherine Douglas, the woman. Long, thick auburn hair pulled into a loose knot; her clothes nothing more than a pair of tight, black running pants, and a loose, blue shirt slipping off her bare, right shoulder. She looked comfortable. *Sensual.* And as slim and toned as she had twelve years ago when they'd met.

He swallowed and stepped back. "Okay then." Not knowing what else to do, he turned and walked the few steps to her front door. Thatcher met him there, wagging his tail. "You'll be happy to know I'm leaving now," he mumbled while grasping the handle.

"David, wait a minute."

He turned to find her walking toward him.

"If you leave," she said, stopping inches from him, "I'll spend the night doing something really insane." She frowned. "Like cleaning every inch of my house while I try to figure out what to do for Daisy's Bouquets."

Their eyes caught while his heart pounded his chest. "But if I stay?" *Could she actually—*

"I'll do something even more insane." She clutched the front of his fleece pullover. "Something like this." She tugged him forward, down, and pressed her lips to his.

It took his brain a few seconds to comprehend this was really happening. But once his brain and body were in sync, he cupped her face, and angled her head back, deepening the kiss.

She released a soft moan that he felt inside his jeans that became uncomfortably tight, but he'd be out of his mind to rush anything about this damn near miraculous moment.

He lifted his right hand off her cheek to brush away wisps of hair, then gently slid his fingers down her cheek as their mouths moved in unison.

His right hand continued its leisurely path down her arm, her side, and when he reached her waist he slipped his arm around her, bringing their bodies together. So close he felt her rapid heartbeat. As her arms went around his neck, he slowly ended their kiss.

Her eyes fluttered open, and they stared at one another while catching their breaths.

"God, that felt good," he murmured. Like he was *finally* where he belonged.

She nodded and whispered, "Please stay." She stepped back, bringing him with her.

"Wait," he managed to say, followed by a deep breath. "Al, are you sure? You haven't been yourself tonight." As much as he wanted this—*her*—he couldn't ignore that fact.

She took another step backward, which put her on the first stair and eye-level with him. "David, I know exactly what I want." She leaned forward. "To be here in the now with you, not tomorrow. Believe me when I say I'd rather do *you* than clean every inch of my house."

He grinned. "Thanks, Al. I'm relieved you'd choose me over cleaning." He followed her up the stairs, but when they reached the top, his conscience again made him pause. "I don't want you to hate me in the morning, because if we do this—"

"We are doing this." She led him down the short, dark hallway. "I won't hate you."

He stopped just inside her bedroom. "I won't leave until you kick me out."

She smiled, tugged him farther into her room, and closed the door on her dog. Who started barking. "Thatcher, stop." He whined for a few seconds before becoming silent, then she said, "I *promise* we're on the same page. So please shut up and kiss me."

He returned her smile before their mouths fused once more.

They stumbled toward her bed where she gripped his pullover, and yanked it up and over his head. His glasses went, too, but he caught them before they fell to the floor.

She grinned. "You know, I won't mind if you wear your glasses."

He laughed and placed them on the nightstand. "Maybe we'll try that later."

She bit her bottom lip while she placed her hands on his bare chest. "How is it you've hardly changed in ten years?" She slowly slid her hands down to rest on his stomach.

Centimeters above the waist of his jeans.

His vision blurred. But it was in that moment it hit him they couldn't do this.

"Shit." He ran a hand through his hair. "Al, I'm not...*prepared* for this."

She gripped the waist of his jeans. "Well, I am. In the nightstand drawer." She undid the button while looking into his eyes. "David, I'm a grown, single, *smart* woman."

"You're right." He brought back his smile. "You can keep doing what you were doing."

She laughed and slowly unzipped his fly.

He lowered his head to the spot where her neck curved into her shoulder and breathed her sweet, familiar scent deep into his soul, followed by a series of kisses and nips up her neck. "You still taste as good as you look."

"So do you." She slipped her hands inside his jeans.

His brain short-circuited and this time he moaned. "You're wearing too many clothes," he managed to whisper into her ear.

"I think that's something you can help me with," she whispered back.

He lifted her arms, slowly raised her soft, light shirt up and over her head, and flung it over his shoulder.

Their eyes locked until he lowered his to admire *her* bare chest.

"How is it you *haven't* changed in ten years?" he murmured while reaching out to gently cup the round, firm, soft flesh.

His body buzzed, then she wrapped her arms around him, causing them both to moan at their bare skin touching. A second later their mouths became one and they fell onto her bed.

He stretched out on top of her, placing himself right between her thighs.

She arched against him, and he inhaled sharply at the desire that swept through him.

Their mouths stayed as one while he slid his hand down her arm, past her elbow, onto her waist, where he hooked his fingers on her pants. Which were gone within seconds.

"Now who's wearing too many clothes?" she asked on a breath between kisses.

His shoes and jeans quickly followed, and he ended up stretched out beside her. His fingers picked up where they left off on her waist, only he slid them down toward her bare thigh.She shivered. "That's making me crazy."

He grinned, then slowly slid his fingers back up. "Good." But he paused when he reached the spot so warm he felt the heat without touching her.

Another round of desire spiraled through him.

"You're still so good at touching me," she breathlessly said.

He lowered his mouth to hers. "You've always been worth touching."

This kiss was slower, more gentle. *He couldn't rush this.* But Al rolled onto her back, bringing him with her so their bare skin once again touched. She then wrapped her legs around his and dragged her fingernails along both sides of his waist.

He jerked left.

She released low, wicked laughter. "You're still ticklish."

He grasped her wrists and pinned her arms above her head. "Something tells me you're still ticklish, too." His eyes traveled the length of her *fantastic* body tangled with his. "And while I have you trapped right now would be the perfect time to find out."

Her humor vanished. "David Preston, don't you dare." She started to squirm.

He immediately freed her wrists and pressed his mouth to hers again.

Her arms went back around his neck and she stretched against him.

He needed to take this slow. But he slid his hand down, paused on her stomach, then gradually continued down, paused again…and gently slipped his middle finger inside of her.

She gasped between kisses, followed by a deep groan as she moved with his finger.

Between that and her damp flesh, he said, "You have two night-stands. Which one?"

He'd take it slow next time.

"Right side, top drawer."

He rolled off of her. In under a minute he was sliding into her snug, wet warmth while thanking the universe his dreams were coming true. He then buried himself deep inside her.

She tightly squeezed him.

Only his dreams were nothing like the reality.

Their bodies moved together like they had from the night their physical relationship began. As if they hadn't been apart for ten years.

David pressed his forehead to hers. "Alyson, open your eyes." He met her hot gaze. "Promise me you won't hate me tomorrow for not leaving tonight."

She met each of his thrusts, her breathing becoming shallow. "I promise."

He pressed his mouth to hers. Ten years of being apart, combined with how perfect she—this—still felt hit him swift and hard, but he held on until her muscles tightened around him. As he let go, his muffled moan joined hers.

Their heavy breathing filled her room for several moments. Then he said, "That didn't last long enough."

"Agreed," she said around a quick laugh. "But it felt incredible."

As had always been their usual. He shifted backward.

She tightened her arms around his neck. "Don't move. You feel too perfect."

He opened his mouth, but she silenced him with a long kiss.

He slowly relaxed against her. "You feel incredible, but I don't want to crush you."

"You won't." She squeezed him so tight he released a breathless laugh. "I just want to stay like this a little longer."

Or until she made him rock hard again. It wouldn't be too long if she kept doing *that*.

"Please don't leave."

He kissed her forehead. "I'm not going anywhere." They sealed his words with one kiss, followed by another, and several more. Like they were making up for lost time.

"Al," he said on a breath, "I really need to get up."

She nodded and released him.

He eased out of her, rolled off the bed, and headed for her bathroom. But when he walked back into her room, now dimly lit from a lamp on her nightstand, he stopped. She was propped up on her right elbow, her hair now falling around her shoulders, and wore his glasses.

He grinned and headed for the bed. Or more like *her*. Once he was stretched out beside her, he nodded. "I think those look better on you than me."

"Hardly." She pushed the frames up her nose. "You're not that blind."

"No." He propped himself up on his left elbow. "Just enough to be slightly inconvenient." She removed his glasses, slid them onto his face…and her smile turned naughty. "What is it about these you like so much?"

She tipped her head right. "They make you look distinguished."

"Which is a nice way of saying *old*."

She shook her head. "That's not the definition of distinguished and you know it." Their eyes came together. "How is it you're here with me right now? And like this?"

He grasped a lock of her hair. "Fate." He twisted the soft lock around his finger.

David's mind rewound to the last time he'd been with Al exactly like this; the night following their hooky day in the city.

Their physical relationship had always been exciting. *Mind-blowing*. Their last night together had even surpassed those words. They'd been one with the universe. As she'd drifted off to sleep, he'd told Al he loved her which she'd sleepily echoed. Then he'd asked her one very important question, but she hadn't heard him. Two days later—

He released her hair, placed his hand on her waist, and guided her toward him.

She ended up on top of him, her hair forming a curtain around them. In spite of his glasses, he buried his face between her neck and shoulder.

"Al, I've missed you so much," he whispered into her neck.

She lifted herself up enough to catch his eyes, opened her mouth, but then pressed her lips together. "We're here together *now,* so let's just be here. Okay?"

He nodded, swallowing the words he'd planned to say next—*give me one more chance.*

She slid her hand down his chest, across his stomach, and lower still where she stopped.

He took a shaky breath. "That's making *me* crazy."

"Good," she murmured, scooting down and lowering her hand even more until—

He moaned as his eyes drifted shut.

"I should drive this time." She kissed a spot below his stomach. "You won't mind, right?"

He opened his eyes that immediately found hers in the dim light.

"No." He returned her naughty smile. "In fact, I think that's an excellent idea."

Seconds later, he once again became lost in the *now.*

Chapter Twelve

ALYSON BROUGHT her knees up and hugged them to her chest as she watched him sleep.

Dammit. He looked good enough to kiss and nibble—again and again—while he slept naked and tangled in her purple sheets.

He'd been *her David* last night…and early this morning. Gentle. Fun. Delicious. Completely irresistible. Everything she'd loved about being intimate with him when they'd been a couple and had missed so much, but hadn't been able to voice last night having been focused on the now. And now it was *tomorrow*, and she had no idea what to do next, outside of prepare for the extremely long work day ahead of her, then focus on her shop's big problem.

He'd offered to bring in his aunt and uncle. No doubt they'd be immensely helpful, too. Then what? She'd be linked to him and his family in yet another way.

She tore her eyes away from the sheets loosely covering his perfect lower half.

That was something she wasn't at all ready for.

Not letting him leave last night had probably not been the best choice, but she'd wanted to lose herself and wanted *him* to get lost with her. Thinking about last night…and early this morning…caused her flesh to rise while remembering his fingertips gliding across her bare skin.

She shivered.

It was as if they'd picked up where they'd left off ten years ago. How was that even possible? They weren't kids in college. They were adults who were barely the same people. So how could he still have that kind of effect on her? How could she lose herself so easily like she had last night…and early this morning…especially when she remembered how he'd, in one moment, obliterated her heart and soul.

Yes, she'd definitely been craving human company last night. It had been a long time since she'd been with a man, too. And she and David had always possessed a strange, potent, very chemical attraction to one another. He also had looked beyond incredible in his glasses.

She fought the strong urge to curl back up beside him and into his familiar, warm, strong arms by hugging her knees as tightly as possible.

"I knew it," he murmured. "You hate me."

She turned to find him watching her through wary, bleary eyes. "David, I swear I don't hate you."

He sighed. "Okay. But your body language is spelling regret."

"I wanted last night as much as you did." She shook her head. "I need to get ready for work." She grabbed her purple quilt, wrapped it around herself, then scooted off the bed.

"Alyson, what are you doing?" He pointed at the quilt.

She lifted her chin. "I'm cold. It's not exactly summertime." Her gaze fell to the sheet now barely covering his perfect lower half. Heat consumed her face, her body, as she recalled his kisses, sighs, moans, and thrusts last night…and early this morning.

He unleashed that damn, devilish smile of his. "What are *you* thinking about?"

"Please stop smiling at me like that."

He rolled onto his back and rubbed his eyes. "Fantastic. We're back to that."

She headed for her bathroom. "I have to get ready, and you should probably leave."

"Why? So your imaginary boyfriend won't catch us?"

She stopped and glared at him. "That's not funny."

"You're right." He threw off the sheet and rolled out of bed. "It's not funny being lied to."

She ripped her eyes off of *him*. "Can we do this later?" *And while we're wearing clothes.*

"I'd love to. How does tonight sound?" He bent down, grabbed his jeans, and pulled them on. "We have a gig in Evergreen. Our first at this place that's pretty popular. Al, I'd really love it if you went. Maybe we could talk afterward?"

She wasn't sure which one was more hot—naked David or the shirtless David wearing only his tight jeans. She pressed her lips together, then replied, "I can't tonight." But she couldn't ignore the fact going to his show and watching him play the piano in his jazz band would be way more fun than what she and Jillian had planned for this evening. "I have to work."

He walked toward her. "Okay. Tomorrow?" He cupped her face. "Al, last night was unbelievable. I know I don't deserve it, but...I only want you to give me another chance."

Their eyes locked.

"Please?" He stepped closer. "We can go somewhere quiet for dinner and really talk." He cracked a smile. "I'll bring you home, make sure you get inside okay, then leave. I promise."

Of course he wanted another chance. And last night had been so unbelievably amazing, as if time had never passed. But giving him another chance came with such a *huge* risk.

He gently brushed her bottom lip with the pad of his thumb. "What are you thinking?"

If she gave him every part of herself again and he pushed her away—she stepped backward, which caused his arms to fall to his sides. "David, is *that* why you really came into my shop that day? Be honest with me."

He raised his eyebrows. "Becs was the main reason I came in that day. But, yeah, I also wanted to see you. I wanted a chance to"—he lifted his shoulders—"explain my behavior that night *and* apologize."

"But you were also hoping for me to…what exactly? Fall into your arms like I did the day we met?" Another reason she'd blurted out the fat lie of having a boyfriend. *It really had been safer*. And all it had taken to fall into his arms a second time was the soulless Marsden Enterprises, sexy glasses on his too-handsome face, and him being *her David*.

He frowned. "I don't remember it going like that."

Utter frustration with herself made her snap, "David, you *destroyed* my heart!"

He angled his head back.

"Don't stand there looking surprised." She pointed at him. "You know what you did because I saw it in your eyes that night before you turned and walked away from me."

He remained silent while all those emotions she'd buried deep inside rose to the surface.

Emotions that desperately needed to be freed after all this time.

"I kept thinking," she continued, "or more like foolishly convincing myself, that maybe once the shock of everything that happened wore off, that when you started thinking clearly again, you'd come back. Call me. Do *something* to reach out." She caught his eyes. "Because no matter how awful you were to me that night, I knew you loved me."

"Alyson, I'm still—"

"And we both knew we had more than some college thing." She stepped toward him. "We had what many people wish *they* could find." She paused before adding, "I didn't just lose a boyfriend that night. You were my best friend—" Her voice cracked on the words.

He looked away.

"You were so much more than even that." She tightened the quilt around her shoulders. "I know this doesn't even compare with what you were feeling then, but I was hurting, too."

He brought his eyes back to hers.

"You know how much I loved your parents and Rebecca."

He nodded. "I wanted to call you. I almost did call you after I got—"

"Then why didn't you?" she nearly yelled.

He leaned forward. "Because I was a lost, scared, embarrassed *kid*!"

Silence fell between them until he released a quick breath and ran a hand through his hair.

"I wish you would've called me," she softly said. "I would've answered. But you waited ten years. And the only reason you contacted me is because your sister found me by *accident*."

His head snapped up. "That's not true. I did search for you, but…" His shoulders fell.

She straightened. "I can't give you what you want, because how could I ever trust you again?" She'd never survive him walking away if heart-wrenching disaster struck a second time.

He cleared his throat. "I'm sorry." He snatched his fleece sweatshirt off the floor and shrugged into it. "For everything." He gathered his socks and shoes, swiped his glasses off her nightstand, and marched toward her still closed bedroom door that he ripped open.

Thatcher backed up, and David darted past him.

She followed. "I don't want apologies. I just want you and your sister to stop feeling guilty." She trailed him down the stairs. "Don't you two get tired of it? Carrying all that guilt?"

He halted at the front door. "What the hell does Becs have to do with this?"

She cringed, hesitated, then said, "Please don't blame her."

"Alyson, what are you talking about?"

As he wriggled his bare feet into his shoes, she answered, "When

I had lunch with her on Wednesday, she told me what happened that morning in her hospital room."

He stopped and his eyes, back behind his glasses, widened. "I don't understand."

Thatcher started scratching the door, but she stayed focused on David.

"Did *you* ask her about that morning?"

"Yes." She raised her chin. "I did."

He stared at her.

"I needed to know what happened."

He finished wriggling into his shoes. "It was none of your business."

She wanted to scream "*Yes, it had been her business!*" Instead she said, "Becca feels responsible—guilty—for what happened between us."

He squinted at her. "Why would she think that? I never told her anything about that night with you. In fact, the only people who know about that night are you, me, and Jackson."

Alyson sighed. "Becca said after you two started…talking again…she asked about me. That's when she found out we were no longer together. She said she just knew it had happened that day."

He opened the door.

She blocked Thatcher before he ran out of the house.

"I can't believe she told you." He huffed. "I've never told anyone what happened that morning. Not even Jackson. The only reason my aunt and uncle know what happened is because they, along with everyone else on that floor, heard her screaming—" David turned from her. "I wish she hadn't told you."

"What's so wrong with me knowing? And why didn't you just tell me—?"

"I didn't want you to know any of that," he threw over his shoulder. "Everything was shitty enough. I couldn't unload all of *that* on you, too."

So he hadn't told her because of wanting to protect her from more ugliness. It was also now clear he *was* still struggling with everything that had happened ten years ago.

She released a heavy breath, then said the only thing she could think of at that moment."David, you have to let it go. *All* of it."

He stepped outside.

"Becca adores you," she persisted, because he needed to hear this and so much more. "She regrets everything from that morning. You have to know that by now. And your parents—"

"Please don't."

"You were upset with them." She leaned forward. "It happens to every kid who doesn't like or agree with what their parents—"

"I wasn't 'upset' with them. I was angry. And said things—" He flinched. "Things I would never want to hear my kid say to me. But what I really can't shake," he continued, staring off to her left, "is that the fight was all for nothing. No, I'm not a teacher and have no regrets not becoming one. But I'm not a full-time musician, either. Because they were right." He shook his head. "There is no real money in music unless you're one of the lucky bastards."

"But maybe you could be now?" She angled her head until her eyes caught his. "With Becca finishing school, getting married, eventually getting a job…maybe it is something you could do full time since it sounds like your band is doing *really* well."

He stared at her for several seconds, some light returning to his dark eyes.

"You've…given me a lot to think about." He stepped outside. "Don't let me, being her brother, stop you from seeing or talking to Becs because she loves you. She always has." He started to close the door. "I promise that as of right now your friendship will have nothing to do with me." And he closed the door behind him.

Less than a minute later, he drove away in his black SUV.

All Alyson could do was hope he *would* think about everything she'd said to him. No one—especially David and his sister— deserved to live in the present, emotionally stuck in the past with guilt as a constant companion. Those two had absolutely been through enough.

Thatcher whined and furiously scratched the door.

"Okay, okay," she grumbled. "Can I get dressed first?"

He barked as she turned and walked back up the stairs.

As she got dressed, she would *not* think of him, moments ago, naked and tangled up in her purple sheets. Nor would she think about his kisses, sighs, moans, and thrusts last night…and early this morning. She wouldn't think about any of hers, either.

She'd done the right thing for David and *herself.*

She would pull herself together, get to work and, tonight, successfully "crash" a fantasy Felicity Mayhew wedding as a possible way to protect her business. Her livelihood. Then she and Jillian would begin the hunt for a new space.

That's what mattered most right now.

Chapter Thirteen

"NOW SHE WANTS the damn kitchen and dining room to be the size of Aspen. I don't have time for this shit. We're already behind because of the snow we've been getting!"

David held the phone away since Bob's voice had risen several notches as his tirade ended, and he stared at his office computer's monitor, deciding now would *not* be the best time to mention he was working on the staircase redesign. He'd also known what had been happening, because Vivienne had called him first about her newest wants, and to whine about Bob's "nasty attitude" and "constant unco-operativeness." But in reality, Bob had come highly recommended from a colleague who'd worked in that area before moving back to Denver months ago.

"At this rate," Bob continued, "I'll be dead before this job is over and I want to die in peace. Far and away from your damn client who's causing me to be behind on my *other* projects." There was another pause, before he heard, "David, I like and respect you, and hate resorting to threats. But if you don't get your ass up here again and put a stop to Mrs. Vivienne Dunne's craziness, I'm taking my guys and we're walking."

And there it was. What he had feared would happen again,

despite extinguishing fire after fire since his last trip up there in mid-January. Queen Dunne had driven Bob Clancy, a veteran contractor, into borderline insanity. Which left him with no other choice.

He leaned back into his chair. "I'll be there by Monday morning."

Bob muttered something that sounded like gratitude and, seconds later, the call ended.

He placed his phone on his desk, right beside Marjorie's stapler he'd lifted on his way up to his office. He'd missed the fun of watching her tear the office apart looking for it. Driving to Aspen to babysit Vivienne and that damn project again had also *not* been on his never-ending to-do list. But remembering the painfully honest and eye-opening conversation with Al only hours earlier, he couldn't help but feel this trip was exactly what he needed.

To get the *hell* out of Denver.

Aspen wasn't Scotland, but it was a beautiful, mountain town at the height of ski season, and almost two-hundred miles away from *this* city, along with the questionable choices he'd made since around 8:00 last night. However, there was his music. Being away from the band, his piano, and for God knew how long, really pissed him off.

He winced, imagining that conversation with Randy.

They had their gig tonight in Evergreen, where they'd be focused more on their bluesy sound, because that was the kind of crowd the joint attracted. They also had their usual gig Thursday night, but the band would only be able to perform covers with a back-up piano player. Which Randy loathed since they were known for their original music. No doubt his head would blow when David told him he had to be gone again for work.

He narrowed his eyes.

He'd really thought Al would say yes to going tonight when he'd stupidly invited her.

He never should have stayed. But, like she'd said only hours ago, he'd wanted last night to happen as much as she did. Recalling his *fantastic* night with her brought him directly to this morning not going at all the way he'd imagined. Especially when he remembered all of her honesty he hadn't been prepared to hear.

He'd actually long since recovered from that horrible morning in his sister's hospital room. Most of the recovery taking place during the hard, highly emotional session with her and her psychologist months later. But he couldn't grasp why his sister had shared such a personal, *rotten* moment, and with Al of all people.

No matter what she believed, she hadn't needed to know any of that rotten shit. Yeah, his words and behavior toward her that night in his bedroom had been cruel and harsh due to his frame of mind and all the damn alcohol. He'd been the definition of a heartless dick. But he really had saved her from his weeks of self-destruction following that day and night.

David should have told Al that this morning after she'd freed ten years of pent up and merited disappointment and frustration. But he hadn't been able to get the truth out because of the shame that still haunted him. Then all he'd wanted to do was leave after she'd added her one, reality-biting admission.

I can't give you what you want, because how could I ever trust you again?

Her blatant honesty, combined with being given the unexpected information his sister felt responsible for his crap choices, only added to the burden he could never seem to shake.

He frowned.

There also was another aspect from that dark time no one knew. In fact, the only other person who would have known was his mom. Possibly his dad.

Oh, yeah. Aspen was looking better and better with each passing second.

"So you look like you were up all night."

His head shot up.

"You listened to Jillian." Jackson leaned against the doorframe. "Who did tell me Alyson is, in fact, single."

David sat up. "No comment."

"Fair enough." He walked into his office. "But, damn, Jillian's good." He stopped when he reached David's desk. "She also has spunk." He stared at him. "What the hell are you doing here on a Saturday morning after reuniting—oh, shit. What has the Queen done? She is the only reason you would be in here right now."

David pointed at his monitor. "I'm working on the staircase redesign because I couldn't deal with cleaning my kitchen this morning." He had, however, soaked all the dishes and pans before taking an almost scalding shower and dragging himself into the office.

Jackson laughed. "Will and I have never figured out how Mom manages to make such a huge mess. It's kind've impressive when you think about it."

He sighed. "Anyway, on top of the staircase redesign—that Bob *doesn't* know about—Queen Dunne now thinks the kitchen and dining rooms aren't big enough for entertaining. I'm sure Bob's ready to say and do something he'll regret. And he *is* ready to walk."

Jackson nodded once. "Then I take it you'll be leaving us again for a while?"

"Yep." He stared at the designs. "I'll leave tomorrow so I can be there Monday morning. On the bright side of *this* lousy morning, I'll be able to charm her out of the staircase in person."

Jackson turned one of David's chairs backward and straddled it. "You know, you really look more like horseshit than up all night with 'the hottest girl you've ever seen in your life'."

He glared at his friend. "Thanks. But do you even know what horseshit looks like? And I don't need to ask why you're in here on a Saturday."

He hadn't seen much of his business partners the past week, outside of their basketball games. Zach was busy with a mixed-use real estate project. Jackson had been shut up in his office, which meant disturb at your own risk, working on an all-too important bid for a highly coveted project. The bids were due Wednesday and Jackson was still in the review phase.

"Jillian also mentioned, after hanging up on you, that Alyson went with you guys yesterday." Jackson paused, then asked, "Becca's doing?"

David nodded.

"What the hell happened?"

He sat back. "Did you ever meet Al's roommate, Tricia, from back then?"

Jackson squinted. "The name sounds familiar, but I don't think so, no."

He quickly recounted the day, including the call Al received from Jillian that ultimately contributed to the day's, and night's, unexpected ending.

"So, yeah," he continued, "I listened to Jillian and went over to Al's place."

His friend folded his arms on the chair's back. "From there, I can put two-and-two together. But what's with the long face?"

How could I ever trust you again?

He concentrated on a clear spot on his desk.

You have to let it go. All *of it.*

"David, I can feel myself aging."

He blinked and said, "I thought…*hoped*…Al and I would be on the same page this morning. But I never should've gone over there." Jackson didn't need any more details than those. "She made her choice, and that is officially that." Even though she'd said several eye-opening things right before he left, Al had made it clear she didn't want to be with him again.

He had to let her go.

"Well, that explains the long face." He frowned. "So what was last night?"

"Huge mistake number two." That hadn't felt like a mistake at the time. *Not even close.*

Jackson released a long, low whistle. "Then it's probably a good thing you're going to Aspen tomorrow."

"Can we talk about something else?" David shook his head. Or more like shaking aside the memories of last night and early this morning. "How'd it go with Jillian?"

"After you stopped calling me, it was great." Jackson grinned. "Fantastic, actually. She's not boring. After dinner, we ended up on the light rail. The line that goes all the way south." He laughed. "We just talked, almost nonstop. And laughed a lot. Going on the roundtrip light rail ride was her idea, too."

David smiled because his buddy's grin had tripled in size while summarizing his date.

"I invited her to your show tonight, but she said they're working." He stood.

Apparently, Al had been telling the truth when she'd said that to him earlier. It had later crossed his mind that she might have used her work as an excuse to avoid him.

"I'm planning on giving her a call sometime tomorrow."

He absently nodded.

"David, I'm sorry. I know Alyson has always been different." Jackson stepped back. "*You* were different when you were together. And before the accident."

He focused on his monitor.

"I know whatever she said to you this morning must've really sucked, but promise me you won't turn into *that guy* again." He gave him a slight grin. "Or I'll be forced to kick your ass a second time."

His memory went to the night he'd shoved Al out of his life. Because it also happened to be the only time he and his best friend got into a brawl. He managed to say, "I know I was drunk as shit that night, but I do remember getting in at least *one* good hit."

Jackson headed for the doorway. "I think my memory of that night is a hell of a lot more reliable than yours," he threw over his shoulder. "I know I'll see you tonight at the show, but in case I forget to say it, don't do anything stupid while you're gone. Try to place nice with Queen Dunne and Bob, too."

Once Jackson left, David picked up his phone.

It was now time he talked to her. He also needed to tell her his travel plans.

"Hi," Becs answered almost instantly. "I'm so glad you called."

"I really need to talk to you, too."

"Okay. But first I have to tell you all about Matty's thirtieth birthday party since he's gone snowboarding with some friends."

Right. Matt's birthday was a month or so after his sister's.

He briefly closed his eyes, then said, "What's going on?"

"His mom and I were finally able to sit down and get it planned out. It's going to be a *surprise* party with an eighties theme." She released a squeal mixed with a laugh. "You know he loves a lot of the movies, and we'll play nothing but eighties music." She paused, then added, "We also decided everyone in the bridal party *has* to dress up in eighties clothing. No exceptions, big brother. Everyone else can dress up if they want to, and I'm sure most people will."

A costume party. *Fantastic*. But he stayed silent.

"Oh, my God, it'll be so much fun." She laughed. "It'll be at our house, so I'm going to ask some of his friends here in Boulder to take him out for a beer. To get him out of the house?"

"Becs," he began, "that all sounds great. Really. But I need to talk to you right now."

There was a long pause before he heard, "What's up?"

"Why did you tell Alyson about that morning in your hospital room?"

Silence. Which meant he'd obviously caught her off guard.

"She asked me about it. I can't believe you didn't tell her yourself."

He tried to rein in his frustration. "You still have such a big mouth."

"David, it was Alyson," she argued. "It's not like I told a *stranger*. She of all people deserved to know—"

"No. I never wanted her to know any of that. It was between *us*." And their aunt and uncle, and her psychologist back then.

Silence fell again.

He strongly suspected she was rolling her eyes.

"I honestly don't understand why you're so upset. It's obvious to everyone, despite how silly you two act around each other, that you're both still—"

"Stop right there." That was the *last* thing he wanted to hear. Especially after everything that had happened between him and Al, from when he showed up at her place through early this morning. "I want you and Al to be friends, but she knows more than enough. You also need to leave me out of your friendship." He sighed. "What she and Tricia did for you yesterday was incredible. But no more bullshit, throwing us together, using your wedding as a reason. Got it?"

Yeah, maybe he'd been a bit harsh. But if he had any chance in hell of moving on with his life, far from *her*, his sister had to stop interfering.

"Okay," she murmured. "I understand."

That led him to his next topic. "Becs," he began in a softer voice, "you can't take responsibility for my bad choices back then. I promise they had nothing to do with you."

She moaned before he heard, "I didn't think she'd tell you *that*."

His sister didn't know a damn thing about the numerous weeks following *that* specific day and night. She would never know, either, because he'd made his aunt and uncle, and the Lovett family, swear they'd never tell her.

"Well, she did and I'm glad. Because your behavior this last week now makes more sense." He paused, then said, "But I'm telling you it has to stop since I know for a fact it's too late. And that's all you need to know," he added, recalling that specific part of Al's honesty. "So whatever guilt you have about *that* morning, promise me you'll let it go."

He heard a long, slow sigh before, "I promise."

His burden lightened a fraction.

Al had been right about many things this morning, specifically all the guilt. Something his little sister didn't deserve or need to be carrying.

He was carrying enough for them both.

"I have to go back to Aspen because there are a bunch of issues going on up there with the Dunne project."

"Seriously?" she nearly squeaked. "But what if something with the wedding comes up?"

He wanted to ask what could possibly happen since the wedding wasn't until August, but said, "Call me, or Aunt Eileen and Uncle Hugh, and we'll deal with it over the phone." He removed his glasses, tossed them onto his desk, and rubbed his eyes. "I have to be honest. This trip is coming at a good time. I need to get out of this city." His trip to Aspen wasn't a vacation by any means, but it would give him a much-needed chance to clear his head. To think long and hard about what Al had said right before he left.

"David, did something happen between you and Alyson yesterday?"

More than you can possibly know.

"You could say that, but it's not important. Don't worry about it, either. I know you guys can't come to the show tonight, so do you need anything before I leave tomorrow?"

There was a long pause, then, "No. Not that I can think of. But text me when you get there? And while you're gone?"

He grinned. "If you insist...*brat*."

She laughed. "I do insist...*loser*."

David tapped the red dot. He had one more person he needed to talk to, but he'd see Randy tonight at their gig in Evergreen. In the meantime, he had a job to do.

As he went back into the staircase redesign, he thought of his piano. His band. His music.

Maybe it is something you could do full time.

He stared at that damn staircase.

Yeah, she'd definitely given him a lot to think about.

Chapter Fourteen

THE RITZ-CARLTON in downtown Denver offered a few options for weddings. But this particular fantasy Felicity Mayhew wedding—the guest list based on the number of chairs pushing four-hundred—was taking place in the ballroom.

Conversations between guests already seated were hushed. Ripples of laughter here and there reached Alyson who stood in the back, the only place left with available seats.

Her eyes widened as her mouth inched open.

Bouquets of white and ivory roses with a hint of pale pink spilled out of tall, gold vases at the end of each row. At the base of the vases, sat arrangements of three lit candles, in three different sizes, and in glass containers. Two of the same floral and candle arrangements had been set up near the front, where the bride and groom would stand with the officiate.

She slid her eyes up to the elaborate, sparkling chandeliers, and back to the full room.

Fantasy wedding? More like epic fairy tale.

Her phone buzzed inside the most expensive purse she owned—a black, Michael Kors clutch she'd bought at the outlet store for less than half its retail price.

She reached into her purse at the same time an older couple, dressed in elegant, black tie attire, brushed against her. They gave her questioning once-overs, which she returned with her best *how-dare-you-stare-at-me-like-that-since-I'm-just-as-rich-as-you-are* look before she pushed her large, black sunglasses up her nose.

Jilly had texted, *I think I can smell the money oozing off everyone in here.*

Jillian's "wedding crashing" job consisted of blending in with the hotel staff working this astounding event, while wearing fake eyeglasses and her hair in braids. Her goal was to track down and get close to Felicity Mayhew's crew; a way to get valuable intel right from the source.

Alyson gripped her phone, walked to the second-to-last row, and lowered herself to the aisle seat. She then crossed her legs and, using her narrow purse as a shield, opened her camera app and snapped a photo of the nearest aisle bouquet. And, dammit, if the bouquets weren't *perfect.* Her next task was to get photos of the bridesmaids' bouquets and, of course, the bride's.

It was vitally important they knew what they were up against in this pretty unfamiliar world of epic, fairy tale weddings. So far, it seemed just a tad overwhelming.

"Excuse me, Miss Golightly, but I was wondering if I could sit on the other side of you?"

She whirled right and looked up.

A man with wavy, russet hair, and dressed to kill in a dark suit, gave her a playful smile that reached his chestnut eyes.

"Oh, yes." She angled her crossed legs left. "Of course."

He eased by her and sat one seat away.

She smoothed each wrinkle of her snug, black evening gown's skirt, and adjusted the matching wrap. Another purchase she'd made at the same outlet mall she'd bought her purse.

"Were you going for Holly Golightly when you were getting ready for this thing?"

She looked at the man, still giving her that playful smile.

Oh, how she was so sick and tired of handsome men and their cute smiles. She said, "Her look in the book and movie is still iconic, so I'm going to say yes and take your question as a compliment." She also had carefully planned this outfit. If she wanted to be in big business with Felicity Mayhew, she couldn't be recognizable after tonight. "I'm also impressed you know who Holly Golightly is. Not many men do."

His smile grew. "Big Truman Capote fan. I'm also an English professor at Red Rocks Community College." He held out his hand. "I'm Scott."

Crap. She hadn't anticipated a handsome *and* flirty man sitting beside her at this wedding extravaganza. But then an idea hit, and she grasped his hand. "Holly."

He laughed. "The beautiful lady behind the sunglasses wants to remain a mystery." He leaned toward her. "I like solving mysteries."

Scott the English professor definitely knew how to flirt.

Alyson managed a half smile and released his hand.

As affable and attractive as he looked and sounded, she wasn't in the mood for this.

"My sister insisted I come to this thing with her," he continued. "Thought I needed a break from grading essay tests. She also doesn't think I get out enough when I'm not working." He grinned. "I'm beginning to think she might be right."

She held onto a sigh. Then her phone buzzed with a text from Jillian.

I'm pretty sure I've tracked down a FM employee. Text soon!

She closed her eyes and breathed deeply through her nose.

They just needed the florist intel. Perhaps Jillian would even find a way to get the person to talk about how a small business joined forces with the likes of Felicity Mayhew? Then they could get the hell out of here and work on moving forward.

"You okay over there, Holly?"

Her eyes flew open.

Holly's admirer was clearly not giving up.

Alyson returned his grin. In the mood or not, she had no reason not to play nice while waiting for Jillian. Or the wedding to start, so she could get her pics and discreetly leave.

"I'm fine. So, where *is* your sister?"

He shrugged. "She's around here somewhere. Probably talking to someone she knows, and she knows way too many people." He faced her. "That's fine with me, though, since Holly Golightly has my full attention."

She shook her head. "You're a shameless flirt, Scott the English professor."

He slid into the seat beside hers. "I've been called way worse. The question is, am *I* capturing the attention of Holly Golightly?"

She fought a smile as his eyes lit up with mischief that matched his grin.

Under completely different and no-David-Thomas-Preston circumstances, Scott would have a fighting chance. And his female students—maybe even some male—had to be in love with him. But she was still reeling from everything that had happened between her and David last night, early this morning, and right before he'd left.

He'd wanted and asked for a second chance. But she'd definitely quashed that *and* him.

She gave Scott a hesitant smile. "You seem like a really nice guy."

He cringed. "Ouch. The kiss of death." He slid back into the other seat. "Where did I lose you? You can be honest."

"You didn't lose me," she insisted. "It's just"—she had no choice but to spill her cover story—"I'm here as a bride-to-be and potential new client of Felicity Mayhew. I'm sure you have no idea who that is," she hastily added, "but she's the most sought after wedding coordinator in the Denver area and beyond. This is one of *her* weddings."

He nodded. "Gotcha. And I'm sorry for throwing all of this at you so fast." He gestured at himself. "But when I see a beautiful woman, all alone, and dressed a lot like a character from an *iconic*

Truman Capote story, I forget how to act like an evolved, civilized man."

She laughed. "Then I suppose you're forgiven."

He tilted his head left. "If you don't mind me asking, why *are* you wearing sunglasses?"

She adjusted the frames and yet another lie tumbled from her mouth. "I had some work done about a week ago. There's still some bruising," she quietly added. She'd probably end up in hell because of all this, but desperate times called for immensely huge risks.

His eyes widened, but then eased into curiosity. "Where's your fiancé tonight?"

"He's out of town for work."

He glanced at her left hand. "Did he forget to give you a ring when he proposed?"

She stared at him.

Scott the English professor's appeal was dwindling. What was with all of the questions? Did he not believe her? Everything she'd said was absolutely believable. As would her next lie. "We designed it together and it's not ready yet." She sighed. "I'm terribly disappointed about it."

What the hell *had happened to Jillian?*

He gestured at their surroundings. "What do you think so far, Miss Golightly?"

She smiled. "It's breathtaking." She angled her head toward the flowers. "The flower arrangements are lovely, too. Though not *quite* as lovely as arrangements I recently saw at another wedding." She leaned toward him. "Between you and me, it wasn't a Felicity Mayhew wedding, but spectacular just the same. *Especially* the flowers. A little shop in the Highlands." *Dammit.* Why was she babbling to him about flowers and her shop? It's not like he cared.

Alyson mentally groaned. Where was Jillian? And why hadn't this wedding started yet?

"I know who did the flowers for this thing, and she would hate hearing all of that." He released a quick laugh. "Would be good for her, though."

She whipped her head in his direction. "You know the florist for this wedding? How?"

He grimaced. "It's my ex-girlfriend's business. Exquisite Professional Events? They do top-dollar event planning and she has a team of florists." He tipped his head toward the nearby floral arrangements. "All of their work looks exactly the same. And I know this *only* because I've been to a few of my ex's events."

Her mouth eased open.

Everyone in the event planning world knew of that company. Of course Felicity Mayhew, who only did top-dollar weddings, would join forces with a business of that caliber. And if that info was made available via her website, Alyson never would have concocted this plan.

"Things didn't end well with her, either. Another reason I was hesitant to come to this thing, but my sister wouldn't take no for an answer." He shuddered. "My ex, her royal highness Stacia Marsden, is also friends with this family. Though I haven't seen her since I got here."

She froze.

No. It couldn't be the same family. Could it?

"I'm sorry did you say Marsden? As in *Marsden* Enterprises?"

He eyed her. "The one and only."

She faced forward.

"She's his youngest daughter."

The ballroom's walls began to close in on her.

The Felicity Mayhew was in business bed with the soulless Marsden family? No. She couldn't be. And how was it she'd never heard that last name until they bought the building? Or maybe she had and it never stuck? No real reason it would have, either.

Scott angled his head left and down. "Did I say something that I shouldn't have?"

She focused on him. "You're saying that Felicity Mayhew, the creator of fantasy weddings, uses a *Marsden* for all of her wedding flowers?"

He opened his mouth, but she stood. At that moment, her phone buzzed with a text.

Got what I needed and leaving. But you're not going to believe what I sweet-talked out of the employee.

Crap, crap, *crap*. This couldn't be happening.

"I'm sorry, Miss," a woman in the last row said, "but could you please sit down?"

Alyson frowned. "Relax. The wedding hasn't started yet." She stepped backward. "I'm leaving." She gripped her phone and purse, looked at Scott, then the woman in the last row. "I sure hope all of you have fun at this wedding created by a woman who's in business with the *devil*. She's also a woman I will never work with or recommend because of that fact."

Scott squinted at her before she adjusted her wrap, turned on her high-heeled feet, and stalked away.

She texted Jillian, *I know. I'm leaving, too.*

Damn Marsden Enterprises, Exquisite Professional Events, and, most of all, Felicity Mayhew. She could be aligned with any florist in this city, supporting small businesses, yet she aligned herself with the daughter of the most selfish *asshat* in Denver? She had to know who she was in business with.

She and Jillian could also have used this time searching for a new space instead of spending it getting ready to "crash" an over-the-top wedding most people couldn't afford. And she'd thought being a part of the fantasy wedding world would be the key to her shop's survival.

No. Daisy's Bouquets was better than Felicity Mayhew *and* Marsden Enterprises.

Her phone buzzed again with, *Okay. I'll be back to pick you up ASAP.*

She had no idea where Jillian had parked. The Ritz-Carlton's valet parking had *not* been an option for a few reasons, so Jillian had dropped her off near the hotel's entrance.

Alyson gritted her teeth.

Dammit, none of this was fair.

Still, they would absolutely figure this out. *They had to.*

What felt like hours later, Alyson slid into Jillian's Subaru.

"How'd you find out?" Jillian asked as she drove them from the hotel.

Alyson removed her sunglasses. "A very chatty guest who started out by trying to pick me up."

"And how did the chatty guest know?"

She rested her head against the headrest. "*Stacia Marsden* is his ex-girlfriend."

Her friend sighed. "How can the Denver metro area be so big and so small at the same time?" She braked at a red light. "So, what now?"

Alyson rolled her head left. "We find an amazing new spot and get the hell out of that building." *Far away from the Marsden name.*

"Okay." The light turned green, and Jillian hit the gas pedal. "Was the chatty guest cute?"

Alyson stared out the windshield. "Yes." Once home and, after changing her clothes and walking Thatcher, she'd jump on her computer to begin the search for a new space.

Absolutely no feeling sorry for herself and...no David showing up on her doorstep in his sexy glasses, checking to make sure she was okay. If he stayed true to his parting words, that would never happen again, either, since she'd made herself perfectly clear.

"But I'm guessing you *didn't* get his number?"

She groaned. "Of course I didn't, Jilly. I wasn't there to find a new boyfriend."

"Great! You're gorgeous right now and Evergreen is calling."

She sat up and looked at her friend. "You can't be serious."

Jillian lifted her shoulders. "We were *both* invited to the show tonight. I'd really like to go. I know you do, too. I'll bet they haven't even played yet, so I'll text Jackson—"

"No, Jillian. Take me home."

"*Me estas volviendo loca.*" She slammed on the brakes at a light and faced Alyson. "David still wants you."

"We're not talking about this."

"I know you feel the same way about him. You're just too stubborn—"

"He made his choice years ago. I've made mine. The subject is closed."

The light turned green, and Jillian pressed the accelerator. "Al, all he wanted was a second chance. You had to already know that when you *didn't* let him leave last night."

Alyson crossed her arms. "Okay. I wasn't quite myself and I—" *Not one part of her had wanted him to leave.* It's not like *he'd* wanted to leave, either. "It happened. We're adults. Now it's time to move on. And where's this coming from?" She narrowed her eyes. "It's not like you're an expert on relationships." Yes, beyond bitchy. But at the moment she didn't care since she was tired of her best friend defending *David Thomas Preston.*

"No, I'm not. But after my date with Jackson last night, I get it now. The chemistry?" She braked at another light. "I've never seen *any* chemistry with other guys you've dated, but the few times I've been around you and David—"

"Jilly, I'm happy you and Jackson like each other and had fun on your date, but please stop talking." She'd meant every word about Jackson, too. She just didn't want to think or talk about *him* or their damn chemistry. In and out of the bedroom.

Jillian followed a car through the intersection. "Al, what are you afraid of?"

She lifted her chin. "That something else will happen in his life and he'll crush me. Again!" *She'd never survive that a second time.* She'd basically told David the same thing. Then watched the light leave his...deep, soulful brown eyes.

"Finally, some honesty," her friend mumbled. "Alyson, that was a *tragic* situation and you know that." She paused, then added, "But apparently he's not the only one who needs to let go of the past."

Alyson's shoulders fell as Jillian's words settled around her.

"And if I were you," she continued, "I know what I would do and where I'd go tonight."

She turned to stare out the window.

"Home or Evergreen?"

Yes, she was still irrefutably drawn to David, and he to her. And, no, it hadn't been his fault heart-wrenching tragedy had caused his life to implode two years into their relationship.

But the choices he'd made *after* had caused a lot of damage.

"I need to start searching for a new space," she finally answered. "That's my number one priority right now." *Not her personal life.* That's exactly how it should be, too.

"*Estás cometiendo un gran error.*"

"I'm not making a mistake," Alyson stated. "But *you* should go and spend time with Jackson, because I really am happy you two have clicked." A bit weird and surreal? Absolutely. However, she couldn't ignore the fact Jilly seemed more than a little taken with Jackson Lovett.

Her friend released a long, weary sigh. "Daisy's Bouquets is mine, too, so no. We're going to find a new spot together." She glanced her way. "We're going to do this together, just like we vowed when we started the business."

She gave her a soft smile. "Thanks, Jilly."

Her friend stayed silent.

Alyson rolled her head right.

Maybe she, like Jillian had said, did need to let go of the past. This morning she'd given David the same advice.

You need to let it go. All *of it.*

But how *could* she ever trust him again with her heart and soul that she'd blindly given him twelve years ago?

Chapter Fifteen

DAVID GRASPED his glass of water as he read through the documents his financial advisor had e-mailed him earlier in the week. This was the first chance he'd had since arriving in Aspen Sunday night to carefully go through them.

The corner of his mouth lifted in a smile.

According to the numbers, walking away from architecture was a very real possibility.

He took a drink and sat back in the leather chair, then scanned the rustic bar of the Hotel Jerome. Being a Wednesday evening, there were only a few other people in the bar with him. But if he was still here come Friday night, the hotel would be packed with people in Aspen skiing for the weekend. The area had received some recent snow, too, with more to come that night. He'd probably get on one of the mountains if still stuck here due to Vivienne and Bob's continued determination to be unyielding. And pissing him off in the process.

He brought his eyes back to the documents and recalled the Saturday night show in Evergreen that had been so fantastic they were playing there again later this month.

The night would have been extraordinary if his sister and Matt had been able to make it.

He frowned.

And *her*.

As foolish as it had been, an uncomfortably big part of him had hoped that after they'd finished working, Al would have changed her mind and shown up with Jillian. Because according to Jackson, Jillian had really wanted to be there. But that, of course, hadn't happened.

He shook his head and concentrated on the documents.

Focusing on his music, becoming a full-time musician, had fallen within his reach. He had *her* to thank, too. He'd been so caught up in being David Preston the architect to support himself and his sister the last several years, he'd failed to really see the fact Becs had grown up. Become a young woman who was on the verge of true independence. She didn't need David Preston the architect anymore. At least, she wouldn't after the wedding. She would only need David Preston, her older brother. So why the hell couldn't he work full time on becoming who he was meant to be? The guy he'd actually once been, minus the real-world experience.

The guy Al had fallen in love with twelve years ago.

He set his glass down.

Okay. She wasn't interested in trying again and that stung something deep inside of him. At the same time, he really couldn't blame her or her blatant fear. He had to move on from Al, from being an architect, from being his sister's primary provider, and not look back.

His eyes again swept over his surroundings.

He liked Aspen enough and this hotel was more than nice and comfortable, but he belonged with his piano at home in Denver. Which meant—

"David, what are you doing here all by yourself?"

He swallowed a groan at the familiar voice and flashed Vivienne Dunne what he hoped was his most charming architect smile. "Hi Vivienne. You're looking lovely as usual." *Please go away now*. It was well after 8:00 at night.

She smoothed the top of her beige pantsuit.

He'd discovered during his times here that when Queen Dunne wasn't demanding changes to her compound and making Bob crazy, she spent her days shopping and lunching with other older widows. And sometimes skiing.

She patted her white-blonde hair pulled up into a tight bun. "Thank you. But you, my darling, are looking more pensive than usual." She sat in the chair across from him and set down a glass of dark liquid.

He managed not to release an irritated sigh and put his papers aside.

She pointed at his glass. "What are you drinking tonight?"

He eyed her drink that had to be good whiskey. Also known as his drink of choice during the darkness that really didn't feel that long ago some days. Right at this moment being one of those times. But he said, "Just a stiff glass of ice water."

She frowned. "You need something stronger than that." She turned toward the actual bar.

"Vivienne, I'm fine with water. Is there something you needed?"

She whirled forward. Probably at his sharp tone. But shit. He was off the clock.

He should have stayed in his hotel room.

She picked up her glass and sipped. "What's gotten into you tonight?" She glanced at his papers. "Bad news?"

Yes. That showed up in an expensive, beige pantsuit drinking equally expensive whiskey.

"Actually, it's very good news," he replied.

She smiled. "Care to share?"

"Not really."

She sat back. "You're an enigma, my darling David."

He grinned. "Thank you. Again, was there something you needed from me?" Why had she decided to come to the bar? He knew for a fact she usually ate in the restaurant at this time.

Her blue eyes sharpened to a point. "I know you're upset with me and the fact you had to come back to Aspen. But I want *my* custom-designed home to be exactly what I'm envisioning."

He stayed silent.

"You're also my architect and I'm glad." She grinned. "I'm really quite fond of you."

He froze.

Oh, *shit*. Was she actually about to—

"Not like *that*." She sipped her drink. "I'm not a cougar." She laughed. "Not yet, at least."

He slowly released the air in his lungs.

"If you were a happy young man," she continued, "I wouldn't hesitate to set you up with my daughter who has decidedly questionable taste in men."

His skin turned hot beneath his thick sweater and he fought the urge to yank it off.

"But it's clear you're not happy and it can't be all my fault. *Or* that Mr. Clancy's."

"Vivienne, I swear I'm fine." He pushed back his chair. "I'm also—"

"A liar," she countered. "I'm guessing a woman is behind most of your brooding, too. If not all of it." She gave him a warm smile. "Despite what that Mr. Clancy thinks of me, I'm a very good listener and have nowhere to be at this precise moment in time."

Something about her words and smile that seemed genuine kept David in his seat.

"What's her name?"

He sighed and sat back. "Alyson." *Alyson Catherine Douglas.* "Al for short."

She settled into her chair and crossed her legs. "And how did you and *Al* meet?"

He absently smiled. "College. Twelve years ago. In an English class I waited as long as possible to take." A decision that had changed his life in a matter of minutes.

It had been fate. Pure and simple.

She peered at him. "I didn't know you were married. You don't wear a ring."

"Because I'm not. I mean, I was." He shook his head. "It's complicated."

"And I promise you I can keep up."

He stared at her. "It's also a long story." *And incredibly painful.*

She looked at the bartender, raised her glass, and the guy nodded. She then focused on him once again. "David, my darling, I have all the time in the world."

She clearly wasn't going to leave him or this alone, so he nodded once. "Okay, Vivienne. You asked for it." And maybe it would be good for him to talk about it with someone who hadn't been there. Something he hadn't done in almost ten years. "After that day in class, we went on a date later that week. And fell hard." *As if free-falling and they'd landed right into each other.*

"All of this is sounding encouraging. But something must have happened?"

The bartender brought her the same drink and took her empty glass.

He swallowed and tore his eyes from the all-too familiar dark liquid he could almost taste. "I was a music major at that time and April of my senior year…there was a car accident." This part of the story always challenged him the most. *In more ways than one.*

Her eyes became round.

"A horrific car accident to be more accurate," he added under his breath.

She leaned forward. "Did something happen to your girl?"

He cleared his throat and reached for his water. "No. My parents and sister."

Her mouth eased open. "Did they…?"

"My—our—parents died." He took a long drink, trying not to wish he had Vivienne's glass. He then said, "My sister, who's five years younger than me, barely survived. But the impact of the car flipping over permanently damaged her spinal cord." He gripped his glass. "She's paralyzed from the waist down and in a wheelchair."

"Oh, David." She stared at him. "It must have been absolutely horrendous to go through such trauma. And at that age?"

More than you can possibly know or imagine.

"You weren't the one…driving. Were you?"

He shook his head. "I wasn't with them." But he and Al were *supposed* to be with them.

Her eyes fell to his hand clutching the glass, then to her glass. Understanding caused her eyes to widen.

"I'm terribly sorry for insisting you needed something stronger. I can have him—"

"It's fine." He released the glass and flexed his fingers. "I swear it's the subject matter, not the drink." *At least it was mostly the subject matter.* "Life changed considerably, and Al and I broke up." And that's all Vivienne needed to know about that ugly, shameful part of his life.

She slowly nodded. "If you two broke up that long ago, why are you focused on her now?" She straightened. "Or did you two find each other again?"

He hesitated before saying, "We did."

She sat back. "That would explain your snippiness with me *and* your brooding since you arrived Sunday night." She caught his eyes. "I took you away from *the one*."

"Vivienne, you definitely took me away from something, but it's not her." *Because she was afraid he'd break her in half again.* "When I'm not being an architect, I'm a musician."

She smiled softly. "That's right. You said you were a music major before—" Her smile vanished. "You are no longer an enigma."

Silence fell as she absently turned her glass; the contents no longer calling out to him.

That's how the cravings always happened. They'd stay only long enough to remind him of how alcohol could turn into him into an unrecognizable, despicable asshole, then leave.

"What kind of a musician are you?" Vivienne suddenly asked.

He blinked and said, "I play the piano. I'm also in a jazz band." *That needed him more than architecture. That* he *needed more than architecture.*

Her smile came back, but with a trace of sadness. "My Phillip played piano. I loved listening to him play. He was quite good, too."

He watched her continue to absently turn her glass.

Holy shit had this night gone in a completely unexpected direction. But seeing this very human, *likable* side of Vivienne Dunne meant that he'd make it through this project without losing his sanity. Now all he had to do was somehow get her and Bob on the same damn page.

She released a quick breath, straightened, and folded her hands on the table. "Now that you're no longer an enigma, what do we"— she frowned—"what do *I* need to do to get you back home to your piano and band and everyone you love in Denver." She paused before adding, "Including *the one.*"

He raised his eyebrows. "Unfortunately, she's no longer *the one.* And did I hear you right?" Had she turned into a mind reader, too?

She waved her hand. "Who told you she was no longer *the one*? And, yes, you heard me correctly." She glanced at her watch. "If it weren't so damn late, I'd tell you to get on the phone with that Mr. Clancy so we could set up a meeting for tomorrow morning."

David stared at his nearly unrecognizable client.

What the *hell* was happening right now?

"Did Al tell you she was no longer *the one*?"

He squinted at her.

"If she did, you should have called bullshit. Like in that card game?"

He lowered his eyes to the table. "It's not that simple."

"Of course it is," she insisted. "Young people love to make everything complicated." She stood and picked up her glass. "The only things I miss about being your age is having a young body, mind, and sex on a regular basis."

He nodded once. Though that had been a little too much information.

"David, my darling, please set up a meeting with that Mr. Clancy for as soon as possible. I'd like the three of us to sit down and talk about how to move forward successfully." She stepped back. "You need to be where you belong, and I need my house to be finished. Believe it or not, I'm quite tired of living in a hotel." She looked at the bartender, watching her. "Even one as fine as the Hotel Jerome." She faced David once more, gave him an air kiss, then turned away.

He couldn't help but smile as he watched her disappear from view. His smile only grew when he pictured Bob's hard hat blowing to the moon, but in a good way, when he told him about Vivienne's request tomorrow morning at the site of her compound.

He stood and swiped the papers off the table.

Considering how unbelievably good their Friday night had been together, he strongly suspected Al *was* fighting her feelings for him. Like his client had all but said.

But he couldn't make her say the truth.

David followed the same path Vivienne had taken out of the bar.

What he could do was get this project back on track once and for all, get home, and get to work on turning his life into what *he* wanted for the first time in ten years.

⸺

ALYSON SPUN in slow motion in the available space that was narrow, but long.

Jillian wandered toward the back; a straight shot from where Alyson stood.

The real estate agent, who also handled property management, said, "There's a sink with a counter at the very back. Other than that, it's really not set up for a flower shop."

No, but none of the other five places they'd seen had, either.

They'd have to take almost everything from their current location and move it to a new one.

She narrowed her eyes and damned Marsden Enterprises for the billionth time.

"That's not a problem," Jillian answered. She turned and looked at Alyson. "I really like how open it is."

She nodded since this space, located a couple blocks off of Colorado Boulevard and a quick drive from The Denver Museum of Nature and Science, was the best one they'd looked at this week. Still, it would definitely need some TLC in the form of a good scouring and paint job. That thought made her ask, "Would we be able to re-paint it to reflect the shop and our brand?"

The woman smiled. "Of course. Not a problem at all." She laughed. "I co-own this space with my soon-to-be ex-*bastard,* and he put me in charge of it." She leaned toward Alyson. "But he owns a bigger percentage, so you can do whatever you want. Graffiti the walls, for all I care."

Alyson caught Jillian's eyes, and her friend smothered a smile.

"I do like the location," Alyson conceded. "You?"

Jillian nodded. "There are definitely worse places to have a flower shop."

They would know, too, since they'd seen a couple this week. Spaces that had looked viable in photos and on a map, but a *huge* disappointment in person.

"I don't live too far away," the agent added. "I also have a new man in my life who knows how to use tools." She sent Alyson, then Jillian, a sassy grin. "If you get my meaning?"

Jillian returned the woman's smile.

Alyson, on the other hand, wasn't convinced this was a good idea. Something about this woman, what sounded like a contentious divorce, and the "new man" in her life, caught Alyson's instincts the wrong way. But the spot was by far their best option and they had to be packed and moved out in less than thirty days.

"I'm sure Oliver—that's his name—would be more than happy to offer his services as a handyman if you need help getting settled in or if anything minor breaks." The woman's smile doubled in size. "He's only available Monday through Thursday right now, though, because he's a ski instructor up at Copper Mountain on the weekends." She laughed. "It's how we met."

Alyson eyed Jillian, who lifted her shoulders, her opinion clear.

What other choice did they have? Outside of looking at more spaces. But they had a wedding tomorrow night and Saturday afternoon to prepare for. Time was *not* on their side.

Alyson smiled. "I guess we just need to talk about the rent?" Another reason they'd contacted the woman about the space was her stating the "rent was negotiable."

"My soon-to-be ex-*bastard* told me what to rent the space for." Her grin turned wicked. "But since he so graciously put me in charge of finding a new tenant because I refuse to give up my stake in this building, I think it's only fair to accept what you're paying at your current location. I certainly don't need the money. And that greedy little prick needs the money even less," she enunciated. "He's a real estate attorney. It's also how we met."

Alyson peered at the woman.

How'd that saying go? If it's too good to be true, it probably is? And did they really—

"We'd like to go for it," Jillian stated. "The sooner the better, too."

She mentally groaned.

The agent led them toward the door. "I'll e-mail you the application, which will have a fee, when I return to my office. The deposit will be due as long as the app results look good."

They followed her out of the space.

She locked the door and faced them. "I had a very good feeling about you ladies as soon I saw you walk up to the building." She shook Alyson's hand, then Jillian's. "I have to get to a showing down in Cherry Hills Village, but expect the application by the end of the business day."

She sauntered right while removing her phone from her black, Prada purse.

Probably getting on the phone to her soon-to-be ex-*bastard* to share the "good news."

"*Jillian*," she moaned, "this doesn't feel right."

They turned in unison and went in the opposite direction.

"I know, I know," her friend replied. "I'm not totally comfortable with the idea of, possibly, getting in the middle of an ugly divorce. But what choice do we have?"

Alyson sighed. "We could keep looking."

Jillian shook her head. "With what time? Al, we have a business to run and that business will be out of a home in twenty-three days if we don't jump on this." She gestured at their surroundings. "This isn't exactly a bad spot to have a flower shop."

No. It wasn't. This older area of Denver was actually quite charming with pricey homes. It looked like their neighbors would be a quaint bistro with outdoor seating, a market with a deli, and a dog grooming place, with the agent's space on the end.

Jillian slipped her right arm through Alyson's left. "Hopefully, she and her ex will keep their divorce to themselves." She giggled. "But I am a tad curious about that new man of hers."

Alyson eyed her. "And what about Jackson?"

"We've *barely* started dating." Jillian shrugged. "I can still look and admire."

David smiling at her with that hint of devil flashed through her mind. She'd met that smile of his the moment he sat beside her in the classroom. After the professor had started class, he'd passed her the cute note she still couldn't bring herself to set on fire.

She'd been a goner and had never looked twice at another guy. Not until *years* later.

"I do have to admit," Jillian slowly added, "I am looking forward to our second date Saturday night."

Alyson's phone burst into the old-fashioned ring tone as they approached her 4Runner. A welcome interruption to where her thoughts had gone no matter how hard she tried *not* to go there. When she saw who was calling, though, she sighed.

"Crap," she mumbled. "It's my mom."

"Since when do you dread a call from her?" Jillian asked while they climbed into the SUV. "You two can't be fighting."

"No, it's just"—she stared at her jangling phone—"they don't know about the building."

Her friend buckled her seatbelt. "Tell her now. We have great news, too."

"They also don't know about David," she blurted out.

Jillian stared at her. "It's not as if there's anything to tell." She arched her right eyebrow. "Unless you feel the need to tell her about your one *libidinous* night together?"

Alyson glared at her and answered, "Hey."

"Hi Sweetie. You never got back to me about Fondue Fun this Saturday night."

She sat back. "I'm sorry. It's been a crazy week." She closed her eyes. "Thatcher and I can definitely make it, but Jillian will be on a date."

Her mom laughed. "Good for her. Where'd she meet him?"

She opened her eyes, glanced at Jillian watching her, and answered, "At a party." Certainly not a lie, either.

"Well," her mom began, "since you'll only be here with Thatcher, would you mind if I also invited this absolutely adorable, *single* man your dad just hired?"

Oh, my God. She was not in the mood to deflect her mom's match-making attempt.

"Please don't do that."

She released an exasperated sigh. "Alyson, you and Steven broke up months ago, and I really think you'd like Alex."

Alex and Alyson? How absolutely adorable. A little like *Jackson and Jillian*. But those two clearly had connected.

"Mom, I can't deal with a blind date."

She fell silent.

Alyson's eyes drifted back to Jillian, making a nudging motion with her hands. "I also really need to talk to you guys, because there's a lot going on right now with the business."

More silence, then, "Sweetie, what's going on? Should we be worried?"

"No." She started the engine. "I promise I'll tell you guys everything on Saturday. We have a job in downtown Denver, but I'll head to Evergreen after I pick up Thatcher. Okay?"

A pause, followed by, "Alright. We'll see you Saturday."

The moment Alyson ended the call, Jillian asked, "Did they ever meet Jackson?"

She carefully pulled out of the spot. "Yes. Once." She frowned. "At the funeral." That fact hadn't even crossed her mind until this moment.

"It's not like I know what's going to happen with Jackson," her friend swiftly added. "But if date two goes as well as date one, on top of all the FaceTiming and texting this week, I think…this could be something, Al."

She nodded. "I already know that." She hadn't seen her best friend this excited about a guy in an *extremely* long time.

Jillian Castillo would never easily give her heart away.

"Which means—"

"I know," Alyson interjected. "And I will tell them. You're right. It's not as if there's anything to really say beyond being reconnected with Becca." She smiled softly. "They were around her a few times back then and thought she was pretty sassy—which she could be— but still liked her as much as they liked David. And their parents." Her smile disappeared.

Jillian reached across the console, grabbed her hand, and squeezed. "Al, you need to keep smiling. You've been so serious this last week. *Everything's* going to be okay."

The last time she remembered genuinely smiling and laughing and feeling normal was a week ago Friday night while with very comfortable, soothing, familiar company.

Crap, crap, *crap*. He'd gotten inside of her again. In *and* out of the bedroom.

Or had he really ever left?

Alyson forced her mouth into a smile. "Yes. It will." She needed to believe that, too.

Jillian released her hand and laughed. "You, me, and Campbell need to go out and celebrate tonight. I'm thinking happy hour at the place down the street from the shop?"

She changed lanes. "Hayley will be crushed we left her out."

"And she knows she can join our celebrations the second she turns twenty-one."

A celebration was exactly what they needed and deserved after becoming a victim of soulless Marsden Enterprises and turning triumphant. And maybe while celebrating with Jillian and Campbell, she'd be able to shake the inexplicable apprehension that continued to shroud her.

Chapter Sixteen

DAVID LOOKED AT VIVIENNE, then Bob, the contrast between them vast.

She wore gray and pink designer ski clothes, her white-blonde hair pinned up into her usual tight bun, and Bob, broad and solid and weathered from his years of being a contractor, had on jeans now dusty from the site, a blue flannel shirt, and work boots.

They sat at a table in Vivienne's suite with a spectacular view of the mountains covered in fresh snow that fell during the night.

The serene view outside her windows in no way matched the tension in her suite.

It had been a long day out at the site of her custom compound while waiting for the inspector to show up. Fortunately, the news had been good and they could continue moving forward with the kitchen changes he'd grudgingly done when he arrived earlier in the week. But now it was time to hold his client to what she'd said the night before.

He focused on Vivienne. "The inspector signed off on the plumbing changes today, which means the new kitchen design is set. It can't be changed. In fact," he stressed, "there can't be any more changes at this point, *including* the staircase."

Bob straightened. "You wanted a new damn *staircase,* too?" He muttered something incoherent under his breath that David suspected his client would not appreciate hearing.

Her blue eyes became slits.

"It's taken care of," David continued, "because it's not even possible at this point. The city won't extend the building permit another time. And we're already way behind on this project. The snow isn't helping, either."

Bob released a half grunt, half huff.

Vivienne continued to glare at the contractor.

David concentrated on his client. "You said last night that you're tired of living in a hotel and want your house finished. That means you have to stop second guessing everything."

Bob flashed him a quick grin that David took as his version of gratitude.

She glanced at Bob and back at him. "The house is going to be my permanent home, and I only want it to be perfect. I don't see anything wrong with that."

Bob released another grunt.

"And it will be," David stressed. "Especially when you and my colleague, Laura, really start working on the interior design."

Despite his unexpected and surprisingly nice time with Vivienne last night in the bar, he planned on celebrating the day he officially turned her over to Laura.

"Okay, my darling David."

"So we're crystal clear?" Bob asked. "No more changes?"

Vivienne went back to glaring at him.

David nodded. "None. Which leads me to now that everything is back on track and we all understand each other, I'm driving back to Denver. Tonight." Unfortunately, he wouldn't make it in time for the band's weekly Thursday night gig. Unless he could get his Audi to go mach speed. But being thrown in jail for excessive speeding wasn't part of his big, new life plan.

They nodded.

"Then we're all set." David stood, followed quickly by Bob.

Now all he had left to do was pack his shit, check out, grab some food, and hit the road.

Vivienne slowly came to her feet and led them to her suite's door.

"I'll wait for you in the hallway," Bob said, then fled the room.

David faced her. "Vivienne, everyone—including Bob—is working extremely hard to get your house done *and* on time." Which would be a damn miracle at this point.

She smiled. "I understand. But I'd like you to do something for me before you leave."

He froze.

Oh, *shit*. What now?

"Promise me you'll call *the one* when you get home and ask her to go on a date?"

He raised his eyebrows.

"Take her out to a nice dinner, bring her back to your home, and play the piano." She laughed. "That always worked for my late Phillip."

He managed a slight grin. "Honestly, Vivienne, I would love to make you that promise."

"Wonderful! I'll be sending you good thoughts."

"But the last time I saw her," he continued, "I said I'd stay away."

I can't give you what you want, because how could I ever trust you again?

She frowned. "Why on earth would you say something like that?"

He opened the door. "No more calls." He paused to look at her over his shoulder. "Unless you absolutely need to hear the sound of my voice." He winked.

She sighed. "David, my darling, you're too adorable."

"Thank you." He started to close the door.

"If you and *the one* can't seem to figure things out, I can always set you up with my daughter."

No chance in hell. But he said, "I'll keep that in mind." He closed the door behind him.

Bob stood several feet away from her suite.

When David reached him, the contractor asked, "How do you do it?"

They headed for the elevators.

"That woman makes me crazier than a bull being released from its chute."

David chuckled. "Lots of patience." He glanced at Dave. "Charm also goes a long way with her." Apparently, so did being an enigma.

Bob pressed the down button. "That's why *you* get paid the really big bucks."

The doors opened, and they stepped onto the elevator.

David punched the button for his floor.

"Thanks for coming up here again," Bob said. "I know you're busy back home and I really appreciate it."

"Actually," he replied as the doors opened to his floor, "this trip was exactly what I needed. So no thanks necessary." He held out his hand, which Bob grasped. "I'll check in early next week. Sound good?"

Bob nodded, and they shook hands.

Seconds later, David entered his room and withdrew his phone from his jeans pocket.

The decisions he'd made while being in Aspen wouldn't be real until he talked them through with the closest person to him, outside of Jackson. Who he'd also have to tell.

"Hi," Becs answered. "So Matty's totally jealous you're in Aspen with all of that fresh snow and doesn't think you've been up there working." She released a squeal, followed by high-pitched laughter and phone jostling. "Matt, *don't!*"

David retrieved his bag from the floor and tossed it on the bed. "Should I call you later?"

"No, I'm here," she breathlessly answered. "And Matt's leaving to go play basketball. Good riddance, too," she said, but at Matt since her voice became muffled.

He sat on the bed's edge. "Becs, I really need to talk to you."

Silence, then, "The last time you said that you were upset with me about what I told Alyson and whatever happened between you two before you left."

He stared at the floor. "This has nothing to do with her, and I promise I'm not upset." The corner of his mouth lifted in a smile. "I'm coming home tonight, but I couldn't wait to talk to you about some decisions I've made while I've been here."

"Okay. What's up?"

He took a deep breath and started at the beginning—with Al's comment before he'd told her he'd stay away and sealed those words by literally closing *that* door.

ALYSON CURBED the strong urge to cringe while her parents and grandma stared at each other with round eyes. An understandable reaction, considering she'd just unloaded *everything* that had been happening in her life since Valentine's Day.

Minus her one *libidinous* night with David over a week earlier.

She tucked her feet beneath her on the couch, nestled deeper into the cushions, and picked up her glass of wine that she sipped.

Yes, she'd shocked the crap out of her family. Still, she did feel a tad better having spilled the truth, even though she had a good idea on how they'd react to the David Preston part.

The heavy, somewhat uncomfortable silence continued. The seconds turned into a minute and beyond. All she could do was sit there, sipping her wine, and wait for their responses.

Her grandma leaned forward and set her glass down hard on the coffee table, which caused Thatcher, lounging on his nearby dog bed, to raise his head.

"I say damn that Marsden company *and* that boy for waiting ten years to contact you."

She sighed. "Grandma—"

"Let's talk about David first," she continued in a gentler tone. "Sweetheart, I understand he had his entire world upended in one very terrible night. And my heart still hurts for him and his sister whenever I think about it." She paused, shaking her head. "Their parents were lovely people and didn't deserve…" She focused on Alyson. "But that never gave him the right to take it out on *you* the way he did."

She couldn't dispute her grandma's statement. But they didn't know the whole story, either. No, David wasn't that suffering, bitter, twenty-one-year old boy trying to numb the pain with alcohol while locked in his bedroom, avoiding everyone in his life. However, he still wasn't free from that darkness. And she couldn't help but think he never would be free from any of it.

Her vision blurred at the thought.

"But he's gone for good now. Right?"

"Ben!" her mother snapped, giving him a razor-sharp look.

"I'm not trying to sound insensitive," he calmly added. "I agree with everything your grandma just said. You know that." He frowned. "But I don't like the fact he came walking into your shop out of the blue, expecting to pick up where you left off years ago."

She clenched her teeth for a few seconds, then said, "Dad, it really wasn't like that." *Not entirely, anyway.* "It was about Becca."

Her mom smiled. "I think it's wonderful he reconnected you with his sister. And I'm stunned she's getting married. The last time we saw her she'd just turned sixteen."

Almost two months to the day before the accident.

"How's she doing? Besides being an excited bride-to-be?"

Alyson grinned. "She's extremely happy. She and her fiancé, Matt, have a cute little house in Boulder that Hugh and Eileen bought for them. David helped them with the remodel, too." Her grin grew. "She's also finishing her Ph.D. in psychology at Boulder."

Her family members smiled for the first time since she'd said David's name.

"And now Jillian's dating Jackson?" her mom clarified.

"Yes." Alyson set down her wine glass. "They seem to really like each other."

"There sure as hell hasn't been a dull moment in the Highlands the last couple weeks." Her grandma paused, then asked, "Sweetheart, are you going to be okay if she and Jackson become serious?"

"Of course." She lifted her shoulders. "Those two being together has nothing to do with me or David." She looked at her grandma, mom, then her dad. "Becca and I have every intention of staying friends, too. David will have nothing to do with *our* friendship."

Their expressions turned dubious. She wasn't certain she believed her strongly spoken last statement, either. Last Friday night had proven she and David should stay far apart. But something about that thought tugged her insides. Probably because everything about last Friday night—in and out of the bedroom—had felt so incredibly *right*.

"Alyson," her mom began, "we understand that your relationship with David was years ago and you're adults now."

She readied herself for what had to be coming next.

"We also know he was very special." Her mom gave her an affectionate smile. "It's no secret where you two were headed before... everything that happened."

Alyson looked away.

"It's admirable what David's done with his life. What he's done for his sister," her dad commented. "But all of us remember how his toxic behavior affected *you*."

"And for how long," her grandma quietly added.

"We just want you to be careful when it comes to him and your friendship with Becca," her mom finished. "Okay, Sweetie?"

She nodded, since they had every right to their concerns.

"And as for that Marsden company," her grandma muttered, "they deserve a special spot in hell for doing business like that."

Alyson couldn't and wouldn't dispute her on that one, either.

Her dad caught her eyes. "You don't seem very happy about the new spot."

She smoothed a wrinkle in her jeans. "It's not that." *Not entirely, anyway.* "I just can't believe all the work we have ahead of us. Between preparing to move, and keeping up with the weddings and general orders, and now we're getting orders for Easter…" She smoothed another wrinkle. "And the new space needs some work done." Another wrinkle gone, but her lower lip quivered. "We're feeling overwhelmed." She most of all, considering Daisy's Bouquets had always felt like it was more hers than Jillian's, and only because the shop had been her idea.

Her mom, sitting beside her on the couch, leaned forward. "Alyson, how can we help? Because that is *a lot* for the four of you to tackle by yourselves. And in less than a month?"

"I'm not needed at work as much," her dad added. "What work does the new space need? We can help you pack, too."

Alyson smiled. "I think the extra help would be really nice." Jillian, Campbell, and Hayley would certainly agree if they were here. She released a quick breath. "Thank you."

Her mom wrapped her in a tight hug, and Alyson squeezed her back.

Yes. Everything would be fine. She just had to take it one step at a time.

Her phone started to ring. She grinned at the caller's name.

Her mom stood. "You answer that." She pointed at her dad. "You come with me. Enough seriousness. It's time to start our Fondue Fun evening."

"And I'll stay right here and keep this handsome dog of yours company." Her grandma settled back into the recliner with her glass of wine.

Alyson swiped her phone off the table and headed for the staircase. "Hi there." She then cringed at the fact she'd used David's preferred greeting. Only it sounded better in his voice.

"Hey!" Becca chirped. "I'm calling about Matty's big surprise, eighties-themed, thirtieth birthday party."

She sat on a step and laughed. "That's quite a mouthful. When is it?"

"Two weeks from tonight, our place in Boulder. I'm pretty sure Jackson's going to invite Jillian, and I'm inviting you. Can you make it? Please, please, *please*?"

She couldn't help but wonder, based on Becca's comment, what David had told his sister, if anything, about their conversation last Saturday morning. So she asked, "Do you think your brother will be okay with that?" Their words to each other before he'd left had been pretty final.

Becca laughed. "Why wouldn't he be? It's not his party, and I know Matt would want you to be there. *Just* like me."

She smiled softly.

An eighties-themed surprise birthday party did sound like fun. Another much-needed break and distraction from real life. They had a wedding that day, but she could put Campbell and Hayley in charge. The only reason to say no was Becca's big brother.

"Please say yes. I promise you'll have a great time," she added in her high-octave voice.

Alyson hesitated before saying, "Then I promise I'll be there." David had said her friendship with his sister would have nothing to do with him.

Becca squealed. "*Awesome.* Oh, and you can dress up in eighties clothes if you want to. The bridal party *has* to dress up." She giggled. "David's not super happy about that rule."

She laughed, too.

He'd never dressed up for college Halloween parties they'd attended, either.

"Ooh, Matt's home," Becca whispered. "Gotta go. I'll see you soon!"

The line went dead.

Okay. She'd be seeing him again much sooner than she'd

thought. And, if he played by the rules, dressed in some eighties outfit.

She smiled at the image. But then her mom's words drifted through her mind.

We just want you to be careful when it comes to him and your friendship with Becca.

Alyson stood.

Her family actually didn't need to worry, because when it came to her heart and soul careful was all she'd known for the last ten years.

Chapter Seventeen

DAVID TAPPED OUT THE ROUGH, final notes of his new song, then looked at Randy, sitting on the arm of his couch. "What do you think?"

His bandmate nodded. "I like it. We needed a new, upbeat song like that." He straightened and, laughing, shook his head. "You sure as *shit* have been full of surprises since I got here." His smile slowly faded. "But I needed to hear some good news since I already heard back from the Jazz Aspen Snowmass people."

David straddled the piano bench. "It was a gigantic long shot."

"I know," he said around a heavy sigh. "Hopefully, the Evergreen Festival gives us a legit shot next year. We may even want to have a serious conversation about recording another CD because of all the new music we have."

David grinned. "Which means my two music epiphanies while I was gone has to mean my trip to Aspen wasn't a total inconvenience for you guys."

Randy walked toward him. "No, but you belong here, especially on gig nights." He crossed his thick arms and looked around David's living room. "Are you really going to be able to walk away from *this* life?"

He shrugged. "It's a house with a bunch of stuff inside of it." With the exception of his piano, several photos, bed, clothing, and shoes, there wasn't anything in this house he wanted.

Randy laughed once again. "Okay, Piano Man. Then I guess the best *is* yet to come."

Al's perfect face lit up with laughter drifted through his mind, but he pushed the image aside and released a quiet breath. "Absolutely." Maybe more like *finally*.

His doorbell ringing seemed to punctuate that thought, and he frowned since he wasn't expecting anyone.

As he and Randy strolled toward his front door, his bandmate said, "We'll start working on your song Wednesday? Maybe we can have it ready for our second gig up in Evergreen."

David started to open the door, but Randy stopped him with, "I wasn't kidding when I said the best is yet to come. I think we'll be able to turn Sixteenth Note into something even better than it is." He paused, then added around a laugh, "Lea and the guys are going to fall over on Wednesday when you tell them your news."

David laughed with him as he opened the door. But stopped when his eyes landed on Jackson glaring at him.

His friend's eyes drifted to Randy and he gave him a quick smile. "Hey, Big Man."

Randy pointed at Jackson's Denver Broncos hoodie. "Loyal to a fault. Even after one of their lousiest seasons in a while." He slapped Jackson on the shoulder. "You need to join us Packers fans so you can know what it's like to be a fan of a team with *real* talent."

"I'll sell my soul to Satan first." Jackson concentrated on David. "But, yeah, that's me. *Loyal*. Even when it's not reciprocated."

Randy glanced David's way. "Alrighty then." He shuffled past Jackson. "I'll see you Wednesday."

Jackson walked into David's house and shoved his hands into his hoodie's front pocket.

"So," his friend began as David shut the door, "I came over to remind you that I'm Jackson Lovett, your best buddy for the last twenty years *and* business partner." He paused, then added, "I'm also technically your boss."

David headed back toward his piano. "As I signed the papers to make the firm official, I knew you would throw that in my face someday."

"What the hell have you been doing since you got back from Aspen?" His friend followed him. "Why haven't you returned my calls? And most of my texts?"

"I told you in a message." He dropped to his piano bench. "I've been working."

Jackson frowned. "On what? Because you never answered *that* question."

He gestured toward his piano. "A new song."

Silence fell between them.

His friend squinted at him for several seconds. Until he started to quietly laugh.

David raised his eyebrows. "And why's that funny?"

"It's not," Jackson replied. "It's just—between you avoiding me and Rebecs being weirdly vague as to what you've been doing since you got back, I thought…" He flinched.

David's shoulders fell. "Right. But don't you think you'd noticed I'd turned back into *that guy* the second you saw me?" It's not like he'd worn *that guy* very well ten years ago. "You also have to know Becs wouldn't hesitate to call you and your family first if I went off the deep end."

"Yeah. I know." Jackson lowered himself to the same couch arm Randy had been sitting on earlier. "The last time I saw you, it was obvious you were upset about what happened with Alyson. Between that, you blowing me *and* the office off when you got back into town, and—" He released a quick breath. "I'm glad you're okay."

What his long-time buddy failed to add was *and sober*.

David shook his head. "I'm better than okay. " *For the most part.* "And we do need to talk." He slid his left index finger across the keys. "It's another reason I've been MIA."

"I knew you were avoiding me." Jackson nodded. "Okay. Give it to me straight."

He paused, since the news he was about to share was a big, damn deal. And would directly affect him, Zach, and the firm they'd created and built as a team.

David faced Jackson. "I'm leaving you guys for my piano." Saying it to his closest friend and business partner caused his shoulders to fall forward, officially free from a weight that had been heavier than he realized.

His announcement hung between them while Jackson stayed silent, staring at him.

"When I was in Aspen, I figured out that I can financially do this and want to."

"What the *hell*?" His buddy leaned forward. "Where's this coming from?"

"Two places." He absently tapped out a tune with his left fingers. "The first one being something you should already know."

He sighed. "Okay. I get it. Architecture wasn't your first choice."

It hadn't become an option until he had to make another choice. But he said, "The second is something Al said to me before I left her house last Saturday morning."

Jackson frowned.

"Everything's been so crazy the last few weeks, I haven't had a chance to tell anyone, with the exception of Al, that the band is playing at the Evergreen Jazz Festival this summer."

His buddy's frown transitioned into surprise, followed quickly by a smile. "Are you shitting me?" He laughed. "You really are a dick. I can't believe you didn't tell me."

He focused on his friend. "That could end up being something, Jackson. A *big* something I can't afford to miss."

"And I get that." He lifted his shoulders. "But the Queen Dunne project should be finished by then."

"And then there might be another project interfering," David shot back.

Jackson's frown returned. "What about Becca?"

He smiled, remembering her ear-splitting response to his news. "She's completely behind me on this." He tapped out another tune. "Al said some things about Becs that never crossed my mind until that morning. She's a grown woman." He finished his tune. "Who's damn near done with school and getting married this summer. Matt makes a good living, too, and she'll eventually have a job. She won't need me anymore. Financially speaking."

"Fine. I'll give you that." He crossed his arms. "But what are you going to do?"

David grinned. "Focus on my music. Work more with Randy on promoting the band and getting us more gigs." Marketing *not* being his strength or favorite part about all of this, but now he'd have the time to learn from Randy. And, possibly, get Matt involved.

"How the hell are you going to survive doing that? Especially in this city?" Jackson stared at him. "Do you guys even make any money?"

"Not a whole lot," he replied around a laugh. "But I've looked at the numbers. My percentage from Vivienne's compound, selling you and Zach my stake in the business, and selling my house will only add to my bottom line." *Significantly.*

Jackson't eyes widened. "You're going to sell the house?"

He repeated what he'd said to Randy moments ago and added, "I also don't need it anymore. Becs and Matt have their own place, and, when Hugh and Eileen are in Denver, they typically host everything at their house."

Jackson peered at him. "David, selling your house seems a little extreme. It sounds like you're assuming too much." He paused, then quietly added, "And giving up."

He leaned forward. "Al doesn't want me, and I'm sure as hell not going to make the same mistake I made with Sara." He stared at the corner of his piano. "I'm not saying I'll always feel like I do." He could very well meet another woman someday…maybe. "But it is what it is right now, and my house is too much for only me." He straightened. "In any case, between all of that, and what I currently have invested and saved—although my savings have taken a hard hit because of the wedding—I'm in *really* good shape. I can do this." He released a quick laugh. "The hardest part will be finding a condo or apartment in a building with an elevator that also has a unit big enough for the piano."

Jackson glared at him. "You're also working under the assumption Zach and I will accept your resignation, *and* want to buy your stake in the firm."

He eyed his friend. "Then you'll find another architect. I've made up my mind, Jackson. I have to and want to do this." Making this huge life change would start him on another much-needed and long overdue path. Something else Al had strongly inferred that morning.

Forgiving and repairing himself.

"And when do you think you'll be leaving us for your piano?"

He tapped out the opening notes to his new song. "When Vivienne's compound is finished, so I won't be taking on anymore projects." He glanced at his friend. "I want to keep this between you, me, and Zach—after I tell him tomorrow—for as long as possible. Agreed?"

Jackson absently nodded.

Yeah, David had a lot to accomplish between now and the endpoint that wouldn't arrive soon enough. There was no doubt his news would continue to surprise everyone in his immediate circle, too. But relief shrouded him, and he grinned at the thought of reaching weightlessness one day. And sooner rather than... well...never.

Jackson looked at him, fighting a smile. "You're a crazy sonofabitch for even thinking this, much less doing it."

David laughed.

"But I have to admit"—he stood—"you're starting to sound and look like my buddy from before the accident. So I say go for it."

"Thanks, man." He also stood. "How's it going with Jillian?"

Jackson smiled. "Damn good. We went out again Saturday night and had a *great* time." He laughed. "This will probably sound insane, but I love the way she says her last name."

David angled his head back. "What do you mean?"

His friend stared at a spot behind him. "She says it with a slight accent. Cas*tillo,*" he attempted, then cringed. "That sucked. She says it way better."

David laughed quietly, shaking his head. At the same time, he hoped Jackson and his workaholism wouldn't blow it with Jillian. Especially since it was clear how much his good buddy liked her; something that hadn't happened in a *long* time.

"Feel like some driveway basketball in Longmont with Will and the kids?"

David's humor transitioned into a frown.

"I'm headed that way for Sunday family night with everyone."

He narrowed his eyes. "You got a guilt trip from your mom."

Jackson nodded and shrugged. "But it's all good. I haven't been out there in a while and neither have you. They'd all love to see you and hear your news."

David slid his eyes to his piano where he'd been working almost non-stop on his new song since coming home Thursday night from Aspen. He could use a break, and it wouldn't hurt to see how his old house was looking *and* spend time with his second family. But he still had to say, "I'm not on kitchen clean-up duty because of last Friday night when your mom was here."

Jackson laughed. "Fair enough."

They headed toward his front door.

"I think we should make the argument that the kids are old enough to wash the dishes."

David grabbed his keys from the table by the front door. "I could get on board with that. Will would probably back us up, too."

Jackson stopped, looked around, then concentrated on him. "This is a great house. Are you absolutely sure you want to give all this up?"

He sounded like Randy had earlier. But Jackson's question caught him sideways.

Give all this up.

"You worked your ass off to get here."

Yeah. He sure had.

"You don't have to decide on the house right now," Jackson continued. "Maybe you should…I don't know…wait and see what happens between now and finishing Queen Dunne's compound? This house in this neighborhood sure as hell isn't going to lose value."

David followed Jackson outside.

Wait and see what happens. Give all this up. Worked his ass off to get here.

His brain rewound to last Saturday morning at Al's house.

All she had really said was that she didn't know how she could trust him again. So what if he was able to introduce her to *this* David —the real one—who had worked his ass off once he'd snapped out of it and gotten sober?

As he climbed into the passenger seat of Jackson's SUV, an idea started to form.

Yeah, he'd be breaking his promise to her, but what if it worked? And that *what if* was enough for him.

"HAVE I mentioned how much I despise packing?"

Alyson yanked her eyes from the laptop monitor to look at Jilly. "Just a few, fifty…*hundred* times."

Jillian carefully placed a clear vase now wrapped in newspaper into a moving box.

Campbell laughed as she carefully wrapped another vase. "I love packing. I find it strangely relaxing and therapeutic."

Jillian stared at her. "And I love you, C.G., but I find *that* pretty insane."

Campbell placed the vase into the same box. "My mom has said the same thing to me." She faced Alyson. "But I think it's cool how much your mom and grandma have helped us the last couple days." She frowned. "I never realized how many vases we had around here until we had to start packing them."

Alyson opened her mouth to reply, but her cell started to ring. She released a quick sigh at the agent's now familiar number. "Finally," she mumbled.

Jillian and Campbell stopped their vase wrapping to focus on her.

They'd been waiting to hear from the agent about setting up a time to sign the lease.

"Hi. This is Alyson."

"It's Tegan. So sorry it took me a couple days to get back with you."

She smiled at Jillian and Campbell, whose faces relaxed.

"No worries," she lied. "When will we receive the lease so we can sign it?" It's not like they had all the time in the world.

There was a pause on her end before Alyson heard, "I wish I had some good news. I'm terribly embarrassed by what I'm about to say."

Her smile became a frown. "I don't understand. In your e-mail on Monday you said we were good to go, we paid the deposit, and all that was left was signing the lease."

With wide eyes, Jillian and Campbell approached where she sat at the desk.

What could have possibly happened between then and now?

The woman sighed. "My soon-to-be ex-*bastard* rented the space out from underneath me to get what he wanted in rent."

Alyson gritted her teeth, then narrowed her eyes.

Crap, crap, *crap*. Bastard? She could think of a stronger word to describe yet another devil of Denver's real estate world.

"I really am so sorry," she continued, sounding genuinely apologetic. "I should have expected something like this from the prick. But I've been drowning in showings and acquired two new listings. I just didn't get you signed fast enough."

Alyson sat back in the chair, the woman's words causing her shoulders to slump.

"I reached out to a few colleagues who are also commercial property managers, but they said they don't have anything at this moment in time. I understand you're on a deadline, too."

She pressed her lips together as the shop's walls closed in on her head.

"But I'd be more than happy to e-mail you their contact info if you're interested."

She cleared her throat, her eyes meeting Jillian's, then Campbell's.

"I appreciate you doing that for us," Alyson murmured. "Yes, you can send their info." Not that it would do them a damn bit of good with having nothing available right now.

"I'll do that. Again, I'm terribly sorry. You'll have your deposit back within two days."

She hung up, dropped her phone, and stared at the moving boxes on the work table.

"What happened?" Campbell asked. "I thought the space was ours."

She couldn't even think it, much less say the words out loud.

What the hell were they going to do? A question so strong she became frozen.

"Alyson?" Jillian leaned down to catch her eyes. "What did she say?"

They had to be out in *seventeen days* and officially had nowhere to go.

She lost her breath.

"Al, talk to us, dammit!"

The bells over the shop door tinkled.

Campbell slowly backed away from the desk before heading into the actual shop.

"Her soon-to-be ex-*bastard* rented the space without her knowledge." She looked up at Jillian. "We have nowhere to go and I"—she struggled for air—"can't breathe right now."

At that moment, a very distinct and recognizable voice reached her in the backroom.

Alyson's eyes widened while she managed to take a deep breath.

No. It couldn't be *him*.

Jillian's eyes also became round as the familiar voice grew closer.

"Oh, my *God*." She couldn't deal with this—him—right now. She had more important things to do. Things that involved throwing the vases that weren't packed just to watch and hear them shatter into a million pieces.

He appeared in the backroom. Of course looking *way* too good in a dark-blue suit.

"I know what you're thinking," David said, watching her as he stepped forward. "But I've been working on something the last few nights and I'm here to give it to you. Then I'll leave and you'll never have to see me again if you don't want to." He paused before adding, "Well, you'll see me at Matt's birthday party. And the wedding. But I promise I'll stay away if that's what you still want after reading what I brought you."

Something about him suddenly being in her shop, looking so incredibly good, yet adorably awkward, combined with his words and the decidedly bad news she'd just received, caused Alyson's insides to snap like a bone-dry twig.

Tears hit her eyes. Then her dam disintegrated.

Jillian and David stared at her for a few seconds before he headed toward her.

"Just stop. Right there," she said around her tears, holding out her left arm, fingers splayed. "I don't…I don't need you to…help me."

Her body shuddered as she noisily sniffed while scanning her desk for the box of tissues.

"Alyson, I meant every word I said, but since you apparently don't want me here—"

"Damn you, David!" she snapped around her tears. "This isn't... about you." *Not entirely, anyway.* "And what happened to the damn tissues?"

Jillian walked to the work table, leaned in front of David to grab the box, then held it out and angled it toward her.

She swiped three tissues and dabbed her eyes still releasing hot emotion.

"Would someone tell me what's going on here?" he quietly asked.

Jillian faced him. "I don't know if Jackson told you, but last week we found a space."

His eyes flitted to her and back to Jillian. "He mentioned it when I saw him on Sunday." His deep, soulful brown eyes drifted back her way. "But it looks like you got some bad news."

She sniffed and lifted her chin. "Yes. We did. Because men *suck*." *Well, not* all *of them.* But she'd definitely had her fill of the real estate devils in Denver.

David nodded once.

"And then you arrived," Jillian finished.

A few more tears escaped as Alyson quietly blew her nose.

He glanced at Jillian. "Can you give us a minute?"

Her friend gave him a tight smile. "Sure."

When they were alone, David walked around the desk and stopped less than a foot away from where she sat. He then placed a composition notebook beside the laptop. "That's for you. It's what I came to drop off."

She sniffed a few times. "What is it?"

He crouched in front of her. "You'll have to read it to find out."

Their eyes caught.

"Al, will you please let me call my aunt and uncle?" He tore his eyes from hers to look around the backroom. "How many more days do you have left here?"

She took a shaky breath and mumbled, "Seventeen." Saying that scary number out loud caused a fresh round of emotion to stream from her eyes.

He stood, grasped her hands, and gently pulled her up and guided her to him.

Not having the emotional strength to resist, she allowed David to wrap her in a hug and rested her forehead on the spot right below his collar. A warm, way too familiar spot that also smelled men's cologne incredible. Just like it had when they'd been together.

She relaxed into his warm, way too familiar arms, and continued to unleash her disappointment and frustration and paralyzing fear of the unknown. "I don't…know what…we're going to do," she managed to say into his chest.

His hold tightened. "Feel like getting some air? It's not too bad outside."

His familiar, soothing voice enveloped her, and in that second she wished them back ten years ago. Weeks before the terrible tragedy that changed their lives and path together.

She sniffed several times, forced her wet eyes to open, and lifted her head from his chest.

He released her and, without breaking eye contact, carefully cupped her face, then used his thumbs to softly wipe the wetness off her cheekbones.

Her head buzzed. Just like it had years ago, seconds before their kisses that had often started like this moment—*without* the tears—currently keeping them transfixed.

"I'm…sorry about all of this." She severed their stare while taking a full step back, which forced him to lower his arms. "Getting some air sounds really good." Once outside she would take many deep, head-cleansing breaths, too.

He slipped his hands into his pockets. "Don't apologize." He shook his head. "But I seem to have exceptionally bad timing."

She threw the used tissues into the trash and grabbed a few more. "What do you mean?"

"This is my second time here, out of three visits, that I've encountered crying women."

A quick laugh escaped while she swiped the tissue underneath her eyes.

He grinned. "I'm relieved you find that funny."

She gave him a weak smile. "It's the second time you've been around for *my* nonsense."

Silence fell between them.

Alyson somehow stopped herself from cringing, since he now had to be thinking about their Friday night together...followed by Saturday morning when he'd asked for another chance.

Her eyes fell to the mysterious composition notebook he'd set on the desk.

You'll have to read it to find out.

"You ready?" he suddenly asked.

She straightened. "Yes. Air. That'll be good." She lifted her coat from the chair's back.

He followed her into the shop's main area.

Jillian and Campbell paused their packing, because they still had to be out in *seventeen days*, and watched them with wide, questioning eyes.

"We're getting some air," Alyson stated. "I'll be back in a little bit."

They slowly nodded.

Once outside, she paused to take her first, deep, head-cleansing breath of crisp air.

"Al, what happened with the space?"

They fell into step beside one another. After a few moments, she opened her mouth and started at the beginning.

Chapter Eighteen

AL SAT BACK and sipped her coffee. "Thanks for the walk *and* coffee break." The corner of her mouth lifted in a smile. "The four of us love this place. They have great coffee." Her eyes went to the window beside them. "We've loved having the shop in this area."

David gripped his cup, now wanting to rip out the black hearts of *two* pompous dickheads, shove them down their throats, and watch the guys choke. But he said, "Al, not everyone does business like Marsden and that other guy." He sighed. "I'm sorry you and your shop have gotten caught up with such assholes."

She glanced at him. "Me, too." She set her cup down. "Those two soulless asshats have to be, for the most part, the exception. Cliff, our former landlord, was a nice, *reasonable* man."

David leaned forward. "So you'll let me call my aunt and uncle?"

She stayed silent.

"Al, I know we're damn near close to nothing more than acquaintances at this point." He ran a hand through his hair. "But I *still* don't like seeing you like this. Or like you were earlier."

She laughed softly as she pointed at his head. "Your hair's sticking up now."

He shrugged. "Yeah, well, I'm not trying to impress anyone." *Except you.*

She nodded. "We definitely need help, so okay. You can call Hugh and Eileen."

Finally. He reached into his suit jacket pocket.

"But not right this second."

He froze with his cell in hand.

"I need to come to terms with the fact that the perfect space for Daisy's Bouquets being magically available in *seventeen days* is not going to happen."

"You don't know that."

She stared at him.

His shoulders drooped. "Okay. I'll admit the timing will be tough. But if you'll let me call my aunt and uncle—"

"I'm going to have to temporarily move the shop into my house," she interjected.

His hand, still holding his phone, fell to the table.

"It's our only option until we, through your aunt or uncle or not, find a new space."

He narrowed his eyes. "Al, you can't be serious. Your house is, what, twelve-hundred-square-feet? Give or take several feet? Where are you going to work? And put everything?"

She tilted her head right. "Wow, good guess. And we can use the garage, too."

He raised his eyebrows. "It's March. In *Colorado*."

"I don't know what else to do, David," she threw at him. "Jilly lives with her sister in a two-bedroom apartment in Wash Park. Campbell also lives in a house. It's bigger than mine, but she has two roommates. And Hayley, who's in college, lives in a sorority house." She crossed her arms. "Not all of us can afford to live by ourselves in a big, fancy, million-dollar home."

He froze for several seconds before the air left his chest.

She pressed her hands to her mouth. "I'm so sorry." The words came out muffled. "You didn't deserve that." Her eyes became hazy while she lowered her hands. "I know you must've worked incredibly hard to get everything you and Becca have."

More than you can possibly know and imagine. But if she read everything he'd written in the composition notebook, she would know.

She blinked several times, picked up the cup, and sipped. "It's been a really tough week. I don't mean to take it out on you." She reached out and slid the tiny vase holding a single, equally small red flower to the center of the table. Then turned it until the flower faced the window.

He dropped his phone back into his suit pocket. "I can take it."

She turned the vase slightly toward her and lifted her eyes to him. "I can't believe you're sitting across this table from me."

Neither could he, but when the notebook idea had hit, he'd become determined to see it through, no matter the risk. Based on everything that had happened since he'd walked into the shop while literally clutching most of the last ten years of his life, his actions had been worth it.

She sipped her coffee and turned the vase a fraction more. "I feel I need to apologize for last Saturday morning." She cringed. "I was pretty hard on you."

He angled his head down to catch her eyes. "Alyson, I needed to hear all of that." The urge to tell her how much her words from that morning had affected him became so powerful he opened his mouth; his news on the edge of his voice. But this unexpected and special moment with her wasn't about him or them.

She peered at him. "You did, but I probably could've been much better with the timing."

David finished his coffee and set down the cup. "It's fine. Really." *At least, it would be. Someday.* He grinned. "I think you need some quality time punching a firm pillow."

Al laughed, which meant her memory had gone to the same place —the day she'd choked on a statistics test and needed to free all of her frustration.

"Are you going to hold the pillow this time, too?"

"I could probably be talked into it if you promised not to punch *me* in the process." Which she had that night when her fist missed the pillow and landed right in his solar plexus.

"It was an accident. And you're the one who taught me how to punch like that."

He couldn't argue with her, so he asked, "I hope you still know how to punch like that?"

Her humor slowly faded. "I wish I could show you I do. I know who I'd punch, too."

And he'd hold the two assholes for her if he could. But he said, "Al, don't make any decisions until I talk to my aunt and uncle first. Okay?"

She nodded.

He glanced at his watch. "I have to get back to work for a meeting."

She blinked. "Oh. Right." She stood. "I need to get back, too." She grabbed her coat.

They walked back to the shop, a few buildings down from the coffee joint, in silence.

The last thing he wanted was to say goodbye again. Especially since this time with her had been incredibly easy. Relaxed. Very *them,* and despite what had brought them to this moment. At the same time, it wouldn't be goodbye for very long. She would be at Matt's birthday party. Unlike him, she'd never minded dressing up in costumes for Halloween parties. As foolish as it was, he couldn't help but look forward to seeing what kind of eighties outfit she'd be wearing that night. Maybe by then she'd be able to see him through different eyes, too? But she'd have to read what he'd written in the notebook if that were ever to happen.

Unable to stop his continued foolishness, he followed her inside the shop, even though he now had zero reasons to be in there.

Jillian pounced on her, which stopped them in their tracks.

"You are *not* going to believe who called while you were gone."

Al glanced at him.

He stepped back. "I have a meeting to get to."

"David, wait a minute."

"Don't do anything until you hear from me, or my aunt and uncle," he said over his shoulder. "I'll see you later." *And please don't forget to read the notebook I left you.*

As he walked away from the shop, he pulled his phone back out.

"Hi, Honey," his aunt answered. "What wedding damage has your sister done now?"

"I'm not calling about the wedding." He stopped when he reached his SUV. "I need you and Uncle Hugh to help me with something. It's important." *More than you can possibly know.*

Silence fell on her end, followed by, "He's in the office. Let me get in there and I'll put you on speaker."

This had to work. But if they couldn't come up with anything, due to the tight time frame, he had another idea.

ALYSON RAISED HER CHIN. "Why would I—any of us—care that Felicity Mayhew's assistant called wanting a meeting?"

Jillian and Campbell glanced at each other, then back at her.

"You're not a little curious about the why *or* the eerie timing?" Jillian softly added.

"And when did we stop wanting to be in business with her?" This from Campbell.

Alyson pulled her hair up and away from her face, twisted it into a loose knot, and fastened it with an oversized clip. And her eyes again landed on the mysterious composition notebook he'd brought her.

You'll have to read it to find out.

At that moment, reading whatever David had written inside was all she wanted to do.

"We found out that Felicity's in business with a member of the

Marsden family," Jillian answered. "The same Marsdens who bought this building and are kicking us out."

Campbell's mouth formed an "oh."

"Which is why," Alyson inserted, "you said no to a meeting with her. *Right*, Jillian?"

Her friend lifted her shoulders. "I said I had to talk to my business partner first and that we'd get back to them soon. I'm sure Felicity Mayhew *never* hears that."

"I don't care." She moaned. "Why the hell would *you* say that?"

"Because of curiosity and the timing," Jillian countered. "It's too bizarre." Her dark eyes widened. "Do you think someone at the wedding actually recognized us? A former bride or customer, maybe? *Santo cielo*," she added under her breath.

Campbell frowned. "Timing? Wedding? What are you two talking about?"

Alyson bent down, grabbed her purse, and the notebook. "I can't do this right now." She walked around the desk and them. "I need to get out of here."

"Al, we have to talk about what to do next."

David had told her not to do anything until she heard from him, or Hugh and Eileen, and that's exactly what she was going to do.

"I need a break, Jilly." She marched into the shop. "For the rest of the day."

"But Alyson—"

"I'll see you in the morning." The door's tinkling bells followed her outside.

Seventeen days. The reality was just too overwhelming.

She walked the handful of steps to her 4Runner. Once inside, she swallowed her scream of frustration. Maybe she did need some punching time with a firm pillow.

She started the engine.

Still, punching a pillow he wasn't holding wouldn't be the same. She'd have to settle with taking Thatcher on another hard, long run, then sinking into a hot bath. She'd turn her phone off, too. Shut out the world for the rest of the day and night. She deserved at least that much. Hopefully, nothing in her immediate world would implode any more than it already had while she got lost in her down time. She couldn't even remember the last time she'd gone off the grid.

At a stoplight, her eyes drifted to the notebook she'd placed on the passenger seat.

It seemed to be calling her name.

What had David written? He'd made it sound like whatever was inside he'd done for *her*.

The question had nearly burned a whole in her brain by the time she was finally immersing her body into hot, soapy water.

She closed her eyes, deeply breathed in the eucalyptus scent, and scooted down until her chin touched the top of the water.

Maybe if she hadn't been so stubborn that Friday night, when David had offered to reach out to Hugh and Eileen then, Daisy's Bouquets would be in a completely different situation right now. His aunt and uncle had always been smart investors when it came to real estate. Their lifestyle twelve years ago, when they'd been in the Denver area full time, had been enviable, particularly all the traveling they'd done and probably still did. What really set them apart was their genuine kindness and humility. They were an incredibly successful power couple, but it had never gone to their heads. Being one of their tenants certainly wouldn't be a bad thing. Still, she hadn't been comfortable with the idea of mixing business with the past.

She took another deep breath and slowly released the air.

Now, almost two weeks after the fact and only *seventeen days* away from her business being displaced, her initial reaction felt pretty ridiculous. It's not as if she—they—would be going into business with David. Hugh and Eileen also had employees who actually managed their properties. They lived in another state, too. It's not as if they'd be around a whole lot.

She sighed, then massaged the knot between her neck and shoulder.

David had made it clear what he thought of her back-up plan. But what other choice did she have? It's not like her plan had never been done before. Yes, it would be tight in the kitchen on days when all four of them were working to prepare for a wedding or event. It would also be inconvenient—where would they put everything, most importantly the flowers and plants?—and impact her living space. It'd be tough and sacrifices would have to be made. She had a business to save, though. Again, what other choice did she have until they found a new space, *not* owned by soulless Marsden Enterprises, that was comparable to their soon-to-be former space?

She cracked a smile, remembering David's slightly more positive outlook on them getting into a new and wonderful spot in *seventeen days*.

Thinking of him, she opened her eyes and they landed right on the notebook she'd placed within reach on a mini shelf that held extra towels and other bathroom items.

She'd never been into reading while taking a bath, but today had not been typical, and she wanted and needed to give her busy brain a break. At that, she slowly sat up and reached for her nearby towel. After thoroughly drying her hands, she leaned forward and grasped the notebook. She then settled back into the hot water, paused for several seconds, and opened it to page one.

She fought a grin at the fact he'd written her a note, which reminded her of *the* note.

Dear Alyson,

If you're reading this, thank you. But you're also probably wondering what's in here and why I gave it to you. You said that Saturday morning you couldn't give me what I wanted because you didn't know how you could ever trust me again, which I understand. The last time we were together, I was a completely different and unrecognizable person. I'm hoping after you read this, you'll be able to forget that guy and want to know <u>this</u> David.

Welcome to (roughly) the last ten years of my life. I promise you won't be bored.
David

Her eyes widened. "Oh, my *God…*" she murmured.

He'd actually taken the time to write about how he'd spent the last ten years? And, if that part of him was the same, writing this much wasn't his favorite thing to do.

She released a quick breath and, with still wide eyes, turned the page.

Chapter Nineteen

DAVID TRIED to concentrate on the custom-home designs Cruz, their associate architect, had asked him to review, but he was struggling to fight through the edginess that had taken over after leaving the Highlands. He couldn't stop picturing Al's defeated, wet eyes. Or stop replaying his conversation with his aunt and uncle. Or stop thinking about what he'd left Al and if she'd, at the very least, read his note and flipped through the pages by now. At the same time, it's not as if reading—roughly—the last ten years of his life would be at the top of her to-do list today.

He needed and wanted to go home and play the hell out of his piano, but he couldn't because of his 4:30 appointment with Tricia and Ethan Albright. Cruz would actually be their architect, but David had agreed to meet with them, since the kid would be given a lot more responsibility once he left, though he didn't know that yet.

There was a quick knock on his office door.

His head whipped up and left, right as Jackson walked inside.

His friend smiled. "So, Zach and I had a thought."

"I'm not in the mood to talk." His eyes went back to the designs filling his computer monitor that were making as much sense as gibberish on a page from a faulty print job.

"Tough." Jackson closed the door behind him. "What's your problem?"

He leaned back. "Nothing half a bottle of Johnnie Walker can't fix." *The good shit he could now afford.*

Silence fell for several second before Jackson said, "That sure as hell wasn't funny."

"It wasn't supposed to be."

Jackson walked toward him with round eyes.

David sighed. "Don't look at me like that. I'm not about to go on a bender." Just like that, the desire left him. Why couldn't his desire for Al—to have *every* part of her again—work like that, too? His life sure as hell would be a whole lot simpler.

His friend stopped when he reached his desk. "Is this about Alyson and the shop?"

Of course Jackson knew what had happened with the space that *should* be theirs.

He nodded. "I talked to my aunt and uncle to see if they could help them out, but they haven't called me back yet." He'd also left Al looking defeated and frustrated, and with roughly the last ten years of his life sitting on her desk.

Yeah. He definitely needed to get home to his piano. But he asked, "What do you need to talk about?" A subject change was necessary because Tricia and Ethan would be there soon.

Jackson hesitated for several seconds, then said, "Zach and I finally had a chance to talk today about your decisions."

He shook his head. "Whatever you have to say, you're wasting your time."

Jackson crossed his arms. "Will you at least hear me out, asshole?"

Knowing his friend wouldn't leave him alone until he said his peace, David grudgingly nodded. "Okay. I'm listening."

"This isn't about shitting on your parade or Randy's." He sat in the chair in front of David's desk. "You're a damn good piano player and everyone knows it. Better than that even, but"—he gestured at his desk—"like it or not, you're a damn good architect, too. You're also the *one* person in this office who can successfully deal with the Vivienne Dunnes we get as clients."

David fought a grin. "Thanks. But where are you going with the flattery?"

"I also know how hard you worked to get through CU's program and this point in general." He leaned forward. "It seems like all of it would end up being a huge waste of time and energy if you were to walk away."

Okay. This was an argument he hadn't really considered. But it didn't change how he felt about the job, and that's all it was and ever had been in his eyes.

"Jackson, what's your point?"

He brought back his smile. "Zach and I came up with an idea. A compromise." He paused, then added, "We want you to stay with the firm as a consultant on special projects. Possibly taking on the occasional, *strictly* local project of your own choosing. For example, being Tricia and Ethan's architect instead of handing it over to Cruz."

David stared at the corner of his desk.

This "compromise" wasn't unreasonable. It would also provide him with a steadier, heftier income than what the band made off their gigs…right now.

Jackson stood. "I don't expect an answer this second, but will you think about it?"

Again, not an unreasonable request. So he said, "Deal."

His friend laughed. "That means Zach owes me a hundred bucks."

David grinned."What was your bet?"

"He laid down money you wouldn't even consider the idea, not trusting my skills as a salesman or the fact I've had years of practice smacking down your stubbornness."

"Don't get too full of yourself. There's a fifty-percent chance I'll say no."

"Your final answer didn't factor into our bet." Jackson stepped backward, his smile fading. "Are you going to be okay tonight? I was going to surprise Jillian by taking her out to dinner since she's pretty upset about losing that space. But if you need company—"

"David," Marjorie's voice came through the phone's intercom. "Tricia Albright is here. Can I send her up?"

"Yeah." To Jackson, he said, "Jillian's more important. I'll be fine." Once he got home, changed his clothes, sat at his piano, and cleared his mind of every damn thing.

He would, however, keep his phone close in case his aunt and uncle called.

"Okay. I'll see you tomorrow." Jackson headed for the door, but then stopped. "Before you leave, would you please give Marjorie back her damn stapler? She's driving me crazy."

David managed to simply frown and ask, "It's missing?"

"You can cut the crap. She's the only one in this office with a bright-red stapler, and I saw it on *your* desk the Saturday before you went to Aspen."

A few forceful knocks on his office door seemed to punctuate Jackson's statement. He opened it to a flushed, breathless Tricia Albright.

David stood and smiled. "Hey, Tricia. Come on in. This is Jackson, by the way. My friend and business partner who also went to CU."

Jackson stepped aside to let her into the office, and they exchanged smiles.

"Huh," she said, holding out her hand, which Jackson grasped. "Your name sounds really familiar. I must have heard it from Alyson back then. And probably David. It's nice to meet you."

"Likewise. I remember hearing your name, too." They released each other's hands, and he added, "I'll leave you to it. But remember what I said about the stapler."

David turned his smile on Jackson, who glared at him before leaving.

"Is Ethan parking your car?" he asked once they were alone.

"He won't be joining us after all," she answered. "He's an ob/gyn, and a patient went into labor about an hour ago. That won't be a problem, will it?"

"Not at all." He grabbed a pad of legal paper and a pen. "Would you like water or coffee?"

"Oh, no thank you." She followed him to a table with two chairs, located near the window. "I'm sorry for being a little late. I got a call right before leaving work, and traffic was a bit awful."

"No worries." He gestured to a chair. "Please have a seat. So, where did Ethan end up going for medical school?"

"The University of Washington in *Seattle*." She laughed. "I was so happy when we were finally able to move back to Colorado."

He grinned. "I'll bet."

Tricia opened her mouth, paused, then said, "I have to be honest. I'm still a little shocked you ended up as an architect. You were incredibly dedicated to music."

His grin slipped. "I still am." *And soon would be full time.* "I play the piano as much as I can. I'm even in a jazz band that I helped form."

She gave him a bright smile. "That's fantastic! Good for you."

"Thanks. We play every Thursday night at the Blues Note here in LoDo," he added. "You and Ethan should stop by some time."

"We'd love to do that." She stared at him. "I'm sorry we never had a chance to hear you play at that jazz ensemble you were in what feels like a million years ago at CU. But I remember Alyson saying it was a big deal because you had to audition for it." She released a quick laugh. "She was so excited for you."

More than excited. After he'd told her the news, she'd jumped into his arms and kissed him until neither of them could breathe. In fact, his family—including his parents—and all his friends had been excited since he'd faced fierce competition getting into the ensemble.

"Is this your work?" She flipped through his portfolio. "These homes are amazing."

"Yes. And thank you." *Like it or not you're a damn good archi-tect, too.* "Before we get started, I want to thank you for helping my sister out. I didn't get a chance to say it that Friday."

She looked up, then leaned back. "It was my pleasure. But I have to also admit I was astonished when Alyson called me that day, asking if there was any way I could help your sister, and by extension you, with her wedding dress conundrum."

He slowly nodded as his memory once again went to the past. Specifically that night he'd turned to the dark side and made the *second* biggest mistake of his life. Despite already knowing what Tricia's answer would be, the part of him still twisted up in the past had to know for certain. "Tricia, that night Alyson came over to my place and I—" He sighed. "She must have gone straight home afterward?"

She narrowed her eyes. "She did."

He hesitated for several seconds before he asked, "How…was she?"

Tricia closed his portfolio. "I don't really think I need to answer that."

Shit. But, yeah, she really didn't need to answer his question.

"What you don't know," she quietly continued, "was that her reaction lasted a long time. We, meaning her friends and family, were pretty worried about her there for a while."

He looked down, now feeling the full weight of Al's honesty from that Saturday morning. Suddenly, he no longer felt confident about his notebook idea and everything he'd written inside moti-vating her to see him in a new light.

"Are you two attempting friendship?"

David forced himself to look back at Tricia, watching him closely. "No." Being the closest answer to the truth, what else could he say? "She and my sister were very close back then, and she was nice enough to step in and help her with the dress." He cleared his throat. "But those two are friends again. I'm really happy about that."

She peered at him, opened her mouth, but he abruptly rolled his chair closer to the table.

It was time to be a professional.

"Let's talk about your ideas for the house." So he could get home and lose himself in music. The first movement of Beethoven's "Moonlight Sonata" would be where he started.

Chapter Twenty

"I KNOW we ordered five additional bouquets. It was just a few damn days ago," Groomzilla said. He eyed his mother, also the "wedding coordinator." "She had me call because all of you were still obsessing over the seating arrangements. Remember?"

Alyson exchanged a quick, weary glance with Jillian.

He hadn't called "a few damn days ago," because it was a call all of them would have remembered. But his Bridezilla *had* called yesterday to verify—at the last minute—what they had in fact ordered, never asking about the five additional bouquets for the buffet tables.

Due to *her* testy mood, Alyson wanted to say the bouquets had clearly not been ordered due to a miscommunication between the couple, but she swallowed the snarky response and eased her mouth into a stiff smile. "Maybe those bouquets are still in the van?" she asked Jillian.

She returned her tight smile. "I'll have Hayley check. Maybe you should call Campbell to see if she remembers taking the extra order?" Jillian removed her cell from her back jeans pocket, thumbed her password, and handed it over since Alyson had left her phone in the van.

"What if they're not in there?" Groomzilla snapped. "We won't pay for your mistakes!"

She gritted her teeth as she turned from them. She then walked several feet away and chose Campbell's number.

The pointless call would disturb her on her day off, but, in the interest of providing *stellar* customer service, she had to make the effort. It was also easier to just call than fake it.

"Hi!" Campbell chirped.

"Hey. I hope I'm not interrupting you?"

"Not at all. Just watching a movie with my roommate. What's up?"

"That sounds like way more fun than being here at The Curtis," she mumbled. "Our Groomzilla is *insisting* he ordered five additional bouquets a few days ago."

Campbell released an exasperated sigh, then said, "Of course he didn't. That couple and their *wedding coordinator* have been so rude I would've remembered them calling."

Her blunt statement was completely correct since they'd never been the happiest or warmest couple. But they'd planned a big, traditional wedding with a huge flower order.

Still, they *never* should have taken this job.

Alyson massaged her left temple. "That's what I thought, but I had to make the call. I'm being watched."

Campbell groaned. "I'm so sorry. Do you need me to do anything?"

"No. Just continue having a nice day off and don't think about this." She hung up and walked back toward the irate young man about to get married, his black, bushy eyebrows almost reaching the ceiling. She breathed deeply through her nose before saying, "Campbell doesn't remember the additional order, either."

"I never said I spoke to *her*," he enunciated.

Jillian appeared at Alyson's left side. "They're not in the van."

Groomzilla's face became hot pink as he narrowed his eyes.

She took another deep breath. "I can see you're terribly upset.

And if there was a miscommunication between us, then I'm truly sorry. But I'm not sure what we can do at this—"

"We'll just have to live with your incompetence!" He waved his phone that held the invoice. "We'll be double checking this to make sure we weren't charged for those bouquets."

He marched away, his mother-wedding coordinator trailing by two steps.

"I wonder what *Mommie Dearest* thinks of the way her bouncing baby boy turned out," Jillian grumbled, falling into step beside Alyson.

They headed in the opposite direction as she handed Jillian her phone.

"What now?" Hayley whispered once they reached her.

"We finish up and get the hell out of here," Alyson muttered. And the next time she received a bad vibe from a wedding couple, she'd listen to her instincts and sprint the other way.

They headed back into the hotel's massive Four Square Ballroom that had amazing natural light and modern art pieces. The Curtis Hotel, a quick walk from the Denver Performing Arts Complex, was typically one of Alyson's favorite wedding venues, too. But anxiousness over the fact she *still* hadn't heard from David, or Hugh and Eileen, and working with such an unpleasant couple made her want to be anywhere but here.

"Aren't the bride and groom supposed to be…I don't know…*happy* on their wedding day?" Hayley murmured while picking up a bouquet of burgundy and purple Gerber daisies.

"Those two were spawned from Satan and don't count. *Dos lunáticas que se merecen,*" Jillian muttered while she lifted another vase off the cart.

Alyson grabbed the second-to-last head table bouquet, an elaborate arrangement of the burgundy and purple daisies, but with some red to give the spray a little pop. In spite of her intense dislike for the couple, the bride had chosen nice colors.

She and Jillian walked toward the head table.

"I know this wedding was good for Daisy's Bouquets, but…" Her friend's eyes swept over the elegant venue. "This seems a bit too magnificent. I understand both families have money and it's why those two act like entitled *asshats*."

Alyson laughed as she set the vase down and shifted it slightly to the right.

"They also clearly know a million people," her friend continued. "But what's wrong with an intimate wedding? Do you remember the pics I showed you of my sister Brynn's wedding?"

Alyson glanced at Jillian. "A little bit."

"Something like their wedding, but instead of in the mountains, somewhere warm and on a beach." She smiled softly. "I think a wedding like that is a hundred times better than all this."

Yes. Standing barefoot on a beach with only the groom, officiate, and close friends and family sounded perfect. And nothing like she'd envisioned as a young, naïve girl back when—her mind went to what David had written in the notebook that she'd finished reading last night.

His *and* Becca's story had definitely been one of the Phoenix rising from the ashes, but with many sacrifices on his part; the biggest one being his music.

I didn't want the piano that had been in my parents' house, so we sold it. No piano meant no playing. My aunt and uncle offered to buy me a new one when I was able to live on my own, but I wanted to buy it when I could.

She'd read those sentences so many times the words were etched in her brain. As were a few he'd written about his ex-wife.

She turned the vase left.

Sara and I met when she auditioned for the band. We hired her, started dating, became engaged and, before I knew it, we were married. But it never should have gone that far.

He'd told her the day he'd walked back into her life they "hadn't worked that way."

Those two revelations and other things he'd shared had made for a long, sleepless night. Just more reasons her mood was favoring crabby.

But now she needed to finish this job so they could leave and *never* see this couple again.

Alyson shifted the vase once more to the right, angled her head back—she needed to stop. This couple and their wedding weren't worth her perfectionism.

With that thought, she faced Jillian, smiling softly while she adjusted the flowers and filler in the other bouquet. Alyson couldn't help but also grin, since it was clear who was behind her friend's sappy smile.

"I find it interesting you of all people are thinking of the perfect wedding."

Jillian eyed her. "Dare I ask where you're going with that comment?"

Spotting Hayley across the room, going from table to table for the final check, she asked, "How was your date with Jackson last night?" At least *something* good was happening in their world full of challenges. "That also makes two in one week."

Jillian giggled. "Awesome. We seem to have a lot in common."

They turned and strolled toward the now empty cart.

"You know his parents are still happily married, just like your parents. I think that's pretty remarkable because of how *miserable* my parents were before they finally split," she added under her breath. "But you knew his older brother, Will, right?"

Alyson frowned. "Barely. I was only around him a few times back then."

Jillian grasped the cart's handle, and they headed for the ballroom's entrance. "Well, he's married now and has two kids." Her grin grew. "Jackson *loves* the Broncos and the Rockies, which I'm sure you already knew. That's a huge plus. We also like the same music." She parked the cart against the wall. "He's outdoorsy, too. Into skiing, hiking, mountain biking—" She flashed Alyson a naughty smile. "It's why he looks edible in jeans and a T-shirt."

The memory of David, shirtless and in his tight jeans that Saturday morning, flashed through Alyson's mind, followed by how edible *he'd* looked right before—she halted that thought. Now was not the time to be picturing David Thomas Preston half naked, especially since she was still processing what he'd written in the notebook that she wanted to read a second time to make sure she hadn't missed anything.

"I'm going to Jackson's place tonight for dinner," Jillian continued. "But I haven't been to his house yet, and I'm a little nervous."

Alyson blinked twice, then squinted at her. "Why? You can't be nervous about being alone with him in his house."

Hayley headed toward them while looking at her phone.

"Based on the way he kisses, *hell* no." Her smile faded. "Al, he's the definition of a bachelor. Everything has been so incredible I'm half expecting something to go wrong. Like maybe he's a slob." She leaned forward. "Is he a slob?"

Alyson released a quick laugh, remembering the apartment he'd shared with David. "He definitely was in college. But he's an adult now. And successful." She grasped her friend's hand and squeezed. "I think you need to relax."

Jillian nodded as Hayley stopped beside her.

"We're finished, right?" Hayley slipped her phone into her pink, sparkly crossbody case. "'Cos my sorority is throwing a huge-ass party tonight and a ridiculous hottie from my sociology class will be there." She grinned. "Gotta have time to make myself just as hot."

Alyson's smile vanished. Apparently, she was the only one flying solo tonight. *But it didn't have to be that way.* He had taken the time to invite her into, roughly, the last ten years of his life. It's not like he'd reject *her*. All he wanted was another chance.

She still had his business card with his cell number. He also had yet to call with news from his aunt and uncle. Not a good sign, but that could be her reason for calling him.

When they arrived back at their delivery van, Alyson slid into the passenger seat. She removed her phone from her purse—she froze at seeing she'd missed a call from a local number. The person had left a message, too. *Dammit.* She should have taken her phone inside. But between Jillian and Hayley having theirs, bringing hers hadn't felt necessary.

She squeezed her eyes shut.

Please be David and *good news.*

As Jillian drove them away from the hotel, she tapped the voice-mail icon.

"*Hi, Alyson. It's me*"—yes, it was David—"*Becs gave me your number. I'm sorry it's taken so long to get back to you...and I wish I had good news.*"

Her shoulders fell forward.

"*My aunt and uncle don't have anything coming available right now. They also reached out to colleagues—that's what took so long—but the commercial properties they have available in the Denver metro area are in places I don't think you'd want to be in. Some are pretty far south and east of downtown.*"

Crap, crap, *crap.*

"*I'm really sorry, Al. But I gave your number to my aunt and uncle, since they said things change rapidly. That way they can call you immediately when something opens up with them or the other management companies.*"

She faced Jillian, watching her from the corner of her eyes, and shook her head.

Her friend released a heavy sigh.

"*Hang in there. Something right for the shop will happen. It always does in real estate.*"

The message ended, and she lowered her phone from her ear.

In fourteen days? *Not likely.*

"Alight," Jillian stated. "All we can do is go to Plan B."

Hayley leaned forward. "It won't be that bad working out of your house. And we'll all get quality time with Thatcher, which he'll love."

Alyson cracked a smile.

"And it's temporary," Jillian added. "Did he say anything else?"

She dropped her phone into her purse. "Like what? He did what he said he'd do and it didn't work out." Outside of saying sorry about the bad news, he'd been all business, too.

As if he hadn't left her a notebook full of incredibly personal stories and thoughts that could not have been easy for him to write about.

"Nothing about offering to help us move or call me if you need me or—"

"Jilly, he delivered the bad news, said he'd given my number to Hugh and Eileen, and hung up." *But it would have been nice if he'd said those other things.*

Still, had she given him a reason to?

Jillian glanced her way. "Al, please don't obsess over all of this tonight."

In fact, that's precisely what she would be doing while figuring out how to turn the first floor of her twelve-hundred-and-seventy-square-foot house into a flower shop. This Saturday night activity would also stop her from thinking about David, his past, and the past in general. And an idea occurred to her, because she didn't feel like being alone with all of this.

She withdrew her phone once more.

"Hi, Sweetie," her mom answered. "What's up?"

She hesitated for a few seconds before saying, "I know it's last minute, but can you and grandma come over tonight?" She slid her eyes to Jillian who gave her an encouraging smile. "It's been a crap week, and I…really need your help with something." Her lower lip quivered.

It was time to face reality head on, no matter how much it hurt.

HE PLAYED THE SOMBER, final notes of "One For My Baby" and stared at his piano's keys while the music faded. During a show, it was a duet with Lea; he played while she sang.

Tonight it simply fit his mood.

David sighed and shook his head.

He'd hated leaving Al that message and hated himself for not having the guts to tell her to call him back because he had an idea. At the same time, she could be even more stubborn than him, so the chances of her going for the idea probably would have fallen right at zero.

He stood and headed for the end table where he kept the remote for his living room speaker. It was time to hear someone else's music. Within seconds his phone was connected via bluetooth and he chose another song that fit his mood, which Vivienne would have defined as brooding.

The opening drum beats of John Hiatt's "Alone in the Dark" exploded from the speaker, turned up as far as he could stand it, followed by bluesy guitar.

He dropped to his couch, stretched out, then bent his right arm and slid it under his head. Once he was comfortable, he closed his eyes and tried to concentrate on the music and lyrics. But a harsh realization wouldn't leave him alone—he'd officially reached pathetic.

He'd asked for another chance following their incredible night together, and she'd told him no out of distrust and fear. Though not liking it one bit, he'd walked away. Then he'd come up with the notebook idea, given it to Al…and hadn't heard a damn thing from her. Not at all encouraging for a few, *big* reasons and was why he'd hoped to get her on the phone. But that hadn't worked out, either. He'd also lost his nerve when it came to sharing his idea.

So maybe all of this made him a pathetic *and* insane coward?

But there was still a significant spark between them. He hadn't imagined any of that. Their private moments together, especially that Friday night and early Saturday, had felt like they could be a new and even better David and Al, if only she could see that. See *him*. Then again, maybe he was expecting way too much from her. It's not as if she didn't have enough to keep her busy when it came to her professional life. Another reason he'd despised leaving that message.

His aunt and uncle had reached out to every contact they had in the commercial property management world. He'd heard the disappointment in their voices when they'd finally called him back earlier in the day, suspecting Al wouldn't want to move her business from the Highlands, an ideal Denver location, to Downtown Parker or Aurora. Or some areas in Denver that wouldn't be the best place for a flower shop.

Shit, he'd really wanted to help her, and damned those two greedy dickheads for the millionth time for doing business like that. His uncle had actually chosen a stronger word to describe Marsden and that lawyer when his aunt left the call.

Al's business—she—didn't deserve any of this, but he only had the one idea to help make it right until a new space that would be perfect for her shop became available at some point. But he couldn't shake the feeling she'd never go for it. Maybe if he'd heard from her about what he'd written in the notebook, he'd feel differently. Have a sliver of hope she'd listen to and trust him. He didn't have that, though. Which brought him right back here to pathetic and alone, but not *actually* in the dark, on a Saturday night.

Jackson and Zach's compromise was also heavy on his mind, tempting him for many reasons, the main one being guaranteed financial security. But unlike them, architecture wasn't his real gift. And would staying at the firm, even part time, really make him *happy*?

"What the hell is this?" a familiar voice shouted above the music.

David's eyes flew open. To find Matt staring down at him, sporting an obnoxious grin.

"At least you're not dead." He grabbed the speaker remote now on the coffee table.

Silence replaced the music.

He hauled himself into an upright position and flung his legs off the couch. "What the hell are you doing here? And whatever happened to ringing the doorbell?"

"We rang the doorbell." Becs appeared beside her fiancé. "But because you were playing that song for the *entire city*, you didn't hear it so we used our key."

David removed his glasses and rubbed his eyes.

"I think we got here in time, based on your music choice," she added.

"It's a great song." But *fantastic*. This moment, like the firework fiasco that happened when he and Jackson were rowdy kids, was something she would never let him live down.

"Now that we know you're okay," Matt said, walking backward toward the kitchen, "I need to eat something because I'm hungry. Do you have any food in there?"

"Check the pantry." As Matt walked away, David looked at his sister. "Becs, what are you guys doing here? Because I know you have better things to do than show up at my house like this. Like maybe feeding your fiancé and working on your dissertation?"

"I know we should've called first. We came into the city for dinner, and it was a last-minute decision to come over." Becs gave him an affectionate smile. "I also haven't seen you since you got back from Aspen."

He cringed before putting on his glasses. "I'm sorry. Between work and the band, I've been swamped." She didn't need to know about him trying to help Al. Or the notebook.

Her eyes roamed his living room. "I love this house. I'll really miss it."

He sat back. "I'm not selling it today."

She focused on him. "Have you decided when you are going to put it on the market?"

"By June. Possibly sooner." He grinned. "Why? Did you and Matt win the lottery and want to buy a new house?"

"No." She laughed. "But it would be awfully romantic. Matty carrying me up the stairs every night to our fabulous bedroom—"

"*Stop*," he groaned. "Becs, seriously, what are you two doing here?"

She hesitated, then answered, "To see and talk to you."

He raised his eyebrows. "Well, you've seen me, so what do you want to talk about?"

She gave him a cautious smile.

This had to be wedding related. But what the hell was left? He'd assumed the dress was the last, biggest, *expensive* wedding item on the list.

His sister's eyes drifted to the kitchen and back to him. "Everyone thinks you should ask Alyson to be your date at Matt's party next Saturday."

He squinted at her.

"It's so obvious to everyone that you two are still crazy about each other."

Where the hell was this coming from? And who was "everyone?"

"I've watched both of you the two times I've been around you," she quietly continued. "You're still magnetic." She paused before adding, "Just like Mom and Dad were."

He crossed his arms, that comment grating his already raw emotions. "Becs, did you and Matt really come all the way over here so you could talk to me about Alyson?"

"It's just one reason, but—"

"Then what are the other reasons you're here? Because we're not talking about her."

She wrinkled her nose. "David, I want you to be happy, and so would Mom and Dad."

Shit. She'd come over, obviously prepared for this conversation he hadn't remotely expected. It also reminded him of his talk with Al after Becs's party. As such, he'd give her a similar response to the one from that night. "I'm not unhappy."

She rolled her eyes.

He clenched his teeth.

"I think everything you're planning to do in the next few months is fantastic. And it's a definite start." She leaned forward. "But you know who you want. Who you've always wanted." She frowned. "I don't care what she says or does, or that she lied about having a boyfriend. I *know* she feels the same way. I've seen the way she looks at you. The way you look at each other," she added under her breath. "Like you're going to miss something if you turn away."

His eyes landed on their last family portrait taken around the Thanksgiving before the accident. Specifically their parents, their smiles wide and genuine and a distant kind of familiar.

Becs was right about them wanting him to be happy. That's all they'd ever wanted for him. *Them*. That's all he wanted for himself and his sister, too.

"You're right. About everything." He dragged his eyes back to Becs, watching him. "But I can't make Al do or say a damn thing." And it hit him. He was mentally and emotionally exhausted when it came to the subject of Alyson Catherine Douglas. "Which makes her a closed topic of discussion from this point on."

Becs glared at him.

Matt, holding a bag of trail mix, walked into the living room.

"Are you done telling him about your job? Because this stuff isn't enough to feed a rabbit."

David looked at his sister and frowned. "Wait a sec, you have a job? Since when?"

"You still haven't told him? Are you kidding me?" Matt moaned. "Baby, I'm starving."

"Matty, calm down." She concentrated on David. "The other reason we came over here is that I wanted to tell you in person that I officially have a job." Her smile came back. "It's long-term contract work. I'll start this summer."

"Becs, that's—" He shook his head. "That's incredible. But why didn't you tell me you were looking for a job?"

She lifted her shoulders. "This fell into my lap after you came back from Aspen." Her smile grew. "My advisor asked if I would be interested in helping her research and write a book that will be for helping siblings go through…what you and I went through."

His eyes widened as he straightened.

She reached out and grasped his right hand. "She said she'll change our names."

He slowly nodded, racking his brain for the right response.

"You're not mad, are you? I probably should've told you sooner."

He scooted to the edge of his couch. "Becs, of course I'm not mad. I'm just…surprised." He stared at his little sister, glowing from her good news, and grinned. "Have you told Aunt Eileen and Uncle Hugh yet?"

"No." She leaned forward and wrapped her arms around him. "I had to tell you first."

They tightly squeezed each other. Like they had that day in her psychologist's office after being estranged for four, extremely long months.

He cleared his throat. "I'm really proud of you."

"Thanks," she whispered. "David, the project will entail many… tough conversations. Will you be up to it? Because I'm pretty sure I won't be able to do this without you."

"Yeah. I promise." He took a deep breath. "It'll be good for me *and* for us." *And probably more than he could possibly imagine.*

Their long, tight hug continued, and he pictured their parents. Then one of their parents' favorite things to do, usually in public if he and Becs had been fighting over stupid shit, popped into his mind. It was something that had felt like their form of warped punishment, too.

He laughed while pulling away from his sister.

She peered at him. "What's so funny?"

"I was thinking about Mom and Dad. And *time for group hug!*" he said, mimicking the way their parents would loudly sing-song it in unison.

She burst into laughter.

"I hate to spoil this brother and sister bonding moment," Matt said with his right hand buried inside the trail-mix bag, "but I'm seconds from leaving to go find real food."

"Alright, alright." David stood as Matt headed back into the kitchen. "In case I've never said this, you chose well." He angled his head to where Matt had been standing. "Mom and Dad would approve and also be really proud of you."

She scrunched her shoulders and released a laugh mixed with a squeal. "I know, right?"

"We need to celebrate your job and feed your fiancé, so dinner is on me tonight. Anywhere you and *Matty* want to go." But first he needed to change out of his basketball shorts and T-shirt, so he headed for the staircase.

"David, we're not finished talking about *you.*"

He suppressed a sigh.

"You deserve to be happy, too. Like me, Matt, and like Mom and Dad were."

Nancy had said the same thing to him that Friday night. Then he'd jumped into his SUV and drove like hell to Al's house that had turned into an unbelievable night which had, ultimately, changed his life. Only not in the way he'd expected.

"I need to change. Stop worrying about me, okay?" he said over his shoulder. "I'm fine, Becs. Really." And he would be fine. *Someday*.

▭

ALYSON TAPED THE MOVING BOX. "Jilly, we don't have a choice. I just don't have the space to house anything more than flowers and filler for weddings and events with smaller orders." She picked up the box, carried it toward where they'd been stacking them by the street door, and set it on top of its twin. "Until we get into a new space, we'll have to stop the everyday orders." It hurt her heart to say the words out loud, since it felt like Daisy's Bouquets was taking several steps backward. But she'd found out, with her mom and grandma's help Saturday night, that David's reaction to moving the business into her home had been justified.

She didn't have the room and, being March in *Colorado*, the garage wasn't an option, outside of storing the cutesy gift items and cards and other miscellaneous inventory.

Campbell frowned. "This really stinks."

Yes. And it was all because of two soulless asshats who deserved to be pitched into hell where they belonged with Lucifer.

Jillian leaned against the counter. "I know the everyday orders don't seem like much, but by the month's end they really add up." She glanced at Alyson. "I think that's going to be a bigger financial loss than we can take. *No podemos hacerlo*," she added.

Alyson sighed, opened her mouth, but the shop's door opening caused her to stop.

A curvy woman, about Alyson's height, with copper hair pulled up into a casual up-do walked inside. She removed her brown, over-sized Gucci sunglasses, and her sharp, chestnut eyes landed on her first, then Campbell and Jillian.

"Hello," she said with the hint of a British accent.

Another beautiful woman with a British accent? Just what she needed right now.

"I'm looking for the owners." She looked at a piece of paper she held. "An Alyson Douglas and Jillian Castillo?"

Alyson's eyes met Jillian's before she stepped toward the woman. "I'm Alyson." She held out her hand, which the woman firmly grasped. "And this is my business partner, Jillian."

Her friend stepped forward, and she and the woman also shook hands.

Alyson smiled. "Are you a bride-to-be?"

The woman's eyes drifted around the shop that had definitely looked better and much more professional this time two weeks ago.

"No, I'm not." She straightened. "I'm Felicity Mayhew."

Alyson froze as silence surrounded them.

Between her current up-do and pastel pink and khaki, boho chic outfit, she didn't resemble the Felicity Mayhew wearing a black power suit with her hair tumbling around her shoulders in the professional head shot on her website.

Alyson glanced at Jillian, whose eyes were round, then at Campbell, whose mouth had inched open.

"I'm so sorry." She looked at their moving boxes. "But is your shop going somewhere?"

In absolutely no mood for a surprise visit from *the* Felicity Mayhew, creator of fantasy weddings who did business with Lucifer's minions, Alyson lifted her chin. "As a matter of fact, we're having to relocate since *Marsden* Enterprises bought the building almost a month ago and gave us thirty days to vacate." She narrowed her eyes. "We have twelve days left with zero wiggle room, even though we've been unable to secure a new space in such little time."

And, no, this wasn't Felicity Mayhew's problem. But she needed to know who exactly she was in business with, and she needed to hear it from victims of the Marsden family.

Jillian shot Alyson a right-on grin, then concentrated on their visitor once more.

Surprisingly, Felicity gave her a ghost of a smile. "You must also be Holly Golightly?"

Alyson's mind went blank. She chanced a glance at Jillian, whose grin had vanished.

"Holly Golightly?" Campbell asked. "What exactly have you two been doing?"

Felicity's mouth eased into a real smile. "It appears successfully walking into weddings with not nearly enough security." She focused on Alyson. "And capturing my brother's eye."

Now Alyson's eyes widened.

Scott the English professor was Felicity Mayhew's *brother*? Still, as she really looked at the woman, she saw the resemblance between them in their hair color and eyes.

"He told me all about a lovely woman he'd met, dressed as Holly Golightly, who went on about a shop in the Highlands that had prettier flowers, but was there to see my work because she was getting married." She tilted her head right. "Scott thought the whole thing was a little peculiar, but felt slightly guilty that he made *Holly* leave the way she did."

Alyson's body became hot and she suddenly felt the need to remove her sweatshirt.

"He also wanted me to know she became quite upset when she found out about my partnership with Stacia Marsden. I believe that's everything?" she asked Alyson.

She slowly nodded and eyed Jillian, who flinched.

Felicity laughed. "Wonderful!" She stepped farther into the shop. "Do you two have time to chat? I'm terribly sorry about popping in like this. But when my assistant, Lynn, told me you never followed up with a meeting, I decided to seize the day."

Alyson desperately tried to wrap her brain around the fact Felicity Mayhew was in their shop, wanting to talk to them, on top of everything else she'd said.

"Do you have a quiet place we could chat?" the woman tried again.

Jillian stepped backward. "Yes. Of course we do. The backroom."

As soon as Alyson sat beside Felicity at their work table and Jillian was perched on the desk, she gave the woman a tight smile. "I'm so sorry about deceiving your brother the way I did." She released a quick laugh. "He was actually very nice *and* charming."

"Yes," she murmured. "He does have his moments."

"But," Alyson slowly continued, "he doesn't have an accent."

Felicity set her red, leather Gucci purse on the table. "That's because I lived in London on and off for several years while married to my now ex-husband who's British." She leaned forward. "I'm almost certain Scott would like to hear you *are* single?"

Heat hit Alyson's face. She slid her eyes to Jillian, fighting a smile.

"I am, but—" She sighed. *But she'd given her heart to someone else twelve years ago and he still had it.* "I'm focusing on other things right now." It's not like that was a lie, either.

"Your displaced business." Felicity's eyes narrowed into slits. "I can't express how sorry I am Marsden Enterprises has done this to you. It's quite the perfect location."

Yes, dammit, it was, and none of this was fair.

"Unfortunately, I can't help you with that," Felicity stated. "But I am interested in partnering up with a new business to provide the flowers for all of my weddings."

Alyson looked at Jillian, her eyes once again round.

Was this really happening?

Felicity folded her hands in her lap. "I was getting awfully tired of Stacia trying to tell me what to do with *my* clients' weddings. And this last wedding—close friends of her family—was enough." She glanced at Jillian and back at Alyson. "She also briefly dated my brother and treated him poorly." Her mouth inched into a wicked smile. "It was one reason I wanted him at that wedding. He is quite the charmer when he wants to be, and I was hoping he'd meet someone new." She laughed. "Right in front of that atrocious Stacia who was also there as a guest."

Jillian smothered a giggle.

Alyson, however, cringed. "I really am sorry—"

"Please stop apologizing, because he'll be fine." She straightened. "I'd already decided to break my partnership with her. Hearing what you said about the Marsdens through Scott made me tell her that day when I completed my job."

Alyson leaned against the table.

This was really happening. Her "wedding crashing" plan had actually worked and all because she'd dressed like the iconic Holly Golightly, then caught the eye of an English professor who loved Truman Capote. And who also happened to be Felicity Mayhew's *brother*.

"Before we make anything official," Felicity continued, "I'd like my assistant to see *your* work and take photos for me. I assume your next wedding is this Saturday?"

How was all of this even possible?

Jillian stood. "Yes, but it's an intimate wedding up at the Boettcher Mansion."

Felicity smiled softly. "I remember, when I was fairly new to wedding planning, running many weddings there. It's such a lovely, romantic place to get married." Her smile slipped. "I no longer work with clients interested in intimate." She went into her purse, withdrew a business card holder, then handed one to Alyson. "Please call my office and leave the time of the wedding with Lynn. She'll only be there long enough to take photos of the arrangements, including the bridal bouquets." She stood. "No one but you will know she was even there. Once I get a chance to look at everything, I'll be in touch."

She shook hands with Alyson, followed by Jillian, and picked up her purse. "I have a very good feeling about all of this." She smiled. "I also hope you find a new home for your shop very soon." She paused, then added, "If this does work out, you might need a bigger space, too."

Alyson stared at her, not certain she'd heard the woman correctly.

Seconds later, she was gone.

Campbell rushed into the backroom. "I heard every word because *of course* I was eavesdropping." She laughed. "I know we're in the middle of moving hell right now, but we have to celebrate. Right?"

"Well," Alyson managed to say, "nothing's official yet."

"But it will be," Jillian stated. "What she said before she left?" She stepped toward Alyson. "Seeing our work is just a formality."

Alyson grinned, then squealed and threw her arms around Jillian and Campbell.

No, things with Daisy's Bouquets were far from perfect. But this was a *gigantic* step in the right direction.

"We are getting *cra-zy* tonight, ladies." Jillian pulled away. "I have to call Jackson, too. I've been a little pissy since we lost that space." She withdrew her phone from her back jeans pocket. "But he's been really nice about it. And supportive."

Jillian strolled into the shop with Campbell close behind.

Alyson sat at the desk.

Nice and supportive. *Just like his best friend.* She wanted to call David, but what would she say, especially when she thought about everything he'd shared with her in the notebook. She probably should have called him by now to say…what? Thank you for writing all of that down and giving it to me? I'm sorry you had to sacrifice so much? I'm sorry you lost *everything* dear to you ten years ago and had to work incredibly hard to get a fraction of it back?

I'm sorry you can't let go of the guilt? That's the part that caused her heart to really hurt.

No, she couldn't call him and say those things. But he would be at Matt's party Saturday night and she *could* suggest they spend the evening together, getting to know each other as adults. Turn the party into the date he'd wanted three weeks ago?

She smiled softly at Saturday night's possibilities and taking another big step forward.

Chapter Twenty-Two

DAVID WALKED into his office building, brushing the snow off his hair and coat.

"Good. You're already here," Marjorie greeted him. "Vivienne Dunne is on the line."

Fantastic. On the bright side, this was her first call since he'd left Aspen two weeks ago.

He faced their office manager-receptionist staring at him, unsmiling. "Good morning to you, too, Marjorie." He headed for the stairs. "Can you transfer the call when I get in my office?"

"Yes. Oh, and David?"

He paused on the first step.

"I thought you'd like to know I've concluded my investigation into my missing stapler."

David somehow managed to simply raise his eyebrows and ask, "I'm sorry?"

"And I have it on good authority *you're* the culprit."

Jackson. The traitor and *bastard.*

Her eyes behind her glasses became slits. "Do you have anything to say in your defense?"

He turned and continued up the stairs. "I have my own stapler,

Marjorie." *With hers, buried deep inside his desk, he now had two.* "But this has been a funny way to start the day."

As soon as he was inside his office with the door closed, he laughed while shaking his head. Until his phone started to ring.

He shrugged out of his coat while speed-walking to his desk.

The woman could not be calling him about changes. She seemed smarter than that.

"This is David," he answered, hanging his coat on the back of the chair.

"Hello, my darling."

He sat. "Hi Vivienne. It's nice to hear your voice." *Why are you calling me?* "What can I do for you?"

"I'm calling for a few reasons, the first one being I have so missed hearing the sound of *your* voice. It is quite nice."

He closed his eyes. "Thank you. But I have a meeting to get to," he lied.

"I also had to call to find out how it's going with *the one*?"

His eyes flew open. Shit, really? It was too early for this. He also needed more coffee.

"It's been two weeks since you left. Surely you've made some progress?"

He swiveled his chair right to watch the falling snow. "Nothing's changed, but I appreciate your interest." He'd also officially given up on the notebook idea working, since he still hadn't heard from Al over a week after leaving it on her desk.

For all he knew, it was still sitting there. Or had been shoved into a drawer.

He cringed at that image.

"I'm so sorry to hear that. I do wish you two could figure things out."

She'd be at Matt's party Saturday night, and he had no idea what he'd say to her or how he'd act. Avoiding her altogether would probably be best for both of them. But any time he ended up in the same place with Alyson Catherine Douglas, an invisible line with magnetic strength pulled him right to her side.

"David, my darling, are you still there?"

He cleared his throat. "Yes. And what was the third reason you called?" *Let her go.*

"I know, you have a meeting." She sighed. "A dear friend of mine is in the market for an architect to design a dream retirement home for she and her husband. Of course, I told her all about *my* brilliant and adorable architect." She laughed. "She can't wait to meet you!"

If he loved architecture, this would definitely be flattering. But it was just a job.

He swiveled forward and stared at all the shit masking his desk—plans and contracts and thick file folders and notes on legal pads. His eyes then drifted to his phone, the red light blinking which meant he had messages. Probably a half dozen at least, and it hit him.

As much as he loved the people in this building, even Marjorie, this was the last place on earth he wanted to be right now. Which meant he had his final answer for Jackson and Zach.

He smiled. "Thank you, Vivienne, but I'm not taking any more clients." And *damn* did it feel good to say that and really mean it. "I'd be happy to refer your friend to one of the other partners, or our associate architect, if she'd like."

"Why on earth would you do that? I promise they're a *lovely* couple."

He straightened. "Well, if you must know, I've decided to leave architecture." He laughed, since it felt even better to say that and really mean it.

She fell silent, and he waited.

Vivienne Dunne always had something to say.

"I hope you're leaving architecture for something that involves your piano and band?"

"Vivienne, you were right that night." His smile grew. "You're a great listener." Despite being the biggest pain-in-the-butt client he'd ever had, he'd meant every word.

She laughed. "You're too adorable. I'm sure my friend will be happy with any of the architects in your office. I'll have her call the main line. But you won't be rid of *me* so easily."

Of course not. But a part of him was okay with that.

"The next time I'm in Denver, I have to hear your band play. And I'll be sending you good thoughts when it comes to *the one*. But if it doesn't work out, my daughter—"

"I have to get to that meeting. Goodbye, Vivienne."

"Goodbye for *now*, my darling David." She followed that up with an air kiss.

He stood as he hung up. Now it was time to break the news to the guys. He might start to float as soon as the words left him, too.

He quickly left his office, went left, and stopped at Jackson's closed door where he knocked twice before pushing it open. "Hey. I need to talk to you and Zach."

Jackson glared at him. "Zach will be in late. He's going with Erica to her doc appointment. And unless you're here to give me good news, I suggest you get out."

David frowned and closed the door behind him. "Jackson, it's not even 9:00. How can you already be this pissed off?"

His friend rubbed his eyes and sat back. "I had an early breakfast with a few guys from CU who went through the program with *me*."

He slid his hands into his pockets and walked toward Jackson's desk. "Okay."

"A couple of their firms also bid on that *big* shopping mall project that we did. That one I submitted right after you left for Aspen?"

"Yeah." He angled his head back. "Have they already made a decision?"

Jackson shook his head. "No, but one of the guys somehow found out who's *really* Downey Development. And it's not good news."

David sat, his frown deepening. "What the hell are you talking about?"

He released a heavy sigh. "It's Keith Marsden."

His mouth inched open. "Oh, *shit*. So, what, he's a silent partner?"

"And *consultant*." Jackson focused on David. "I have a rotten feeling that Nelson Downey, the CEO, is really Marsden's mouthpiece."

David nodded.

"We can't be in business with that dickhead."

"We're not," David threw back. "It's not like they've made a decision."

"I'm not trying to be an arrogant ass," Jackson replied, "but our bid was damn good."

"And you know that doesn't mean a damn thing in this business."

Jackson hesitated, then asked, "But what if they do choose us?"

He stared at his friend. "Is this about the shop and Jillian?"

"I don't want to get involved with Keith Marsden, but, yeah." He cracked a grin. "David, I really like her, and she despises everything Marsden related. I don't blame her, either. They still haven't found a new space and will, most likely, have to move the shop into Alyson's house until they do find one."

So they were still moving forward with that plan.

His jaw tightened at the unfairness. Even though he had an idea, he had to stay out of it.

"But if our bid is chosen," Jackson continued, "how could I pass on this, professionally speaking? The project would be a huge-ass win for the firm."

David stopped where his thoughts had gone and leaned forward. "Jackson, you need to slow down. We don't have the job. I get you really like Jillian, but you two are only dating." *Plus, you're a workaholic.* But he asked, "Unless something's changed?"

Jackson smiled, his first since David walked into his office. "No, but I think this could be something." His smile faded. "She won't be okay with us being in business with Marsden. I'm not sure Alyson would, either."

"You don't know for certain how they would react, so stop

worrying about it. And I know you're feeling good about the bid," he added, "but it's no guarantee."

His friend stared at his desk for several seconds, then straightened. "You're right. I won't go there unless I have to." He concentrated on David. "So, are you in here to give me bad news?"

He smiled.

"You're an asshole."

"An asshole who's leaving architecture." He stood, feeling hundreds of pounds lighter, which made him laugh. Again.

Jackson glared at him once more. "It's not funny. That compromise was solid."

"You're right. I appreciate it and knowing the firm will be here if I need and want it again *someday*." David lifted his shoulders. "But right now I want out, and I can do it."

He faced his computer. "Then I guess it's a good thing the real reason I had that breakfast meeting was to get an idea if they, or anyone they know, are looking to make a change in firms."

"And?"

"I got a few names." Jackson glanced at him. "But you're still an asshole."

"I know it." He stepped backward. "So are you for telling Marjorie I swiped her stapler. I'll never confess to the crime, either." *Because her reaction was too much damn fun.*

"Whatever. I'm out of it. So you're dressing up for the party Saturday, right?"

His humor vanished. "Only because my sister said she'd only let me in the house if I was wearing one." Which had made him almost tell her he wouldn't be there. But Matt was his future brother-in-law and had also become a good buddy. "I have to pull something together. What about you and Jillian?"

Jackson's grin came back. "She loved the idea. And you know I don't have a stick shoved up my ass about wearing a costume. Which has always made *me*"—he pointed at himself—"the badass in this friendship."

"Whatever you say." He headed for the door.

"Alyson's going to be there."

He held on to a sigh. "I know that."

"So be her unofficial date."

Why wouldn't his friends and family leave him alone about this? *Her*?

"I'll see you later." He left and closed the door behind him.

But it wasn't exactly a bad idea. If Al, by some miracle, sought him out at the party, he'd follow her lead. He'd fight that invisible line, though, since she had to make the first move.

Alyson Catherine Douglas knew exactly *who* he wanted.

With that thought, he walked back inside his office and closed the door.

The first thing he'd tackle were the voicemail messages, return calls if necessary, then sort through the mess on his desk. And, maybe later, he'd create a count-down calendar as another way to prepare for his new life.

Chapter Twenty-Three

ALYSON ZIPPED UP HER TIGHT, sleeveless, purple mini-dress as her phone started to ring.

She scooped it off her bed and frowned at the unfamiliar, Florida number. She was about to hit ignore when she recalled David's voicemail message from a week ago.

I gave my aunt and uncle your number. They lived in Florida.

With an unsteady breath, she tapped accept. "Hello?"

"Hi, Alyson! It's Eileen Preston. You have to be getting ready for the big party tonight, but do you have a few minutes? It won't take long. Hugh and I came back to Denver for the party, and I have to finish getting ready, too."

She squeezed her eyes shut.

Please, please *be good news.*

"Yes. Of course." She lowered herself to her bed's edge.

"I know we'll see you tonight, but I have some news that couldn't wait." She laughed. "I also thought it would be a little difficult to discuss business at an eighties-themed birthday party. And the news I have is a mixture of good *and* bad."

Her stomach, already in knots at the thought of seeing David in less than two hours and suggesting her get-to-know-each-other-again plan, flipped, and she suddenly felt nauseated.

In spite of Felicity Mayhew turning their week upside down in an absolutely amazing way, she wasn't certain she could handle any more bad news when it came to new spaces.

Jillian, who was in her bathroom, poked her head out and mouthed, "Who is it?"

"The good news," Eileen continued, "is that one of our tenants gave us notice today."

Alyson froze.

"Her husband received the news yesterday that his company is transferring him to the San Francisco bay area."

Her eyes locked with Jillian's and she waved her friend forward.

Had Eileen Preston really just said all of that?

"The space is in the Sloan's Lake neighborhood, near 29th and Tennyson."

"Yes," she answered a tad breathlessly. "I know the area very well." It wasn't terribly far from their current location in the Highlands.

Oh, my God. Was *this* really happening?

Jillian walked toward her, now wearing a very short, slightly frayed, snug denim skirt and a neon-pink shirt that barely sat on her shoulders.

She sat beside her on the bed.

Alyson angled her phone out so her friend could hear.

"It's not a terribly large space, so I'm not sure it'll work—"

"We'll take it," she blurted out as Jillian quietly clapped.

Eileen laughed again. "Well, I'd really like you to see it first before you make that decision? Like I said, it's on the small side."

Alyson grimaced. "You're right. It's just that it sounds pretty perfect." But Felicity had suggested if everything "worked out," to get into a larger space.

"The woman in there now owns and runs a boutique tea shop. It's very charming. But here's the bad news," Eileen slowly added.

She looked at Jillian, who had her hands folded and pressed against her mouth.

"It won't be available until the end of May. Probably around Memorial Day."

Her shoulders fell.

Crap, crap, *crap*.

"It could be sooner, depending on how much work needs to be done. She's been there for a few years. We really won't know until she's moved out, which will be in about six weeks."

Dammit. Could they really go that long working out of her home *and* without the everyday orders? She hadn't expected the shop to be displaced for just over two months.

"David mentioned your back-up plan. Of moving the business into your house?"

"Yes," she murmured. "But my house could best be described as quaint."

Jillian nodded and shrugged.

"Hugh and I would love to have Daisy's Bouquets in that space, but that's a long time to be operating a flower shop out of your own home."

Alyson sighed. "We don't have a choice. And believe me when I say we would *love* to have Daisy's Bouquets in a space you two own." After dealing with one Lucifer minion after another, every part of her meant those words.

Silence fell on Eileen's end, then, "David told me when I was on the phone with him moments ago that he hasn't had the chance to tell you about his good idea on another place you could house your business until you found a new space."

She frowned, looked at Jillian, and said, "David has an idea? Really?" And if so, why hadn't he mentioned it to her? Not that they'd been in close contact since that day he'd come into the shop with the notebook.

In hindsight, maybe she should have reached out to him after reading it?

"Hugh and I have a home in the Country Club neighborhood. It's now our second home. Because of that, we don't use it as a vacation rental, so it sits empty quite a bit. But always under the watchful eyes of our lovely neighbors."

Alyson shook her head. "I'm sorry, but I'm not following."

"Because your house is *quaint*, David asked us if we'd be willing to let you ladies turn our home into a temporary flower shop. The kitchen is quite spacious, and we have a finished basement with a kitchenette. You'd have all the room you needed to store supplies and fill orders."

Jillian's mouth dropped open as she leaned backward.

Alyson looked at the floor. "*David* suggested that?" And he hadn't brought it to her? Still, would she have taken him seriously if he had?

"He was pretty insistent your house, though perfect for you and your dog, wasn't big enough or set up to really accommodate your business, even temporarily."

She certainly couldn't argue with his opinion, either.

"I should get going and let you go, too, so let's plan on you and Jillian looking at the space Monday morning. We'll set up a time later. If you're interested, we'll work out the details and discuss you moving your business into our house as a better back-up plan. Sound good?"

Alyson stared at Jillian.

What was happening right now?

"Alyson?"

Jillian snapped her fingers in her face.

"That sounds great. Thank you so much, Eileen."

"It's my pleasure. We'll see you soon."

The line went dead.

Jillian squealed. "I officially love your ex-boyfriend." She hopped to her feet. "I'm going to tell him just that when I see him at the party tonight."

Alyson stood as she reached a staggering realization—she was such a stubborn *idiot*. "I have to talk to him."

"Well, you're in luck because you'll see him at the party."

She stepped into her bright-white heels. "What I have to say can't wait." *She'd waited long enough.* "And trying to have a serious conversation with him at an eighties-themed birthday party is *not* going to work for me." She grabbed the black, waist-length leather jacket that completed her eighties outfit. "Can you and Jackson get Thatcher to your sister?"

The original plan had been Jackson picking them up here, leaving Thatcher with Jillian's younger sister at their apartment in case it was a *very* late night, then heading to Boulder.

Once at the party, she'd planned on turning the rest of the night over to fate.

"Yeah, but—"

She threw her arms around Jillian. "Lock up for me, too? I'll see you later."

Seconds later she was in her 4Runner and bringing up David's address via Google Maps's memory while begging the Heavens he would still be at home when she arrived.

He'd done everything right since walking into the shop the Monday after Valentine's Day. He'd been calm, affable, and charming, yet respectful of her space; interested in her business; concerned for her and the business; and so incredibly patient. He hadn't even really been that upset she'd lied to him about having a boyfriend. At least, not in front of her. And after she'd unleashed her emotions and rejected *him* that Saturday morning, he'd taken it and walked away. Then there was the notebook.

She braked at a stoplight.

He'd written in his note, *I'm hoping after you read this, you'll be able to forget that guy and want to know <u>this</u> David.* Page after page after page, he'd shared so many highs and lows of the last ten years of his life.

Graduating from CU, high. Graduating with a BS in Architectural Engineering, low.

Finally buying a piano, high. Not having time to play due to long work hours, low.

Forming the band with a man named Randy, high. Getting involved with Sara, low.

Starting the firm with Jackson and Zach, high. Even longer work hours, low.

Becca meeting Matt, high. Separating from Sara, low.

Band becoming popular with locals, high. Divorcing Sara, low.

Becca and Matt becoming engaged, high. Feeling stuck in architecture, low.

Alyson remembered her question for him following Becca's birthday party.

Are you happy?

Reading everything he'd written—twice—she hadn't heard too much happiness, outside of being happy because of his sister's happiness. Big, past mistakes or not, David Thomas Preston did *not* deserve to live that kind of life.

He had, without a doubt, been through enough for one lifetime.

She frowned.

Most of her choices the past month certainly hadn't helped either of them. But that was about to change. And as she approached his house, she spotted his black, sporty SUV in the driveway. After parking behind him, she released a quick breath. "Thank you," she whispered.

Trembling, she slowly climbed from her 4Runner and closed the door. She forced her wobbly, high-heeled feet to move toward his front door, where she paused because of the music.

She quietly giggled.

He was playing the piano. Something upbeat and jazzy, too.

She leaned right, toward his living room window, since she couldn't remember the last time she'd heard him play. But could distinctly remember the first time she'd heard him—he suddenly stopped, and what sounded like in the middle of the song. Within seconds, though, he was playing the same notes.

It was time for both of them to finally put the past right where it belonged.

The music stopped again, and she, on a deep breath, rang the doorbell.

Alyson ran her fingers through her hair hanging loose, not having had the chance to give it an eighties style before her unexpected phone call. And departure from her house.

The door flew open.

She lowered her arms and smiled. "Hi there." She was nearly eye-to-eye with him, too, due to her three-inch heels and the fact he was barefoot.

They continued staring at each other until his eyes drifted down her body.

Her skin became the temperature of boiling.

His eyes reached her face once more and he grinned. "Are you blushing?"

She stepped forward. "I really need to talk to you. Can I come in?"

He stepped aside.

As she walked into his foyer, she felt him watching her closely.

"What are you doing here?" He closed the door.

She stopped and whirled toward him.

His grin turned devilish. "I'm not complaining, considering how you look right now."

She folded her hands. "Thanks, but I need you to be serious."

His grin transitioned into a frown. "Okay."

The longer she stood there, staring into his deep, soulful brown eyes full of curiosity, the more she wanted to leap into his arms and show him exactly who *she* wanted. But she had a few things to say first. "Your aunt called me about a space being available in a couple months."

He nodded. "I know. She called to tell me what *I* hope you think is good news?"

She stepped closer to him. "She also mentioned your idea."

He slipped his hands into the pockets of his shorts. "Good."

She stared at him. "That's all you have to say? Really?"

"What else am I supposed to say?" He exhaled through his teeth. "Alyson, tell me what you're doing here. Both of us have somewhere to be tonight."

She gestured at him. "You're not even dressed."

"I'm not exactly naked, either."

She leaned forward. "I came to say thank you."

He leaned forward. "For what? You knew I went to my aunt and uncle. It was only a matter of time before something would open up." He smiled. "They were right when they said things can change rapidly."

"For your idea," she softly said. "It was incredibly thoughtful."

He stepped closer. "You're welcome, but are you going to do it?"

She shrugged. "I'm—*we're*—going to meet with your aunt on Monday to see the space and talk everything out. But that's not the only thing I want to thank you for."

Their eyes locked.

"I read the notebook you left me." She paused before adding, "Twice."

He angled his head back. "You really found the last ten years of my life that interesting?"

She grinned. "You did write in your note I wouldn't be bored."

He slowly nodded. "True."

"Thank you for doing that." She took another step closer. "I liked feeling close to you again. But what I really want to thank you for is not giving up on me. *Us*. Especially after I—" She flinched. "Would crushed you that Saturday morning be about right?"

He took another step closer. "Yeah, that phrase about covers it. But you had legit reasons, and I told you I needed to hear all of that."

Silence fell between them.

Why was he acting so…unaffected? Hadn't she made herself perfectly clear?

"So you came over here just to thank me, knowing we'd see each other at the party?"

She lifted her shoulders. "I know it's ridiculous, but I wasn't sure if we'd really have a chance to talk—"

He reached up, cradled her face, and lowered his mouth to hers.

His soft lips persuaded hers to open beneath his, and she released a low moan. His mouth so familiar. So delectable. Just like it had always been.

Her legs trembled as their mouths moved perfectly together. Then her purse fell from her shoulder and hit the hardwood floor.

He gradually ended the kiss and pulled slightly away. "Al, I promise *that guy* is gone."

"I know."

He slid his left fingers down her neck and stopped at the base to caress the delicate skin. "And I swear to you that I will never let him come back."

She guided his head closer to hers. "I believe you."

"So how about if *this* is where we start a new beginning?"

She smiled. "I would love that." *Just as much as she loved him.*

He brought back his devilish grin right before their mouths picked up where they'd left off seconds earlier.

"But we have a problem," he said between a kiss.

"The party?"

"Yeah."

They leisurely broke apart.

"It's Matt's thirtieth birthday and he'll be a part of my family soon."

She nodded. "Yes, he will."

"But you," he continued, "the only woman I've ever wanted who looks *incredible* right now, just showed up on my doorstep. Then told me things I've wanted to hear for weeks."

Their mouths fused for several seconds until she leaned back to look into his deep, soulful brown eyes shining with affection, frustration, and clear desire. "We've lost ten years."

He opened his mouth, but she silenced him with a quick kiss.

"I didn't say that out of blame."

He stayed silent.

"David, I just want to be with *you* tonight." She nuzzled his nose. "I also don't want to waste any more time. Do you?"

The corner of his perfect mouth lifted in a grin. "Absolutely not. I also have a strong feeling no one would really miss us tonight. Do you?"

When she remembered Becca throwing them together on dress shopping day and Jilly making her feelings clear many times on the subject of David, she laughed. "Absolutely not."

Their arms became locked around each other.

"Then we no longer have a problem." He lifted her up, slowly turned them, and headed for his staircase. "Matt will have another birthday next year."

When they reached the staircase, he lowered her to the first step. He covered her mouth with his once more, while gently backing her up a step. Followed by another. Then two more.

Before she knew it, they had reached the landing, where they stumbled backward until she was pinned between him and the wall.

"Where the hell did you get this outfit?" He slipped her jacket off her shoulders.

"A vintage-clothing store Jillian found." She hooked her arms behind his neck, hoisted herself up, and wrapped her legs around his waist.

"I don't think I want to take this dress off you," he said around another breathless kiss.

"Then don't. Bedroom?"

He turned them right and walked into what had to be his room.

After he took a few, long strides, they tumbled onto his bed.

He slid his hand up her thigh, reaching the bottom of her tight dress. He wiggled his hand underneath the fabric, sliding his hand farther up. When he reached her waist, he hooked his warm fingers on the elastic of her black leggings.

She kicked off her heels as he ended their kiss to remove them and, within seconds, her legs were bare.

He gave her a naughty grin. "No panties?"

She returned his grin. "Not when I wear leggings."

Their hungry mouths joined again.

She managed to yank his T-shirt over his head. His skin was hot. She wanted to tear off her clothing to feel his bare skin against hers. But that need vanished the moment his hand went back underneath her dress and cupped her bare, left cheek. He gave it a quick, playful squeeze, then leisurely slid his hand right.

The moment his fingers touched her moist flesh she gripped his shoulders.

His hushed moan echoed hers before he whispered, "Give me a sec."

Keeping her eyes locked on him as he stood and removed his shorts, she bit her lower lip while admiring every inch of his bare, lean physique. He'd filled out a bit with age, but other than that he'd changed little in ten years.

David opened his nightstand's drawer. A moment later he gently spread her bent legs, then press...press...pressed into her; their moans replacing the silence. But then he paused, releasing a slow breath as he lowered himself down until their chests were barely touching.

She slid her arms around his waist and whispered, "Why are you stopping?"

"I'm trying to take this as slow as I can because you look and feel —" He finished his sentence by pushing himself fully inside of her, making her gasp.

Their breathing became labored with each thrust. One after another. And another. Their kisses became greedier, more breathless, the longer their bodies kept moving in perfect synchronization. The tingling deep within began from being close. So close that a few more powerful thrusts later, she tumbled off that edge; David not far behind.

As their heavy breathing quieted, he pressed his forehead to hers.

"Holy shit," he said on a breath. "We need to stop coming together like that."

"Why?" she replied, trying to catch her breath. "Do you hear me complaining?"

"No." He laughed. "But it'll be *much* better next time."

He stayed inside of her as they exchanged a series of airy kisses that lasted until he said, "I don't want to get up, but I have to get rid of this thing."

She grudgingly released his waist.

"I'll be right back." He gently pulled away. "Don't even think about moving."

Alyson closed her eyes, her body still buzzing from their fierce, *delicious* union. She knew this was only the beginning of a long, decadent night together, with many more to follow.

They did have to catch up on ten years of separation.

She smiled, stretched, and released a quick laugh.

"That's a pretty wicked smile."

She opened her eyes to see his equally wicked grin.

"I'm ready for that dress to come off."

She raised her arms, and he grasped her hands to pull her upright. The second she stood in front of him, he pinched the zipper, and, very slowly, lowered it until her dress was open.

"Promise me right now you'll never get rid of this dress."

She laughed. "I think I can do that. But where's your eighties outfit?" She placed her hands on his warm, solid chest. "Or were you *not* going to play by the rules?"

"I have an outfit." He slipped the dress off her shoulders, then rested his hands on her bare waist. "It's in my closet." He slid his hands up to her black bra. "I was actually about to head upstairs to change when you rang the doorbell."

The flimsy garment fell away.

Their eyes snapped together.

"And what *was* your outfit?"

He placed his right hand on the back of her neck, wound his fingers through her hair, and pulled her toward him. "White suit and pink shirt. I was going for James Spader."

"*Pretty in Pink.*" She nuzzled his neck once their hot skin was again touching. "A small part of me is wishing we were going to the party so I could see you dressed like that."

He lowered them back onto his bed. "If you ask nicely, maybe I'll put it on for you *later*."

His lips explored the sensitive area beneath her right ear.

She released a tiny whimper, which made him quietly laugh.

That had always been one of her hot spots.

His mouth continued its unhurried exploration before stopping at her shoulder. He lightly brushed his lips across her skin and down her upper arm. When he flicked his tongue against her nipple, she gripped his hair and arched her back.

With each gentle kiss and flick, her body once again became *hot*. Something he must have sensed—still able to read her—since he lifted his head and captured her mouth.

He gradually ended the kiss and said, "We need to slow down."

"*David,* we both know we're going to be up most of the night."

He laughed. "I don't want to rush it this time." He sealed his statement with a leisurely kiss while sliding his fingers down her waist where he paused on her stomach. "I still can't get enough of your skin."

She lightly dragged her nails up his smooth back, and he shivered.

"The feeling's mutual," she whispered into his ear.

David gave her a naughty smile and started to inch his way down. He paused to drop soft kisses on her belly and abdomen.

Her eyes drifted shut.

He continued inching down until he reached his destination. The second he placed his lips on her warm, damp skin, she released a deep moan.

His tongue tasted and teased the sensitive spot.

The pressure within began to slowly build. But he paused, making it clear he wasn't ready to let her go…and brought her close again…waited…and she heard his muffled laugh in response to her second whimper of the night. The third time he didn't pause.

Her climax reached every inch of her body.

He inched back up and laid his head on her stomach.

She released a series of giggles.

He turned and rested his chin on her stomach. "I'm not finished with you yet."

"I hope not," she murmured. "Even after *that*."

Less than a minute later, he eased into her wet warmth.

She closed her eyes as he again buried himself inside of her—as far as he could go—and she tightened her arms behind his neck.

"*Alyson*, open your eyes."

Still savoring her previous climax, she couldn't open her eyes. All she could manage was tightening her muscles around him as he languidly slid in and out of her. In…and back out.

He pressed his lips to her jaw, then placed a trail of airy kisses to her mouth; their kiss lasting until they were forced to break apart for air.

"Al," he breathlessly whispered into her ear, "open your eyes."

She forced her eyes to inch open which instantly connected with his.

"What if this is a dream?" she asked around a shallow breath.

Her head became fuzzy. Lightheaded.

"Dreams don't look and feel like this."

Her body started to ready itself for the inevitable release.

"But you feel too perfect to be real."

Several moments later, their eyes still on each other, they fell in unity.

Chapter Twenty-Four

DAVID STARED AT AL, her head nestled into his other king-sized pillow. He could also see in the light from his bedside lamp the green in her eyes, lit up due to the *crazy* story she'd just told him. "You crashed a wedding at the Ritz-Carlton dressed like a character from a movie?"

"I was *technically* invited." She shrugged. "Either way, it was necessary and worked."

He shook with laughter.

"And it wasn't just any character," she continued. "It was Holly Golightly."

He laughed for a few more seconds before asking, "Why does that name sound familiar?"

She scooted closer. "I know I made you watch *Breakfast at Tiffany's* with me."

He grinned. "If we were alone, I promise I wasn't *really* paying attention to the movie."

She shook her head. "In any case, that's how Daisy's Bouquets will, most likely, be partnering with *the* Felicity Mayhew very soon."

"That was pretty gutsy stuff, Al. I'm impressed." He leaned

forward and gave her lips a light kiss. "I know I said this before, but I'm really proud of you."

"Thanks." She smiled softly. "I heard you playing when I got here. It reminded me of the first time I heard you play the piano. Do you remember that day?"

He returned her smile. "I remember everything from then." He paused, then said, "Except watching that movie with you."

Her smile became shy. "I never told you this, but I arrived about ten minutes early and stood outside the music room, listening to you rehearse 'Memory' for the musical review with that girl. She had such an amazing voice."

He nodded. "Samantha. Yeah, she was crazy talented."

"You both were…are," she amended. "I'm sure she's somewhere in the world, stunning people with her singing. That reminds me, what were you playing? I didn't recognize it."

Her question caught him sideways; a reminder he had so much he needed to tell her. And not all of it had to do with his career decisions. But he wanted to keep moving far from the guilt and shame. Which meant he had to let her into his time stuck in the darkness.

"David?" She ran her fingers through his hair. "Where'd you go?"

He blinked and said, "It's something I started working on a couple weeks ago. It'll eventually be one of the band's numbers."

She caught his eyes. "I'm incredibly proud of *you*."

He'd needed to hear that from her, too. *More than she could possibly know.*

"Al, there's so much—" His phone, on the floor inside of his shorts, burst into the piano riff. He sighed. "That has to be my sister or Jackson."

"Time for us to face the music? No pun intended," she hastily added.

He gave her a swift, yet thorough kiss, then rolled onto his right side. He bent down, and the piano riff grew louder as he lifted his shorts to retrieve his phone from the pocket. "It's my sister." He sat up and scooted back until he was against the headboard. "Come here," he said, patting the spot next to him. Once she was curled into his side, he tapped speakerphone and answered, "Hey."

"Don't *'hey'* me!" Becs snapped. "Where are you? Did you forget there was somewhere important you needed to be tonight?"

"No, I sure didn't. And I'm at home."

Silence fell before, "You better be joking."

"Not joking. Something pretty unexpected and *big* came up." He winked at Al.

She buried her face in his shoulder while shaking with quiet laughter.

"Are you not here because you had to dress up in eighties clothing?"

He whispered, "Say hi."

"Hi, Becca," she said around her laughter.

Another moment of silence, followed by a shriek, followed by, "Alyson? Oh. My. God. What's going on?"

He eyed Al. "Becs, we're not going to make it to the party."

She laughed. "And that's *all* I need or want to know."

"So tell Matt I'll make it up to him, have fun tonight, and we'll talk next week."

"Okay. *Bye Alyson*," she all but sang.

He ended the call, extended his arm right, and dropped his phone. "That should leave us with zero interruptions between now and Monday."

Al rested her chin on his shoulder. "How long do you think it'll be before everyone at that party knows about us?"

"Thirty seconds. *Max*." He shifted onto his left side and brushed his lips against hers. "Please tell me you don't have to work tomorrow."

She smiled. "You're in luck, David Thomas Preston, since I thought I'd be up late due to a surprise birthday party. Jillian and I put Campbell and Hayley on wedding duty tomorrow."

He nuzzled her nose. "What about your dog that hates me?"

"He'll warm up to you and he's with Jillian's sister tonight. So you have me all to yourself." She gave him a naughty smile. "What *are* you going to do with me?"

What if this is a dream?

He concentrated on her mouth curved into that smile. His gray sheets loosely covering her body. Her long, now messy hair tumbling around and past her shoulders.

"I have an idea if you don't."

No. None of this unforgettable, very unanticipated night with her was a dream.

"Oh, I have lots of ideas," he finally said. "But being a gentleman, you go first."

Her smile doubled in size. "Music."

He squinted at her. "You want me to turn on some music?"

"No, silly. I want you to play the piano for me. Please? David, I've missed hearing you play so much." Her smile slipped. "I've missed you, *too*."

Dammit, if that wasn't something else he'd needed to hear from her, as well. Music was also a good idea, since it would give them time, away from this bed, so they could talk. Or more accurately, he would talk while she listened. So he said, "Okay."

Their mouths came together for as long as they could stand it.

He reluctantly pulled away and scooted out of bed. As he pulled his shorts back on, he caught her watching him while loosely biting her lower lip. "Or we could stay right here."

She caught his eyes. "No. I absolutely want to hear you play. But do you have something I could wear?" She pointed at the floor where that *fantastic* dress had fallen. "I know you love it, but it's not terribly comfortable."

At that moment, he remembered he did have something for her to wear. "Yeah, I do." He went to his dresser, opened the bottom drawer, and pulled out the familiar clothes that he presented to her as she stared at him with round eyes.

"Oh, my God. I knew I'd left them at your place." She took her

CU Buffs, cross-country team sweatpants and gold T-shirt. "I can't believe *you* kept these all this time."

He sat beside her still tangled up in his sheets. "They've been washed. I almost donated them a few times, but something always stopped me." He kissed her forehead. "Now I know why." He leaned back and grinned. "But they won't look as good on you as that dress."

She fought a smile as she whipped off the sheet.

David somehow managed to keep his hands to himself while she dressed. But once in her sweats and T-shirt, she looked almost exactly like the eighteen-year-old girl on the cross-country team he'd fallen for and *never* stopped loving.

None of this was a dream, but it sure as hell felt like it should be.

"So, what are you in the mood to hear?" he asked once they were seated on his bench.

"Surprise me."

He placed his fingers on the keys…and played "Chopsticks" with one hand.

She groaned. "Ha, ha."

"Not what you had in mind?"

"David, be serious."

He stopped, stared at the keys, then said, "This is the song you heard me working on before you rang the doorbell. It's still pretty rough, though, so don't expect too much."

He played the first seven notes, paused, and played three additional notes before he launched into what he had so far of his song. He tapped the keys and turned his head slightly right, focusing on the window and using only his trained ear to work through each note. It would definitely sound more enriched once the other instruments were integrated. And he knew this only because he'd been hearing the completed song in his head for the last two weeks.

When the last note he played faded, he faced her. "That's all I have right now."

"Does it have a title?"

"Not yet. I think titles have a way of emerging when they're ready."

She grabbed a handful of his T-shirt, pulled him toward her, and gave him a long kiss.

"You liked it that much?" he asked once they broke apart.

"I loved it. *And* watching you play." She straddled the bench. "The only thing missing from this moment is you wearing your glasses."

He copied her actions. "I guess that means I'll have to wear them more often."

She laughed, shaking her head.

"What's so funny?"

"This." She gestured toward his piano, then the living room. "And it's not *funny*, just"—she stared at him—"I can't believe everything you've done to get to this life you have."

Sometimes he couldn't believe it, either. But she'd given him a damn good opening.

"When's your next show?"

"We have a weekly gig Thursday nights at the Blues Note in LoDo." He grinned. "And if you're not busy crashing a wedding *next* Saturday night—"

"You're not going to let me forget I did that."

"Never. But we're playing up in Evergreen again."

"I might go." She lifted her chin. "If you behave yourself between now and then."

He clasped her hands and linked their fingers. *It was now or... well, now.* "Al, when I wrote *roughly* in my message to you in the notebook, that meant I left a few things out." He sighed. "Things from when I was stuck in the darkness that I didn't put in there, because I wanted to tell you in person if we got to this point." *And here she was, sitting beside him.*

Her smile vanished. "David, it's okay. I don't have to know everything." She squeezed his fingers. "Unless you *really* want to tell me."

" And I do now. It's just…" The shame swept though him, but he forced himself to say, "I know I was a cruel asshole. But it's a damn good thing you weren't around after that night."

She leaned forward. "I think I understand."

"No, you don't. And if you think the drinking I was doing before that night was bad, it wasn't. Because after that night, I became—" The words failed since he despised reliving that time of his life. "My drinking became so bad that I woke up really early one morning in that Jeep I had. It was…haphazardly parked in front of the apartment Jackson and I were still sharing." He frowned at the cloudy image. "I had no memory of getting home. I still don't."

Her eyes widened.

"I was unbelievably lucky to walk away from that, accident free. And also not get pulled over and thrown in jail." *Two miracles that had saved his life.* As was the next admission. "The next day, my aunt, uncle, Jackson, and his family planned and implemented an… intervention." His eyes drifted to his piano. "Jackson talked me into going to his parents' house with him, using the excuse they really wanted to see me. And they did, but not for the reasons I thought." He shook his head. "I don't remember much from that time too clearly, but I do remember how all of them were looking at me." He eyed her. "Al, they were scared. And that scared *me*."

She lifted their joined hands, and kissed one, then the other.

"So when I made it clear to everyone that same day I agreed with them, my aunt and uncle put me in a rehab program that lasted about a month."

She released his hands and hooked her arms behind his neck. "Because you don't drink anymore, I wondered if Hugh and Eileen had intervened." She pressed her forehead to his. "David, that's only another part of you. An insignificant part now, considering your self-discipline." She gave him a light kiss. "You're amazing. But Becca doesn't know any of this."

He pulled away enough to catch her eyes. "No, and she *never* will."

"I understand."

He placed his left hand on the piano keys and absently tapped out a tune. "Did Becs go into the details about that day we finally reconciled?"

"No." She lifted her shoulders. "She was pretty vague about all of it."

He focused on her. "I'd long since pulled myself together by then, but I still wasn't prepared for her honesty that took a long time to come out. Between her crying," he slowly continued, "she told me if I had been with them nothing bad would've happened. That she'd always felt safe when I was with her. She kept repeating herself, and I…lost it." He cleared his throat. "I remember pulling her skinny, fragile body into my arms. She tried pushing me away, but I wouldn't let go. I can't remember how many times I apologized. Begged for forgiveness."

She pulled him close, and he slid his arms around her waist.

He still wasn't finished sharing all the ugliness; something he'd never told anyone.

"Al, my mom called me about Becs's game that night. *Twice.*"

She released him just enough to look at him.

"You had already left the apartment by then." *Rightfully pissed off at him.* "I let her calls go to voicemail." His vision blurred. "I can still hear her disappointment and sadness in those messages, asking me to put aside the argument because Becs was counting on me—us —to be there. Messages I didn't listen to until it was too—" He took a deep breath. "The last things my mom *and* dad said to me were out of frustration and disappointment, and some anger." He stared at her. "How can I ever let go of something like that?"

She placed her hands on his face. "David, you need to stop this. You don't deserve to spend the rest of your life beating yourself up with guilt, especially after *everything* you've done for yourself and Becca." She paused before adding, "Things your parents know you've done."

"I know. And I'm trying." He breathed deeply through his nose, then released the air. "Another reason I wrote everything down in the notebook was a way of…moving forward." He pushed a lock of hair behind her ear. "But I do have good news I want to tell you, too."

"Okay. Keep going."

"Not to bring up more bad memories, but I took your words from that Saturday morning to heart. About Becs being close to true independence and pursuing music full time again?"

Al nodded.

"After finding out that I could financially do it, I've decided to leave architecture."

Her eyes widened, followed by throwing her arms around him with such force they almost fell off his piano bench.

"Whoa." He hugged her tight while straightening them. "If I'd known you'd react like this, I would have told you the second you stepped into my house earlier."

She leaned backward. "What are you planning to do? Tell me everything."

And he did, including his sister's job news that only reinforced he was doing the right things for *himself*.

"I'm still a few months away from leaving the firm because of an existing project." He smiled, imagining Vivienne's reaction when he told her he and *the one* had finally figured it out. "But I've stopped taking new clients."

"David, this is so exciting."

"Thanks. But what I'm planning to do won't be easy."

"Of course it won't." She squeezed him. "But it'll be worth it."

She seemed to be on the same page with him, but he had to know for certain.

"Then are you absolutely sure you want to do this?" Their eyes caught. "Be with *me*?"

Silence surrounded them for the first time since they'd sat at his piano.

His breathing slowed while he waited…and waited…and waited some—

"I'm happy you walked into my shop that Monday."

He smiled, then sealed her words with a gentle kiss.

"There's always been a part of me that hoped we'd somehow come back together, since I've always loved you." She grinned. "From the second I read that note you put on my desk."

They shared a quick laugh.

"And you have to know by now that I've never stopped loving *you*."

She twisted her fingers through his hair. "I do, but this unexpected second chance we're taking comes with a caveat I need to make sure you understand."

"Anything."

Al placed her head beside his and whispered, "If you break my heart again, I'll have no choice but to have you killed."

He nodded once. "Understood."

She leaned back and gave him a wary smile. "I'll be honest, my mom will probably be the easiest one for you to win over. My dad and grandma on the other hand…"

"Also understood." And not surprising when he recalled what Tricia had told him when they met in his office.

"But I know they'll come around."

He had no choice but to accept her words, too.

"Will you play another song for me?"

"I can do that." He faced his piano, paused, placed his fingers on the keys, and went right into the second movement of Beethoven's "Moonlight Sonata."

Tonight, with Al right beside him in his favorite spot, it fit his mood.

Epilogue

SHE AND DAVID danced in time to Peter Gabriel's "In Your Eyes" Becca had requested be played in honor of their parents since it had been their wedding song.

Alyson spotted the glowing newlyweds on the crowded dance floor. Matt cradled Becca in his arms, who looked stunning in her shimmery wedding dress she had, with some help, designed back in late February, almost two weeks after *he'd* walked back into her life.

Her eyes wandered back to David's—that deep, soulful brown—and he unleashed his devilish grin.

How could life change so drastically with one choice, in one moment?

"So," he murmured, "I've been thinking about something *a lot* since I opened my groomsman gift from Becs and Matt last night."

She returned his grin. "And what would that be?"

With his hand on her lower back, he guided her even closer to him. "That three-fold picture frame has two spots accounted for. The pic of our parents on their wedding day is already in there, and Becs and Matt's pic will go in there once they give me a print."

She nodded slowly. "Which means you'll have an empty spot."

"And that would look a little strange."

"I completely agree with you."

His smile deepened. "I was hoping, after the excitement of their wedding settles down and they get back from their honeymoon that, maybe, we could have our own most important day of the twenty-first century?"

She fought a smile as she said, "David Thomas Preston, is this your way of proposing?"

He angled his head back. "You know me better than that."

Yes. Every single part of him, too.

"But is this your way of saying you'd be okay with me proposing…someday?"

She giggled. "The odds are definitely in your favor."

He slipped his arms around her waist, and she loosely hooked her arms behind his neck.

"Okay. That's all I needed to know." He paused, then added, "Al, I've proposed to you before. That last night we were *together*. After our hooky day in the city?"

Her mouth inched open.

"You'd already fallen asleep and didn't hear me." He exhaled through his teeth. "I let it go, then fate…"

She hugged him close. "So, I'll give you the same answer I would've given you that night if I had heard you." She placed her head beside his and whispered, "Yes."

David dipped her, gave her a long kiss, then brought her up. After twirling her once, she glided back into his arms and they continued dancing.

"It's not fair my parents aren't here." He pressed his forehead to hers.

"I know."

"But I can feel them."

She smiled. "Of course you can."

He tightened his hold, and Alyson nestled her head into the curve of his shoulder.

This unforgettable day and night had officially reached extraordinary.

Author's Note

I hope you enjoyed Book One in the Timing is Everything Series that will continue with *First Time We Laughed*.

If you have a moment, please feel free to leave a rating and brief review at wherever you purchased the book. Authors always appreciate and need honest reader reviews.

About the Author

Christine Miles is a full-time writer living in Albuquerque, New Mexico.

An avid reader and writer since elementary school, her passion for literature inspired her to pursue a BA in English and an MA in Creative Writing. She writes YA and Adult Contemporary Romances with sassy, independent heroines and swoony heroes who love them for their strength.

When not writing romances, she loves traveling, binge-watching shows on streaming apps, reading mysteries and thrillers, listening to music, and spending quality time with her family, friends, and dog.

You can find her on Facebook and Instagram. Sign up for her newsletter to get ARC's and updates at www.christinemilesauthor.com.

facebook.com/ChristineMilesAuthor

instagram.com/christinemilesauthor

amazon.com/author/christinemilesya

bookbub.com/authors/christine-miles

goodreads.com/christinemilesauthor

www.ingramcontent.com/pod-product-compliance
Lightning Source LLC
Chambersburg PA
CBHW061620190726
48288CB00007B/2398